S. S. BAZINET

IN
the
CARE
of
WOLVES

MY BROTHER'S
KEEPER

Renata Press
Albuquerque, New Mexico

Published by Renata Press
Albuquerque, New Mexico
www.renatapress.com

Visit the author's website:
www.ssbazinet.com

ISBN: 978-1-937279-21-9

For all those who enjoy an exciting thriller about family ties that can't be broken.

Acknowledgments

My deepest appreciation goes to Laura Christine, my beloved, genius editor. She was a guiding light throughout the editing process. My profound thanks go to Gene Hoglan who spent so much time meticulously going over the manuscript. I am so appreciative of his loving dedication to detail. I am so grateful to Anna Marie for her early editing inputs and wisdom, and for her continued support, and to George for his strong and caring presence. Thank you to Julia Ann for all her thoughtful guidance, counsel and perfect recommendations, and to Rick, a true and wonderful sounding board and enthusiast. Thank you to Gabriel! His shoulder was my crutch when I was mired in self-doubt. He always insisted on turning me back in a positive direction. Thank you to Ashley Barnard for her very helpful, editing contributions. Thank you to all my family and extended family who are always there for me, no matter what the circumstance.

Chapter One

"Daniel! Wake up!"

Daniel opened his eyes with a start and sat up. He shivered as he searched the dark corners of the holding cell. "Who's there?" His voice was thin and ragged, and his question came out in a breathless whisper.

"Daniel, it's me."

"Father?"

"Yes."

The word was soft and comforting, but it did nothing to drive out the numbing cold that had hold of Daniel's body. He clasped his arms tight around himself and began to rock.

"Daniel, you can't give up. Believe in who you are. Don't let them take that away from you."

"But I know what they're going to do to me!"

"You have to find a way."

"How? I don't know how!"

Daniel came awake again, this time in the safety of his bedroom. He grabbed his chest, still gasping. He tried to switch on his bedside lamp, but his hand was too shaky. The recurring dream had haunted him since he was a boy.

"Ever since they got hold of me, and they—"

He couldn't let himself go there. He was a twenty-six-year-old man, not a helpless boy of twelve. He couldn't let his nightmares or the past get the better of him. He had to stay focused on the present.

He had to make sure no one ever suffered the way he had suffered, the way his baby brother had suffered.

He put his hands over his ears and took deep breaths. "I can still hear his screams."

Daniel didn't remember how he got away from the monsters who tortured him. He did remember the pack leader's kindness afterwards. Wolfgang became his substitute father. Daniel's own parents had been murdered. With Wolfgang's nurturing hand to guide him, Daniel slowly came back to himself.

But now, many years later, Wolfgang couldn't understand that his role as a leader wasn't aggressive enough. He believed in peace. He couldn't see the danger that was always ready to destroy their kind. His attitude left Daniel with no choice. He had to adopt a militant attitude and challenge Wolfgang's role. A new kind of leadership was necessary if the pack was going to survive. However, he needed to talk to Wolfgang. He had to explain that he wasn't trying to overstep his position in the pack. His intention was simply to do what he knew was best.

Chapter Two

Wolfgang pulled the Mustang into the driveway of his two-story, suburban home and turned off the engine. He was relieved that his wife, Amelie, gave him a short list of errands. He didn't mind picking up groceries or mailing a package, but his patience factor for extended, everyday tasks was at an all-time low. Besides, he'd been late three times already that week, and he'd promised Amelie he wouldn't be late again.

He threw open the car door and got out. He was about to retrieve some items from the back seat when he jerked upright. He heard something, the hushed sound of a footstep barely scraping the pavement. He swung around, searching the shadows.

"Can I talk to you?" A familiar voice called out to him from the darkness.

Wolfgang relaxed ever so slightly as he turned in the direction of its owner. "Daniel, what are you doing here?"

A tall man stepped forward into the light of a nearby street lamp. It accentuated his youthful but stern features and his light brown hair. "I want to apologize, that's all. I was out of line when I argued with you at the last meeting."

Wolfgang huffed out his reply. "Apologize? That's a surprise."

"Why?" Daniel moved closer. As usual, he was impeccably dressed, wearing a light gray, custom-tailored suit, and an expensive, designer shirt. His facial hair was neatly trimmed close to his face. When he spoke, his intense, probing gaze took on a more conciliatory softness. "You know me. I'm not unreasonable."

"You've been determined to have your way for a long time."

The younger man grimaced. "We all do what we feel is necessary."

Wolfgang's face reddened as if Daniel had reprimanded him. How could he argue the point when he knew the younger man's background? "Yes, that's true."

Daniel turned and walked over to the Mustang. He glanced back at Wolfgang as he ran his hand over the back fender of the 1964 1/2 collector's model. "Still holding on to the same car, I see. It looks as sharp as it did when I borrowed it years ago."

"You mean when you took it out without my permission?"

Daniel's eyes sparked defiantly, like those of the teenager he'd been at the time of the incident they were discussing. "You left the keys on the table. I didn't think you'd mind."

"I trusted you, and you ended up nearly killing yourself playing chicken from what I heard afterwards."

"Give me a break. I was sixteen. I was young."

"Whatever."

Daniel used the fierce glare of his dark eyes to press home his point. "Look, I came over here to make peace. I don't want to rehash the past."

Wolfgang could see what was behind Daniel's uneasiness. Once again, he was staring at the boy who was sneaking back into the house after returning the Mustang, and he'd been caught. "I miss those days, Daniel. Even when we disagreed, we could talk it out. But it hasn't been that way for a long time. You've been fighting me for years. Why would you want peace now with your following growing stronger every day?"

Daniel lowered his eyes with a flush of embarrassment. As he paused, a shot rang out. Its loud retort punctuated the night air with a deafening sound. The gunfire came from a car moving slowly down the street.

Wolfgang clutched his chest in surprise and shock, trying to remain upright. He could feel his hand getting wet as a bright, red stain soaked his tan, button-down shirt.

Daniel jumped in front of him, acting as a shield. "Get back," he yelled.

When Daniel pushed him towards the shadows, Wolfgang tried to obey. All his instincts told him to move, to protect himself, but a numbing weakness took over. He only staggered a couple of feet before he crumpled to the ground. He heard the car on the street pick up speed, wheels burning the asphalt as it sped away. A moment later, Daniel was kneeling at his side. His horrified eyes were wide and questioning as he put his hand over Wolfgang's wound and applied pressure.

"Don't try to move," Daniel said in a hoarse whisper.

Wolfgang stared back with disbelief as his mind grappled with the facts. He knew a bullet that missed his heart didn't have the capacity to do what this one was doing to him. His biology, his gifted nature, could survive such a missile. But something told him this was a lethal wound. Glaring at Daniel, his gaze narrowed in pain and disappointment. "Why?"

Daniel's face flushed red. "You don't think I wanted this, do you? I swear on my life, I didn't want them to hurt you."

Wolfgang wanted to trust the younger man. No, it was more than that. He needed to trust him. He tried to stay focused as he probed Daniel's mind and his heart for the truth. Daniel offered no resistance to the intrusion. When he searched for hidden deceit, Wolfgang found nothing but distress and a need to help. His eyes softened. It was probably his last chance to reach out to Daniel, to let him know he held no grudges. He lifted his free hand with difficulty. The simple gesture took all his strength. "The past is past. Promise me you'll take care of Amelie and Prissy."

Daniel grasped Wolfgang's shaky offering, bringing it to his mouth, kissing the sapphire ring on his finger. "I swear! I'll do everything in my power to protect them, but it's not going to come to that. You're going to be okay."

"You and I both know that's a lie," Wolfgang gasped. As he tried to keep his attention on Daniel, everything was spinning. A powerful force had hold of him. It was robbing him of his strength and his ability to think clearly.

Daniel acted quickly and gathered Wolfgang in his arms. He held him close. "I know what I'm talking about," the young man whispered. "Just hold on, we have a couple of hours to get the antidote. You're going to get through this."

Wolfgang tried to believe him. He tried to cling to life as blackness blotted out Daniel's face. "I've always loved you like my own son," he gasped. He fought for breath as the world slipped away.

* * *

As Wolfgang became dead weight in his arms, Daniel couldn't stop thinking about what the older man had said to him. The words twisted in his gut, making him sick with guilt and regret.

I can't believe this is happening!

But he couldn't give in to his emotions. He had to stay sharp and focused on the situation. If Wolfgang was to have any chance of survival, Daniel had to know the extent of the man's injury. Luckily, with his unique nature and with the training he'd had, Daniel was quite adept when it came to that type of assessment.

"Don't die, please." He allowed himself to utter the needy words before he went into a more clinical role. He held Wolfgang's body tight against him, closed his eyes and concentrated. Shutting out his thoughts took longer than usual, but within a few moments, he was clearheaded enough to let the vessel in his chest take over. His heart was an amazing instrument, one that could seek out the facts, tuning into organs, cells, and Wolfgang's overall state of health. It did the job better than a battery of medical tests, and it was fast. It didn't take long for Daniel to know the truth. Wolfgang was correct about dying. His body was shutting down. The bullet's toxic effects were doing their job beautifully.

Daniel was sick again when the full impact of the situation hit him. Wolfgang was so much more than just the pack leader. He was Daniel's family. When Daniel was just a boy, a boy without parents, Wolfgang stepped in. It wasn't an easy job. Daniel was never an easy child after his father and stepmother were killed, and he was taken by their murderers. Yet Wolfgang refused to give up on him. He became Daniel's teacher and his friend. He was the one person Daniel could trust. If it hadn't been for Wolfgang, he would never have had the strength to become a leader in his own right.

Now, he stared at the person who had cared for him, who had loved him no matter what and remembered it had only been a couple of days since he'd criticized Wolfgang. At the last pack meeting, Daniel had been harsh and uncaring in his speech. He'd tried to tear down the very person who had believed in him and given him another chance at life.

"I've been so stupid." The words were repeated as Daniel rocked the pack leader gently and recalled their bond. All of his ambition, all his desire to take over, fell back into an abyss of dread. Looking skyward, he howled for the first time in years.

* * *

Amelie sat on the sofa reading one of her favorite, mystery novels. She was caught up in the story and paid little attention to what sounded like a car backfiring outside. A few minutes later, a mournful wail made her throw her book aside. Every nerve in her body came alive. She jumped to her feet, recognizing the sound and its implications. The pack rarely used the somber warning, but she knew it was a signal that one of their own was down or dead. She was already bracing herself for the worst when Prissy came running in from the kitchen. She was shouting as she ran for the door.

"That's Daniel! I remember the sound of his call from when I was a kid!" Prissy yelled. "He must be in trouble!"

Amelie was right behind her daughter, moving fast enough to snatch up Prissy's shirt. "No! Don't go out there! It might not be safe!"

Prissy had her hand on the doorknob, but she did as she was told. Her kind learned early on to obey their elders in times of crisis. It was the one rule that couldn't be broken without severe penalties.

"But Mom, what if he's hurt?"

Amelie's knees went weak when her mind broadened the inquiry to include Wolfgang. She expected her husband home any minute. What if something's happened to him?

She couldn't let herself go there. She had to think of Prissy, of her daughter's safety. "Stay here. I'll investigate."

"Please Mom, no!"

Prissy's caution made Amelie hesitate. Being a normal human, a woman from Georgia who spoke with a Southern drawl, she knew how frail she was in the world of werewolves. "You're right. We have to think this out before we do anything."

As Amelie nervously weighed out her options, someone kicked the door so hard it shook.

"Let me in! Now!" The shout was delivered by a loud, masculine voice, Daniel's voice.

Amelie quickly obeyed, turning back the lock and opening the door. "Oh lord, no!" She couldn't hold back her anguished cry when she saw Wolfgang limp and unconscious in Daniel's arms.

Daniel ignored her, moving forward briskly, issuing a loud order. "Shut the door and lock it!"

"Daddy!" Prissy's shriek filled the room.

Amelie sobered as soon as she heard her daughter's cry. "Come here, sweetie!" she urged as she quickly gathered Prissy close and held her protectively. Prissy's breath was heaving and fast, but she didn't try to push Amelie away. Amelie used the moment to steady herself. She couldn't give in to panic. No matter what, she had to remain alert and helpful. She learned that much from being Wolfgang's wife. "What can I do?" she asked.

Daniel paused in the middle of the room and carefully deposited his burden on the white, wool carpet. "Just stay back, okay?"

Amelie did as she was told, but she needed information. "What happened to my husband?"

Daniel gave her the briefest glance as he retrieved a small case from his pocket. "He has a bullet wound, and he's been infected with a virus. Thankfully, I had my emergency medical kit in my car," he said as he took a syringe out of the case. He threw off his jacket and rolled up his sleeve. "I've developed an immunity to the virus, and I'm a universal donor. I can give him some of my blood. Hopefully, it'll slow down what's happening to him until I can retrieve the actual antidote."

"Is my dad going to be okay?" Prissy's voice was small and needy now.

It reminded Amelie of the times when her daughter had nightmares. Wolfgang usually got to Prissy's bedside before Amelie had a chance to help. He was always gentle and quiet. He had a knack for dispelling Prissy's fears and getting her back to sleep. Now, Amelie had to be that comforter. "Daniel knows what he's doing," she whispered as she cradled Prissy closer.

After she reassured Prissy, Amelie tried to remind herself that Daniel was extremely competent. She had to trust him. She couldn't let herself think about her husband lying in front of her, looking dead already. Still, nothing could stop her from feeling like her life was in Daniel's hands too. If Wolfgang died, how could she go on living?

Daniel looked up with hard, inquiring eyes. "Do you know a place close-by where we can hide out for awhile? A place that the pack doesn't know about?"

As Amelie tried to think, Prissy pulled herself out of Amelie's arms and stepped forward. Prissy had always been stubborn and willful. Now that she'd just had her sixteenth birthday, she acted as if she'd left childhood behind her. She clearly wanted people to see her as an adult.

"I know a place. I know someone," Prissy announced in a confident tone. "He's not one of us, but his parents are on a two week cruise. We can go to his house."

Daniel's reply was skeptical and challenging. "What makes you think he's trustworthy?"

Prissy stiffened. "Theodore's a friend, a nice person. Besides, he likes me. He'll do what I tell him," she snapped back.

Amelie spoke up. "Do we have a choice if this is pack-related? I don't know of any other place," she croaked. Wolfgang lay bloodied and still on the rug. She kept hoping to see him move a hand, a finger, to open his eyes. With his long, blond hair spread out around his handsome face, he looked like he was sleeping, but his color was gray and his chest rose and fell in ragged breaths. Her world began to shatter. She was going to lose him, she knew it.

Daniel cut into her misery with a sharp response. "Amelie, I need you to stay calm," he said as he stared at her knowingly. "We'll have to use Prissy's suggestion."

"Should I call Theodore?" Prissy asked as she put her arm around Amelie, reversing their roles, becoming the strong one.

"No." Daniel threw Prissy his keys. "Go out to my car and start the engine, but don't turn on the lights. Amelie, go with her and keep an eye out for people driving by."

Chapter Three

Theodore sat in the living room, enjoying the quiet. With his parents gone, he had the house to himself. He thought he could enjoy his favorite book on astronomy, but he couldn't keep his mind focused on a page describing star nurseries. His problem was Prissy. If he really stretched his imagination, he could pretend she was sweet, that she might even like him.

"You have it really bad," he frowned. "Going for the scariest girl in school isn't very smart."

How could he have let himself fall for such an impossible person? Yet their last meeting had surprised him. Prissy was almost nice when they met at the malt shop. He'd even had the guts to reach out for her hand. She allowed the gesture, but only for a moment. Then she jerked her hand away and gave him a look that could have come from a school principal. He ended up leaving the diner feeling like a reprimanded second grader.

"You're crazy for even thinking Prissy could fall for you." He put his book aside and stood up. He needed a bowl of ice cream or some chips to help him forget his misplaced desires. He was halfway to the kitchen when the doorbell rang. He stopped and frowned. It was nine o'clock at night. Who would be visiting at that hour? He didn't have time to ponder the question. A voice called out from the other side of the door.

"Open up, Theodore!"

"No, it can't be!" He recognized Prissy's voice. Before he could decide about what to do, the bell rang several more times.

"Theodore! Where are you?"

"Coming," he said in a squeaky tenor. He thought his voice had changed, evening out into a deep, mellow tone, but now, when he heard himself, he wasn't so sure. Moving quickly to the door, he barely had time to get the locks undone when the door was thrown open and Prissy was standing in front of him.

"Hi—"

One syllable of speech was all Prissy allowed him. After that, a number of unexpected visitors came marching in. Prissy was in the lead, roughly shoving him against the wall as if he was an irritating obstruction in her path. He only saw her face for a brief instant, but that was enough. Her expression was even scarier than before. It was filled with an admonition. She was on a very short leash, and if it snapped, she'd have him for a late snack.

A tall, imposing man followed Prissy. Entering the house without hesitation, his handsome face was spoiled by a sinister look. Unlike Prissy, the man's true power was more concealed. This guy didn't have to physically express his lethal potential. It radiated out from him like a wave that came with a warning. "Stay back, or you'll learn things about me you'll wish you never knew."

The man was carrying someone in his arms. The person appeared to be unconscious. Theodore stared wide-eyed with recognition. He'd seen the man on Prissy's birthday when she'd insisted Theodore take a walk with her.

They ended up in an alley, and Prissy suddenly became someone who frightened him. Five-foot-two, honey blond with delicate features, she had the flighty look of a real, live Tinkerbell. Yet, in that alley, she taken hold of his jacket. Her powerful grip and her intense, almost glowing eyes were paralyzing. It was a humiliating moment that ended when Prissy's father came speeding down the alley in an orange Mustang. Prissy was quick to release Theodore and follow orders to get into her father's car.

Theodore's heart skipped a beat as recognition and the present moment came together.

I'm sure that's Prissy's dad, the guy I saw on that horrible night in the alley.

Theodore's savior appeared to be in very bad shape. His skin was ashen, and his body was limp and lifeless. He reminded Theodore of his great-uncle when he was lying in a casket at the funeral home the year before.

A woman brought up the rear. Theodore's heart jumped again when he saw her. It wasn't because she frightened him. It was because she was so beautiful. With lovely, porcelain skin and thick, black hair, she had the most striking, emerald-green eyes Theodore had ever seen. They filled with tears when she stopped to speak to him.

"I'm so sorry we have to barge in on you like this," she said softly. "Please forgive us."

The lyrical sound of the woman's voice and her kind words remained in Theodore's mind like the notes of a sad song. They made him want to help her in spite of the fact that his body had been rendered immobile. He didn't know what his visitors wanted, but his gut told him there was trouble ahead.

* * *

Prissy sat in a chair across from the king-size bed. Her father was laid out on its gold, brocade comforter. Her mother was sitting next to him, caressing his face and looking almost as pale. Prissy fought back her tears. Her dad would probably never regain consciousness. She'd never get a chance to say goodbye to him.

"He's going to be alright," Daniel said, reading her thoughts as he hovered over the edge of the bed. His voice was low and edgy despite his words of encouragement.

Prissy tried to stay calm. She had agreed to sit quietly, but how could she keep that promise when Daniel was in charge. She looked up to him when she was still in pigtails and he lived with them. In her childish, fairy-tale dreams, he was her prince charming who rescued her from villains. But recently, he was the villain, the person who brought chaos into her father's life.

She knew her mother had her doubts too. Prissy could feel Amelie's emotions coming to a head as the minutes slipped by and the man she loved remained as still and quiet as death.

"Who's responsible for this . . . this . . . horror?" Amelie asked. Her furious, demanding eyes were a total contrast to her whispered tone. When they settled on Daniel's face, he looked away.

"There was a secret group in the pack. They were trying to be helpful, but they turned out to be fools."

"And you? Were you one of the fools?"

"Not in the way you're thinking—"

"I'm thinking that my husband, Prissy's father, is dying. Daniel, if you had anything to do with the people who wanted to murder—"

"No! I swear I never wanted anyone harmed."

"Liar!" Prissy yelled as she jumped up from her chair. She couldn't sit passively by and listen to Daniel defend himself. "You wanted my father's position. You wanted him out of the way!"

She followed up her statement by lunging at Daniel. Her frenzied assault might have been a brave one, but her hundred pounds of fury were no match for him. With lightning-quick reflexes, he had her by the wrists, holding her at arm's length. Considering her wrathful kicks and the all-out attack she launched on him, his grasp was firm but not overly rough.

Amelie was quick to intervene. "Let go of her!" she shouted as she stepped in to separate the two. She tried helplessly to push Daniel back.

Daniel's expression remained impassive, but his jaw tightened as he stared at Amelie. "Control her, or I'll lock her in the closet. We don't have time for her juvenile outbursts. I'm trying to save your husband's life."

Prissy used all her strength to fight Daniel, blistered the air with obscenities, but she wasn't any more successful in getting her way than Amelie.

"She told you to let her go," another voice called out.

Prissy glanced over at the doorway. Theodore was standing there. He looked scared, but his fear hadn't stopped him from challenging Daniel. She was impressed by his bravery, but she knew he was being an idiot. He was clearly still more of a boy than a man. And even a man would have little chance with Daniel.

* * *

Theodore gripped the keys to his father's car as he stepped into his parents' bedroom. He was under orders from Daniel, the man in charge. He was supposed to fetch an antidote for Prissy's ailing father. Supposedly, the antidote was the wounded man's only hope. But when Theodore entered the bedroom and saw Prissy struggling helplessly with Daniel, he knew he had a more pressing obligation. He needed to rush in and help. He wanted to be Prissy's chivalrous liberator, but his legs were as weak and rubbery as that time when he'd had the flu for a week. Instead of rushing in, he sort of stumbled in Daniel's direction.

"Let her go!" he cried with as much volume as he could manage.

Daniel frowned back. "Why are you still here, kid? I thought you were gone already!"

Theodore stopped a few feet from the bed. "I'm not going anywhere unless you stop hurting Prissy."

"You'll do what I tell you. I'm trying to save her father's life," Daniel yelled back.

Prissy stopped fighting Daniel long enough to ask a question. "Does my dad really have a chance of getting better?"

"Yes, he does, if your boyfriend gets a move on and brings me the antidote."

Prissy's face turned scarlet. "He's not my boyfriend!"

"Calm down, Prissy."

The three words were barely audible, but they got everyone's attention. All eyes immediately focused on Wolfgang.

"Dad?" Prissy jerked free of Daniel and hurried to her father's bedside.

Wolfgang smiled weakly. "I told you losing control doesn't help."

"Sweetheart, thank goodness, you're awake!" Amelie's voice was filled with relief as she reached out for Wolfgang's hand.

Theodore was as surprised as the others by the sudden turn of events. He tried to get a closer look at Prissy's father. His movement was enough to catch Wolfgang's attention. The wounded man's gaze traveled from his wife and daughter's faces to Theodore's. As Wolfgang studied him, Theodore watched the man's smile fade. It was replaced by a look of bewilderment and something else. Wolfgang's pale blue eyes lit up with an unnatural glow.

It scared the breath out of Theodore. He'd never seen eyes like that. Instant panic made him want to run from the room, but he couldn't budge an inch. Wolfgang's power to hold him in place made Prissy's ability seem miniscule. That was bad enough, but the older man's abilities went beyond freezing him to the spot. Wolfgang began to probe Theodore's mind. He could feel Wolfgang searching carefully, but with purpose, invading his privacy, going into places that should have been off-limits.

At first, Theodore resisted the new and demeaning experience. It triggered his anger and resentment. Yet as Theodore stared back, he was also drawn to the person who had hold of him. The man's eyes held no malice. There was no harm intended, only Wolfgang's desire to understand Theodore better. Their connection didn't last very long, but it was enough to fill Theodore with a deep longing for something he knew he was missing in his life.

"It's you, isn't it?" Wolfgang finally asked, unable to hold his eyes steady any longer.

Theodore's chest tightened. There was so much sorrow in the man's voice. It went beyond the borders of physical pain. This torment came from some inner well of misery. Theodore didn't know how to respond or how to help.

Wolfgang stirred again. "I'm so sorry," he gasped. He tried to reach out to Theodore, but his strength gave way. His hand fell limp on the covers, and he lost consciousness again.

Prissy stared at her father and then at Theodore. "How do you know my dad? Why did he say those things to you?"

"I don't know your dad," Theodore insisted. His limbs were coming back to life. He started to move towards the door. He didn't get very far.

Daniel grabbed hold of his arm and glared at him. Unlike Wolfgang's compassionate gaze, Daniel's dark eyes were narrow and demanding. When they invaded Theodore's mind, there was no sense of caring or concern about Theodore's feelings. Daniel was looking for facts. But more importantly, he was actively searching out Theodore's flaws and weaknesses. Theodore tried to avert his eyes, but again, he couldn't break the connection. He was forced to bear the humiliation that flushed his cheeks and told him how inadequate he was.

After Daniel finished his inquiry, he pushed Theodore towards the door. "You're supposed to be on your way to my house. Get moving."

Theodore nodded. He tried to do as he was told, but when he looked back at Daniel, he saw Daniel's disappointment. The man's contempt was etched in his deeply furrowed brows and sullen expression as if he'd had just handled something base and disgusting.

Theodore told himself Daniel's opinion shouldn't matter. He tried to hold on to the pieces of himself that Daniel had discarded as useless. Instead, his gut ached. He felt sick.

Daniel yelled again. "Go, *now!*"

Theodore moved towards the door. Prissy was right behind him, practically pushing him into the hall. He stopped outside the room and held his ground. "I'm not good with directions. I need to see where I'm going. I better check out a map on the computer."

"You don't have time!" Prissy insisted.

Theodore blinked at her, swaying slightly and backing up to the wall for support. He took a much needed breath. He didn't understand what was going on, and he wasn't being given time to figure things out.

23

Prissy snapped her fingers in his face. "What's wrong with you?"

Her overbearing tone brought him back to his task. "You don't want me to get lost, do you?" He pointed unsteadily. "My father's office is right there. It'll only take a minute to look up Daniel's address."

"Just use your phone!"

"My phone's been quirky lately. If I look at a map, I'll be fine."

"Great, anything to get you moving."

* * *

Theodore watched Prissy at the computer. Her fingers were rigid with purpose, entering Daniel's address on the keyboard with hard, staccato taps. Her eyes were fierce and determined. Theodore stepped away and tried to swallow, but even that took energy he didn't have. When he was around forceful people like Prissy, he became the weak, bumbling misfit. He morphed into an alien presence, a being who didn't understand the harsh world he was in.

In his confusion, he remembered Wolfgang's eyes. In spite of the man's condition, they had a glow that felt warm and comforting. He looked at Theodore with compassion and concern. They were virtues Theodore hadn't known before, but he liked how they affected him. Theodore's chest expanded ever so slightly. He could breathe a little easier, and his initial anger was replaced by a primal need to be part of something bigger. Connecting with Wolfgang served as a soothing balm for his body and his mind. The man had even apologized to Theodore.

I know there's something wrong with me. Prissy's dad knows it too, but he was really nice anyway. If a person like Prissy's father can think something good about me, maybe I'm not as hopeless as I've imagined.

So why did he feel so horrible now? If Wolfgang could offer kindness, why didn't people like Daniel and Prissy?

"Theodore, pay attention! I found a map. Look at it and get going!"

Prissy's searing impatience hit Theodore just as he was seeing life with more clarity. Her voice became his mother's voice, his father's voice, and countless other voices. People were always yelling at him, always telling him what to do.

"Are you listening?" Prissy asked insistently, this time in his ear.

It was too much.

"I'm trying my best!" he shouted back. His whole life he'd held himself in check, as if he deserved to be hurt by other people. His gut tightened with outrage. His furtive, cowering eyes blinked up, and filled with an unmasked resentment. "Leave me alone!"

His bitterness was delivered with so much volume it frightened him. He'd never been allowed to raise his voice, much less act out his emotions. But he couldn't stop himself. Too much had happened in too short a time. Strangers had invaded his home and ordered him around like he meant nothing to them. Then Prissy's father and Daniel stirred up feelings that made his world fly apart, leaving him in confusion and chaos.

Prissy took a step backwards. Her face was red and scowling, but after a moment, her eyes softened ever so slightly. "I'm just scared about my dad. Can't you understand that?"

He stared at her, not with adoration or even fear like before, but with a new sense of how much he'd had to endure every day. No one ever gave him a break. "Yes, I understand. Show me the map, and I'll go."

Prissy's scowl gave way to another kind of intensity. Her eyes remained unwavering but more fluid. "I'm depending on you, Theo, and you seem so—"

"I'm fine! And don't worry, I'll get the antidote if I can." Whether Prissy knew it or not, he wanted to help. Wolfgang's fate had been placed in his hands, and he'd do everything he could to save the man.

But why? Why should I risk myself for a person I don't even know?

He grabbed the car key off the desk. He didn't have an explanation nor the time to worry about it.

Chapter Four

Daniel never left Wolfgang's bedside. He observed each labored rise and fall of the older man's chest. His own breath was shallow and quick as he calculated Wolfgang's chances. Their leader was barely holding the line between life and death. How easy it would be for him to slip over that line, to leave the world behind, to leave Daniel behind. The antidote was Wolfgang's only chance. Why hadn't the boy come back with it? What was taking him so long?

The boy.

Daniel's fingers closed on themselves, making tight fists, but he couldn't hold back the questions that loomed in front of him. Why hadn't he allowed himself to know the boy's identity as soon as they met? Why had he ignored him?

Don't be an idiot. You know why. He could destroy you!

Theodore's face flashed in front of him.

So young and pure.

But Daniel knew what was behind those soft, brown eyes. The truth made his breath catch. His lungs stopped working.

Don't go there!

Suddenly, he wasn't worried about death. A part of him, that blameless boy he'd once been, knew what could happen if one were alive. Except for his nightmares and those times that wouldn't be ignored, he hadn't allowed himself to think about that part of his life.

You buried all of it for a reason! Don't dredge it up now!

He forced a ragged breath, forced himself to take in those tiny increments of air that kept his body alive. But his chest was constricting, fighting back, remembering. It was so hard to breathe when the fear took over, when he dreaded the next moment.

You're not that child anymore. Let it go!

He had to keep breathing, to think about where he was, to anchor himself in the chair where he sat. His fists slowly unclenched, but he couldn't completely calm his mind. It rested in silence, like a thin pane of glass. If he dared any movement, the glass might shatter. Everything resting below its smooth surface might be loosed on him, breaking through the numbness that kept his life together.

But he wasn't the only one who could shatter the glass. Amelie sat a few feet away. He could feel her eyes boring into him. He was trapped in her gaze. He couldn't escape her thoughts or his ability to read them. They were like small metal hammers, poised and ready to strike the thin, brittle barrier that protected him. He had to steel himself for whatever Amelie decided to do. Otherwise, he might not survive.

* * *

Amelie eventually succeeded in convincing Prissy to take a break. Her overly passionate daughter had been wearing out the carpet. All her pacing was adding more tension to the situation. Finally, Prissy had agreed to watch television in the other room. Amelie remained sitting in a corner of the bedroom, praying. She petitioned heaven, asking for help, hoping her husband would be strong enough to hold on until the boy got back. In the meantime, she was grateful for the blessing she'd been given earlier. Wolfgang had regained consciousness for a few minutes. His eyes had brightened when he looked at her. Their message was clear. No matter how wounded he was in body, his heart and his soul were still full of love, a love she cherished above all else. How would she live without that love?

Don't even think about it! Focus on something else before you go crazy.

She thought about Theodore. Wolfgang reacted so strongly when he saw the boy.

How are they connected?

Glancing over at Daniel, the answer slipped in quietly, but it came as a shock. For years, Wolfgang had searched for a lost child. Now, she knew he'd found him.

But that means Daniel is—

She stopped and stared at the younger man again. More disturbing questions surfaced. How could he sit there so calmly, so unruffled? How could he be so unmoved by what Wolfgang's remarks signified for him?

What's wrong with you, Daniel?

As soon as the question came to mind, she went red with shame. She'd forgotten to shield her thoughts from him. Her inquiry hit Daniel like a physical blow. She could feel how he made himself take the punishing attack with barely a flinch. But she'd hurt him deeply. She knew it.

"I'm sorry," she said quickly, trying to reverse what she'd set in motion. It was too late. Daniel continued to ignore her, but she observed the slight tremor that shook his body. It was a response to inflicted pain, to her question. Amelie could feel his tremendous control, how hard it was for him not to react. She hadn't simply hit Daniel, she'd ripped open a grievous wound from his past. She didn't know how to repair the damage.

"Again, I'm so sorry," she said as quietly as possible. "It's not my business."

After years of doubt and lack of faith in her, Daniel was just starting to open up a little. With one thought, she feared she'd destroyed the small headway they'd made.

A long silence followed Amelie's second apology. As the minutes ticked by, Daniel did everything in his power to compose himself, to contain the hatred Amelie had unleashed in him. A rage coursed through every fiber of his being when he thought about how cruel humans could be.

Just get the hell out! Get away from here, from everything.

He wanted to run from the room and keep running, but if he did, Wolfgang would die as surely as if Daniel shot him again, this time through the heart. When he could finally speak, his voice felt rough and weak, like someone had tried to strangle him, closed off his air.

"You think I haven't got any feelings about that thing? You're right," he said.

Amelie raised her eyes and stared at him. "Dearest Daniel, Theodore is your brother."

Daniel's body went rigid again, but this time, he wasn't able to contain the words that came out in a rush of sorrow and disgust. "My brother is dead. That walking zombie is what's left after the WKA murdered him."

Amelie shuddered at the mention of the WKA.

It was something they agreed on. They shared a profound abhorrence for the organization. It instilled fear in all who knew its mission and its methods. If the WKA had its way, all of the pack would be dead. On one of their raids, the WKA abducted Daniel. He was twelve. They also took his baby brother. When the pack finally recovered Daniel, he was too traumatized to ever talk about what had happened to either of them.

"Daniel, I'm sorry about everything you endured. But Wolfgang has been hunting for that child for so long."

"Wolfgang's a misguided—" Daniel blurted out the words, but he stopped himself in mid-sentence. He'd said too much already. He'd let himself feel too much. His gaze solidified into a wall of unyielding stone. "There's nothing to find."

30

"But Theodore seems sweet," Amelie insisted.

"What do you know about him? Were you there when they took him, when they did what they wanted with him?" Daniel tightened his jaw, trying to keep his voice steady. "If the WKA let him go, there's a reason. He's been programmed. He's a programmed lab rat."

"Why do you feel like that? They let you go, and you're—"

"Me? You want to talk about me now?" Daniel pushed himself out of the chair and walked over to where Amelie was sitting. "What could you possibly know about me?" His tone was filled with unbridled bitterness, meant to hurt her back. But as he stood over her and she looked up at him with pleading eyes, eager to understand him, he backed away.

Amelie dropped her gaze and studied the floor. "I'm sorry you never felt like you could trust me or confide in me."

"Confide what? What did I have left when they let me go? I can't remember half of what they did to me. I have to watch everything I do, everything I say, examine every motive."

"Your mind and your intentions are pure, Daniel. You lived with us. You're family. I can't read your thoughts like you can mine, but I know the kind of person you are."

"I only know I've tried to prove myself with every decision I've made." He looked at Wolfgang, letting a weak smile replace his frown. "After what happened to me, your husband became my mentor, the only person I had left to hold on to. He told me to believe in myself so many times. So I tried my best. I wanted to be my father's son, and I wanted Wolfgang to be proud of me. But our ideas differed in how to best safeguard and protect those we care about."

Amelie smiled too. "Wolfgang was right about you."

"Yet you questioned me, didn't you? My loyalty—"

"I don't know why I doubted you. I know you've done everything possible to help Wolfgang. Maybe I needed to take out my anger on someone, and it ended up being you. I don't have your strength. I'm only human."

Daniel shot her a scornful look. "Is that your excuse, being human?"

"It's been hard. You've caused a lot of problems for Wolfgang, for the pack."

Daniel knew Amelie had tactfully left out the part about their relationship. When he was growing up, he'd never been able to accept her. He walked to his chair and braced his hands on the back. His anger was replaced by a deep down weariness. "I'm sorry if I've caused problems, but I've tried to do what I think is best. Would you want less from me?"

"No, I wouldn't want that." Amelie stood up and approached his chair. She stopped herself before she got too close.

Daniel knew she wanted to comfort him. When his body stiffened, she crossed her arms, signaling that she understood. It was an old pattern from the past. When she tried to touch him as a child, he always got sick. His body had a profound dread of what a human touch could mean. He tried, but he couldn't hide the terror he felt, the shame that came with what had been done to him.

Amelie's voice was soft again. "I think you're wrong about the boy."

Daniel's grip tightened on the chair. "Don't you think I'd want that more than anything?" His chest rose and fell in short, strained breaths. After a moment, he found enough strength to go on. "I scanned him, looked at what was left. I searched for my brother, but they took everything from him. They robbed him of what he was and could be. Is that clear?"

Amelie started to reach out for him again. Finally, she let her arms drop to her sides. "Daniel, please don't give up on Theodore. Sometimes we only find what we expect to find."

Chapter Five

Theodore parked his father's black Lexus sedan around the corner from Daniel's house. It was a normal, suburban neighborhood located a couple of streets off the freeway. But the innocent setting did nothing to calm his dread. What was he facing? Who might be waiting for him? He sat in the driver's seat, trying to get his heart to stop racing. His anger was gone, replaced by an old familiar feeling. He was frightened again.

I don't have time to worry about it! There's too much at stake.

The thought made his hand shake harder as he tried to open the door. It was a small triumph when he was able to stumble out of the vehicle. Closing the door as quietly as possible, he glanced up and down the street. He knew what to look for. Daniel briefed him before he left. The renegade group who had launched the attack on Wolfgang had a simple outlook on the people around them. A person was either with them or against them. Since Daniel hadn't reported in, he would be listed as a threat and a suspect.

"These guys are very edgy," Daniel insisted. "So stay calm if you see anything suspicious like someone watching my house. They don't have any reason to think you're helping, but they're smart. Be very cautious. And one more thing, shield your thoughts or at least think about something else if you're approached."

"Think about something else," Theodore repeated as he began walking. That was an easy order to obey. As he got closer to his objective, visions of being shot like Wolfgang kept playing out in his mind. He even saw a graveyard and his own tombstone. Its inscription was as hopeless as trying to be calm when his body was a quivering mass of panic.

Here lies Theodore, the coward, the person who never had an ounce of courage.

But Wolfgang's life was in his hands. He had no choice. He had to help. A bout of dizziness made him lean against an old oak. When his vision cleared he surveyed the dark street in front of him. His stomach gurgled ominously as he started walking again. He swallowed hard, managing to push back the bile in his throat.

Prissy has more courage in her little finger than I have in my entire body.

The thought of being so timid was humiliating. It made him walk a little faster as he counted the houses he passed. Daniel's was the fourth down. He was in front of the third house when he saw a parked car. As he moved forward, it turned on its high beams. Bright light flooded the area. He'd been exposed.

"Oh crap!" He was sure the person in the car was one of the people Daniel had been talking about. He couldn't move forward. He became a stationary target for the bullet that would soon tear through his flesh.

So this is it. I'm dead.

But another thought edged in before he completely gave up. He'd had the courage to confront Daniel, and he'd survived. He had to find a way to confront what was waiting for him.

Just walk past the house and keep going. Remember, they don't know who you are.

But this time no matter how hard he tried, his body resisted. His legs wanted to buckle. He couldn't stop staring at the car. After long moments, a tall, muscular man stepped out of the vehicle.

"Hey! Do you live around here?" the man asked.

Theodore tried to answer, but his voice failed him too. A squeaky grunt was all he could get out.

The man yelled again. "I asked you a question!"

Theodore stood mute and rooted to the concrete sidewalk, watching the man move towards him. He tried to swallow and couldn't manage that either. Instead, his gut grabbed. It was another familiar feeling.

He went from being petrified to totally nauseous. He clutched at his stomach. It was churning with the spaghetti dinner and chocolate cake he'd eaten a couple of hours before. He gave the man a quick glance. "I'm warning you . . . stay back," he moaned.

The man quickened his pace and stopped in front of him. "Warning me? Are you kidding, you little punk?"

Taking in short gasps of air, Theodore kept trying to swallow, but it was no use. "I'm . . . I'm . . . going—"

The man squinted back at him with dark, menacing eyes and grabbed Theodore's shirt. "You're going to what?"

"Throw up," Theodore whimpered as his stomach lurched. The next minute he was vomiting, but not in the normal way. His way was dramatic, a scourge that his mother had been dealing with for years. Projectile vomiting wasn't a pretty sight. In this case, the guy in front of him was immediately covered in Theodore's dinner and dessert, along with the chips and dip he'd had for a snack. The man's face was dripping with a horrifying, putrid liquid.

The man shrieked out in surprise and anger as he backed up. "You little jerk!"

His shout hit Theodore's solar plexus with so much force, he threw up again. He could taste the bile spewing out.

The man screamed with new outrage. "Freaking hell!"

They were standing in front of a two story home. Its porch light came on as the guy continued to bellow out his rage. A burly, overweight man came out of the house and stood staring from the stoop. "What's going on out here? What's all the yelling about? Do I need to call the police?"

The questions were acknowledged by the man harassing Theodore. He shoved Theodore in the chest, throwing him backwards. With a final, unbelieving look of loathing, the man turned and ran towards his car. He continued to curse the whole way. Before he got into his vehicle, he tore off his jacket and threw it on the road. Once he was in his car, he quickly gunned the engine and sped down the street.

* * *

When Theodore got back home, smiling faces were waiting for him. Amelie was full of relief and welcome. She hugged him and called him her hero. But he didn't feel like a hero. It had been easy to retrieve the antidote once the stranger was gone. He had Daniel's house keys and instructions that were simple to follow. But even Prissy acted happy to see him.

"Good job, Theo," she said with a smile.

Daniel wasn't nearly as welcoming as he came out of the bedroom and quickly joined them. "Did you have any trouble?"

Theodore's deep blush of embarrassment was Daniel's answer. "A little trouble, a guy was waiting in a car."

Daniel's eyes narrowed as he grabbed the vial from Theodore's outstretched hand. "Tell me he didn't follow you back here."

Theodore felt his empty stomach lurch precariously again. "No, it's okay. He drove away before I went into your house. I was careful to go out the back door when I left. I snuck through a couple of backyards instead of going back out on the street."

Daniel's face registered the smallest glimmer of appreciation. "Good," he said as he turned away.

Theodore watched the tall man move hurriedly towards the bedroom. When a hand clasped his shoulder, he swiveled anxiously. Prissy was staring at him.

"That was very brave of you," she said. "Thank you."

He shook his head. "No, I'm not brave at all. The guy left me alone because I threw up on him."

Prissy's eyes lit up playfully. "Really?"

"Yeah, I did." After a moment, he began to smile too. "Word of warning, Prissy, if I look like I'm getting sick, move out of the way really fast."

Chapter Six

Theodore's eyes darted around his parents' bedroom. Sitting in a corner, on the floor, he felt like an intruder. He'd never been allowed to spend any time in the large cheerless quarters, but that was a good thing. The dark mahogany furniture, hand-me-downs from his mother's side, was old and depressing. The grey-green curtains were always closed against the sun and any feeling of warmth. The dismal atmosphere wasn't helped by the present situation. Two hours had passed since Daniel administered the antidote. So far, it didn't seem to help. Wolfgang was still unconscious. The minutes ticked by as he continued to fight for life. Prissy and Amelie kept vigil by the side of his bed.

Daniel was pacing, but he paused to address the two women. "The group who developed the antidote never used it on anyone who'd been shot with the virus. I still believe it'll work."

Amelie looked up at him with tired, questioning eyes. "Why, Daniel, why would you of all people be a part of a group that would invent such a thing, something that could kill your own?"

"We didn't invent the virus. We discovered it when we infiltrated some of the WKA's database. We've been working to develop an antidote for the past eighteen months. Recently, a splinter faction, a few individuals, started acting suspiciously. I've pretended to be part of their group so I could keep an eye on them."

"That's a bunch of crap!" Prissy cried out. "You wanted to take over my dad's job. Admit it. And you'd use whatever means available."

Daniel glared back, but his tone was calm and measured when he answered. "That's not true. I never wanted your father dead. If I did, would I be here? If you were more capable of using your abilities, you'd know I was telling the truth."

Amelie put down Wolfgang's hand and turned to Prissy. "I know how upset you are, but Daniel saved your father. He's trying everything he can to help."

Prissy leveled her fiery gaze at Daniel again. "I'm trying to trust you, but you know my abilities come and go at this stage. So give me a break."

As Theodore watched them argue from his lowly vantage point, he interjected a question of his own. "What's the WKA?"

Prissy turned her anger on him. "An organization that wants us dead. They're the ones who are responsible for many of our pack . . . I mean our group, being killed. They murdered Daniel's father years ago."

Theodore's eyes went wide as he gaped back at her. "Did you just say 'pack' and what abilities are you talking about?"

"Don't worry about any of that," Amelie pleaded. "It's not important."

"Sorry." Theodore had no intention of upsetting Amelie. Not only was she the most attractive woman he'd ever seen, she certainly was the kindest one. His own mother was nothing like Amelie. "I'm not trying to bother you, but I'd like to know what's going on, please. I think I deserve to know who you are, and why people want you dead."

"No!" The word was a shouted whisper. It came from Wolfgang as he opened his eyes. "Don't tell him anything—"

"Daddy!" Prissy leaped out of her chair. "You're awake!"

Amelie jumped up too and leaned over Wolfgang. "Thank goodness!"

Wolfgang blinked at each of them, as if he needed time to ground himself in the moment. At last he managed a smile too. "I didn't think I'd see either of you again."

Daniel was immediately at Wolfgang's side. He put his hand on the ailing man's chest. A shadow of joy spread across his face as he finally relaxed. "Your heart is stronger. Welcome back."

It was the first time Theodore had seen Daniel smile. It changed his appearance drastically. Instead of being poster material for a wanted mobster, Daniel actually looked cultured and refined. Theodore sighed.

Good, it looks like they all got their wish. They all look relieved and happy.

Theodore knew he wasn't part of that happiness. He was the outsider. He stood up and began to ease himself out of the room. He needed to put distance between himself and the family reunion. It was an automatic response. He was used to not being wanted. Even when his mother and father were around, he didn't seem to have a place in their lives. He was a mouth to feed, a kid who added laundry and upkeep to his mother's chores.

His father had reached out once a couple of years before. As the president of his own small, electronics company, he was always working, but he'd had a rare day off. Sitting in a lawn chair drinking a few afternoon cocktails, he was more relaxed than usual. "It's okay to raise a little hell at your age," he confided in an unguarded, mildly-drunken tone. "I was on the football team, and it was natural to step outside the bounds a bit. You know what I mean?"

Theodore's reaction to his father's counsel was one of alarm. He furtively glanced around for his mother, hoping she hadn't heard his father's remarks. He didn't want to witness another scene between his parents, especially since his father would be on the receiving end of his mother's sharp tongue.

His father saw his response and looked away quickly. A flush of shame spread over his face. He was giving his son advice on letting go. Yet they both knew neither of them was allowed such liberties when Theodore's mother was anywhere near. After that brief conversation, his father never had much to say.

Growing up, Theodore didn't know what a real family was all about. When he observed Prissy's family and Daniel, he was beginning to understand. They shared a bond Theodore would never be privy to. Wolfgang made that clear with his recent instructions. Wolfgang gave the others explicit orders, "Don't tell him anything."

I was so wrong about what he thinks of me.

But he hadn't just been wrong. He'd been a fool. He'd been taken in by Wolfgang's riveting eyes and supposed kindness. He'd had the ridiculous idea that he mattered to someone. He had to accept the awful truth. No one gave a damn about him. The fact was so hard and hurtful it brought tears to his eyes. He quickly swiped them away as he let himself out the back door. He couldn't believe he was actually crying. He despised the weakness that made his chest cave and his throat tighten.

I hate them all!

He jogged across the backyard, heading for the large expanse of woods and rock that backed up against the property. It was a private game preserve that afforded quiet, natural surroundings. As a child, he'd always found solace there. He played a game about space visitors and how he'd been dropped off on Earth for a while. Someday his true parents would come back for him. He was sure of it. He scanned the night skies looking for their ship, a grand flying machine that would take him home. Of course, it was a child's story, and he was always disappointed in the end. But he wasn't a kid anymore. He needed to face reality.

As he made his way into the thicket of evergreens and bush, his cell phone rang out with his mother's ringtone. It was late, but she knew he loved to stay up when they were away. He quickly dug into his jeans pocket and retrieved the phone. His mother didn't like to be kept waiting.

"Hello, Mom?" He paused to listen to her usual barrage of questions. "Don't worry . . . yes, I'm keeping everything clean, just like you told me. Yes, I'll remember to vacuum. Yes . . . I know . . . I will."

When his mother was satisfied and Theodore's answers were the right ones, he was able to disconnect. Afterwards, he stared at the phone. He'd just come from a room where Wolfgang, Amelie and Prissy all interacted with each other with unrestrained affection. That kind of fondness seemed foreign to Theodore when he thought about his mother.

Does she really care about me?

Her greeting was always the same when he came home from school. She granted him a sterile 'hello' that was as cold as her bedroom. It never included a welcoming smile like Amelie had given him.

Never.

Maybe his mother didn't know how to smile. Maybe she was only capable of handing out orders with a miserable face. "Take off your shoes! Wash your hands! Do your homework! Can't you see how tired I am taking care of you and your father?"

But wasn't there supposed to be some demonstration of love, some gesture of kindness? Wasn't a mother supposed to offer a little warmth to her child?

Has she ever once hugged me?

His mother always gave him the impression he wasn't measuring up, so he tried harder, with chores, with school, and with his attitude. None of it made any difference. Things never changed.

What does she want from me?

His hand tightened on the phone as he squared his jaw against a reality he lived day in and day out. His future was clear. It would be more of the same, just like it was for his dad. The thought was such a horrible one that he hurled the cell phone into the brush.

* * *

"Theodore! Where are you?" Prissy had searched everywhere in the house. She called out the back door and hoped Theodore was in the yard. He'd mentioned that he liked to sit outdoors and gaze at the stars. "Theo! Answer me!"

Amelie joined her at the door. "Still no luck?"

"No." Prissy crossed her arms. "I thought I saw him sneak out of the bedroom, but where could he have gone?"

"Maybe he was hungry and went out to get something."

Prissy looked at the clock on the microwave. "At this hour?" She went to the refrigerator and opened the door. "Look at the shelves. I don't think he needed to go out for food. He said his mom arranged for a grocery delivery twice a week."

"His mother must really care about him."

"Mom, he's sixteen. He can go shopping for himself. His mother must be a control-freak. That's probably why Theo is so nervous all the time."

"Did you find him?" Daniel asked as he walked into the kitchen. He headed towards the coffee pot and frowned when he saw the empty carafe.

Amelie went over to where Daniel was standing and began looking in the cupboards above the counter. "Theodore has vanished."

"He's probably hiding somewhere."

Amelie handed him the coffee and filters.

"Thanks, I could use some caffeine for this headache." He rubbed the back of his neck. "It's been building all evening."

Prissy noticed how strained Daniel's face looked, but she immediately shielded her thoughts. She couldn't let him know she remembered their times together when she was a child and he was like her older brother.

I really looked up to you, Daniel.

How different it was then. He could be so kind around her. His hard barriers were softened by a gentle quality. Once, when she'd had a bad spill on her bike, he carried her all the way home. He'd held her carefully, soothing her cries with his calm, caring voice. She had clung to him then, enjoying how protective he could be when she was in trouble.

Why did you have to change?

She walked over and stood behind him. "Let me massage your shoulders. It always helps Dad."

Daniel glanced back in surprise. "That's nice of you."

She started kneading his tense muscles, feeling the knots of worry and stress, trying to work them out. "Dad needs you to be in good shape, that's all." Her hands were small but strong. She knew how to use just the right amount of pressure. After a moment, she could feel Daniel's shoulders relax a little.

He sighed. "You're very good at this."

Amelie smiled proudly as she took the coffee pot to the free standing water dispenser in the corner of the kitchen. "Prissy can be very tuned-in to people. She has a lot of intuitive abilities when she wants to use them."

"Good, then tune into your friend, Prissy. Your dad is asking to see him."

Prissy let go of Daniel's shoulders and returned to the back door. "I don't know where that little jerk went. I can't believe he'd just leave us. What if we need him again?"

Amelie poured the water into the coffee maker. "Maybe he went for a walk in the neighborhood."

Prissy shook her head. "No, he went this way, into the woods, I'm sure of it."

Amelie looked up at Daniel. "Maybe you should go after him. He might be upset."

Prissy spun around. "Why would Theodore be upset? He's not the one who has a father who some maniacs want dead."

Amelie's face was thoughtful and petitioning. "Prissy, my dear, Theodore has been dragged into our mess, a mess he hasn't a clue about. And yet he took a chance with his own life to help us."

Prissy stood her ground, bringing her brows into a hard line of defiance. "I told him I was grateful. I should think that's enough."

Daniel gave her a disapproving glance as he walked over to the door and stared out. "Listen princess, you may think the whole world revolves around you and your family, but it doesn't. That hole in your father's chest is proof of that."

Prissy started to protest, but Amelie stepped forward before she could reply.

"Daniel's right, Prissy. We're all still in danger. We need to stay aware of that fact and pull together. We also have to be considerate of each other's feelings." She looked over at Daniel. "What do you think we should do about Theodore?"

Daniel moved away from the door. "If the kid has run off, maybe he'll do us all a favor and keep going."

* * *

Wolfgang lay propped up on several pillows. He could breathe a little easier now that the antidote had started to take effect. Fortunately, Daniel had enough medical training to retrieve the bullet from his chest. It was lodged in muscle and hadn't affected any vital organs. The deadly, viral agent was the problem. Most wouldn't have survived its effects, but he was stronger than most. Daniel's quick delivery of his own blood had also helped. But Wolfgang wasn't thinking about his recovery. He was thinking about Theodore and how careful he wanted to be in telling the boy about who he really was and about what had happened to him. The boy was so nervous and unsure already. Wolfgang would approach the subject in a way that didn't frighten him more than necessary.

Theodore looks so young and unprepared for being sixteen, but that's understandable.

Theodore's genes and body chemistry had been a plaything for the WKA. Yet the boy's eyes still held something the WKA couldn't change. They reminded him of Daniel and their father. Their dad was Wolfgang's best friend before he was killed. As Wolfgang remembered the man's strength and courage, Daniel walked into the bedroom.

"What is it?" Daniel asked as he put a large mug of steaming coffee on the bedside table. "Feeling better?"

"I do, but I'm smiling because I'm looking forward to talking to the boy. Where is he?"

Daniel shrugged and sat down. "The idiot ran off."

Wolfgang winced at Daniel's tone. "Why are you acting like this? Is your heart so closed you can't even care a little about your brother?"

"I already had this argument with Amelie. He's a lost cause."

Wolfgang knew it was useless to dispute the issue with the determined, younger man. "Where do you think he went?" he asked, trying to sit up.

Daniel gave him a warning look. "Relax, your body needs time to recuperate."

"We don't have time. This is the boy's house. So the WKA must have put him here."

Daniel's face lost all color. "You're right. Oh hell!" He stood up and began to pace. "Why didn't I think about that?"

"Don't be so hard on yourself. You've had a lot on your mind." Daniel's self-condemnation was obvious. He'd been so busy trying to forget who Theodore was that he'd been negligent in his appraisal of the situation. "Do you have any ideas about what the WKA is up to?"

"I'm sure they're monitoring him in some way, maybe not constantly, but at least sporadically. They also have some mind scanners who are talented. Let's hope they aren't too efficient or too interested." Daniel paused, running his hand through his hair, his eyes shifting rapidly as if he was sifting through his knowledge base on the WKA. "He's probably got a tracking device implant too. We don't dare take him with us."

"Are you crazy? He's coming with us."

Daniel scowled back. "You have to let him go. He's nothing but trouble at this point."

Wolfgang tried another attempt to sit up. Daniel wasn't the only one who could be inflexible. "I won't give up on him."

Unfortunately, Wolfgang's body wasn't able to go along with his conviction. His body was heavy and lethargic. It took all his effort to swing his legs over the side of the bed. He grabbed hold of the mattress to keep from falling over. Once he was stable, he used what breath he had to issue an order. "Find the boy, now."

"Yes sir, you're the boss."

Wolfgang gasped in a breath trying to maintain his balance on the edge of the bed. The world was spinning. He quickly braced a hand on the headboard. "Do you want to take over? If that's what you really want, why did you save me?"

45

Daniel blinked back a couple of times as if he had to clear away the pain the question evoked. "Do you think I could let you die?"

"If you have a clean conscience, it would have made things easy."

"I do have a clean conscience. I also have a sense of what's right. I don't want to be leader by default. I want to lead because it's best for the pack."

"Then start being a leader now. The boy is one of us. Help me get him back where he belongs. After that, we'll go after the group that did this to me. If all goes well and we're successful, I'll be happy to let you take charge if that's what our people want."

"You'd step down?"

"When my father died, I felt it was my duty to lead. But if you're better for the job, that's fine."

"What about Prissy? Someday, you could hand the reins over to her."

"That's the old way, Daniel. Yes, my family has ruled this pack for three hundred years, but now times are different. You might believe I don't think in those terms, but I do."

Daniel stared back in surprise. "I'll do everything I can to retrieve the boy, but don't expect me to care about him."

"Leave him to me. I promised myself long ago that I'd bring him home if he was still alive. After all these years, I'm getting a chance to keep that promise."

"I hope you know what you're doing."

Chapter Seven

Tracking Theodore was the last thing Daniel wanted to do. At least the chore was an easy one. With his enhanced ability to see in the semi-lit darkness, he picked up the boy's trail of heavy footprints and broken brush. After ten minutes at a fast lope through the woods, he could sense Theodore's immediate proximity. He could almost feel Theodore's heartbeat. But the end of the trail went around in circles, in and out of the trees like the kid had been pacing and thrashing about aimlessly. The undergrowth was a mess of gouged-out dirt where he'd obviously been kicking at his surroundings.

The kid's an idiot, just like I thought.

From the looks of the trail, the boy was also confused and upset. Daniel would have to be somewhat diplomatic if he wanted his retrieval task to go smoothly. "Theodore! It's Daniel," he called out in a firm but patient voice. "I've come to take you home. Prissy is asking about you."

A stirring breeze and the sound of rustling grasses answered as he paused and listened. "Theodore!" he called again.

It would be easy to tune into the boy's mind and thus his location, but Daniel refused to subject himself to experiencing Theodore's thoughts and his inadequacies a second time. "Listen, kid, save us both some trouble. I'm tired. I don't feel like having to hunt you down."

"Leave me alone," a voice cried out from above.

Daniel looked up. Theodore sat on a thick limb of an old tree. His chunky body was silhouetted against a starlit sky. "Come down here now!"

"Why? So you can send me on another errand? What do you need now?"

"Listen, smart ass, I'm trying to protect you. Your house isn't safe. We have to go somewhere else, and I'm wasting time standing here having this discussion."

"Just go. I'll be fine. I'm planning on leaving home anyway."

"Oh really? When did you decide that?"

"I've been planning on it for a long time."

Daniel let out a worn sigh of disgust.

Like you'd last five seconds on your own.

Still, he was dealing with an immature teenager, one whom Wolfgang insisted on reclaiming.

Stay calm and use a little psychology.

He recalled his college days and the course he'd taken in human interaction. "Fine, but Prissy wants to say goodbye."

"Really, she said that to you?"

"Yes, she likes you."

Theodore let out a loud, contemptuous laugh. "You're hopeless as a liar."

Daniel narrowed his eyes. "If you're not down here in thirty seconds, I'll be up there to drag you down by the scruff." He moved back several feet as he spoke. "And don't think about throwing up on me, or you'll wish you were dead and buried."

Silence followed Daniel's threat, but he could feel the boy's mind working. Theodore got the message, loud and clear. Finally, the boy shifted his weight on the limb above and began to climb down the tree. His movements were slow and cumbersome.

Daniel watched with disbelief. When he was Theodore's age, he was extremely agile, able to scale trees, boulders, or whatever else was in his path. Gauging from Theodore's present abilities, he was sure the boy would be ready for a walker by the time he was forty. "Are you just being difficult or are you really that pathetic?" he asked as Theodore jumped the last three feet and landed in a crumpled heap.

Theodore's eyes narrowed, but his face flushed red. He was the kid who was used to being the butt of jokes at school, the person people dismissed as inadequate. After he dusted himself off and started towards the house, his backward glance in Daniel's direction was one of resignation.

Daniel moved past him and took the lead. "Don't fall down again. I don't feel like carrying you back."

Theodore stopped abruptly. "It must be so easy being you. You're strong and tough, and you know how to get your way by pushing others around, people like Prissy. But people like you suck!"

Daniel kept going, refusing to be goaded by the boy. "Think about me any way you want, but I'm the guy who'll have to save your butt if things heat up. Then you'll be happy that I'm tough."

"Maybe, but tonight I had to save yours. Obviously you didn't want your friend to die."

Daniel turned around. "You ran a quick errand. What's the big deal?"

Theodore's face flushed again. He lowered his gaze and scuffed the dirt. "I guess you're right. I'm just a coward."

Daniel felt a rise of anger. He was doing everything he could to forget who Theodore was, but somewhere, deep in his memory banks, he remembered his baby brother. He was a happy little boy, a strong healthy child who laughed easily and loved his big brother. *Now look at what he's become.*

He cursed under his breath as he walked back to where Theodore stood. Being a good four inches taller and ten years older, he needed to give the boy some advice. "Stop acting like some helpless, little kid. You're going to be a man soon. Behave like one."

Theodore slowly lifted his eyes. But once their gaze connected, he didn't flinch. His fists tightened as he studied Daniel for a long moment, as if he was gauging Daniel's counsel and Daniel himself. When he turned away, he began to run through the woods, moving with the grace of a lumbering bear. His awkward gait was painful for Daniel to watch. Still, he had to admit that the boy, who thought he had no courage, had spunk enough to stand up to him. Maybe Wolfgang was right. Maybe the WKA hadn't completely ruined his brother.

Stop it! He's nothing to you. Leave it that way, or you're going to open yourself up to a hell of a mess.

* * *

The group decided to vacate Theodore's house in favor of a safer location. Theodore sat nervously in the back seat of the vehicle they were using for travel. "Do we have to take my mom's SUV? She's going to be very upset if anything happens to it. She just got it six months ago."

"Again, I'm sorry about all of this," Amelie said. She reached across Prissy, who sat between them in the back seat. She put her hand on his. "I wish we had another option, but we don't have much choice. Daniel's car is too small for all of us. And we have to stay together."

Her reassurance made Theodore pull back with embarrassment. Why should he be concerned about his mother's car when people's lives were at stake? Why did he always worry about everything?

Daniel, seated in the driver's seat, stared back in the rearview mirror. "We're going to a friend's cabin. There's nothing to worry about. Now put the blindfold on," he ordered as he backed the car out of the driveway.

Theodore obediently put his mother's silk scarf over his eyes. What choice did he have? On the other hand, he was glad Daniel insisted he come along, that he wasn't still stuck in the woods. After running off earlier, it felt kind of good to have someone come after him. Of course, he must have looked pretty dumb when he was discovered up in a tree. Still, his lofty perch gave him a unique perspective. When he looked down, the waning moonlight made Daniel's face look surreal in a powerful, confident superhero sort of way. It was hard to admit, but he admired the older man. At the same time, he knew there was definitely something different about Daniel. Was he an alien too? The ridiculous idea reminded him that he was great at making up stories. But he was too old for that. Like Daniel said, he had to start acting like a man. But how would he manage that impossible feat?

Just go to sleep and forget it all.

He gave himself the suggestion and became instantly alert. Instead of relaxing, his mind came alive with an attentiveness that was very different than his normal way of thinking. It was almost like he was waking up after a long, drugged sleep. He ignored the feeling, knowing it was probably just his nerves acting up again.

Chapter Eight

Prissy was stuck between Theodore and her mother in the back seat of the car, but her focus was on Daniel. Did he believe what he'd said about everything working out? Did he really know what he was doing? She tried to tap into his thoughts and had to give up after a few minutes. Like most adults in the pack, he could easily shield his mind from an inexperienced person like herself. She crossed her arms with annoyance. Her father insisted that Daniel was loyal. She hoped it was true.

"Everything is going to be fine, sweetheart," Wolfgang said in a breathless tone. He was in the front passenger seat and was obviously monitoring her thoughts with ease.

"I know," she said sharply. She didn't want to react disrespectfully, but his remark made her feel like a child who needed daddy to make everything all better.

Wolfgang tried to reply, but his words were cut short by a bout of coughing.

Daniel glanced over at him with concern. "You have to try to get some sleep. You shouldn't even be out of bed. This virus has done a lot of damage."

Prissy knew Daniel was right about one thing. Her father's condition was precarious at best. She had watched him earlier, trying to stand up and nearly fainting with the effort. It seemed all he could do to sit upright in the passenger seat. By the time they were a few miles out of town, he'd blacked out again.

Please, please don't die!

The words kept repeating in Prissy's mind as she stared at her father's hand lying on the console. It was still and lifeless as he slumbered between life and death. How many times had that hand been there for her, wiping away her tears, touching her face to reassure her? How could she even think of life without that constant guiding hand showing her the way? Her mother was sweet and supportive, but Prissy felt like her true strength came from her father. She'd known others who'd lost a parent, seen the hollow way they went through life afterwards. But to think it could happen to her was the worst thing she could imagine.

A soft touch on her knee brought her out of her morbid reflections. She turned to look at Theodore. "What is it?" she whispered.

He withdrew his hand at once. "What's going on? Is your father sleeping?"

She swallowed hard, happy that Theodore was blindfolded and couldn't see her tears. "Yes, he's just napping."

She lied, trying to spare him. Theodore seemed very concerned about her father earlier. While Daniel was attending to other duties, Theodore practically carried her father to the car. His hand shook as he helped put on her dad's seatbelt. She caught a glance at his eyes. They were kind and considerate as he cared for her father.

Theo can be irritating, but he does have his moments.

So why should she get him upset now, by telling him the truth? He was already too jumpy. In fact, she'd never met anyone who was so constantly on edge. Was that why she liked him, because she was the strong one around him?

I don't think so. Theodore might be stronger than me.

He once told her he felt like he'd been alone his whole life. But instead of becoming bitter, he still kept trying his best. If she were in his shoes, she doubted she would have been that capable.

* * *

Daniel watched the miles slip away as he drove out of the city. Wide expanses of empty land lay on either side of the highway. There was almost no traffic, only an eerie calm as the car sped forward into the darkness. It was quiet inside the car as well, giving him time to think. He had to make sure he stayed ahead of the WKA from now on. He had taken precautions with the borrowed SUV before they left. He switched license plates with a neighbor's vehicle. It wouldn't be easily tracked. Daniel also tidied up the house, making sure there was nothing left behind to indicate they'd been there. There was one other issue to ponder, his agreement with Wolfgang. The more he thought about being the future pack leader, the more he realized he'd made a mistake.

I must be crazy to want the position.

He was starting to understand what Wolfgang really dealt with. The people side of leadership was a wearing responsibility. Amelie and Prissy were clearly in a state of panic over Wolfgang's condition, especially when he passed out again in the car. It seemed like a constant battle just trying to reassure them. Presently, both mother and daughter were exhausted, and their ability to cope was nil. Getting them to calm down was an achievement. As for Wolfgang, Daniel could only hope he'd rally. The antidote wasn't a sure thing. There was still a chance the pack's leader wouldn't make it.

And the boy? He's my problem until Wolfgang recovers, if he does recover.

As soon as Daniel focused on Theodore, the questions started to pour in. How had all the genetic tampering affected the kid? Had he been engineered to accept the WKA's programming completely, but on a subconscious level? Was he programmed in some way to betray his own blood?

Daniel could only hope Theodore had some of his lineage intact, that he wouldn't turn on them all. If he did, Daniel would be forced to put him down like a mad dog. How would he do it? Shoot him? Give him a fatal dose of poison?

Listen to yourself. You're thinking about killing him, but why? The fiends got hold of you too. Why can't you remember more about what they did to you? You might be the one who's programmed. Maybe that's why you feel so cold when you look at him? You called your brother a thing. That's how the WKA refers to our kind.

* * *

Amelie sat in the back seat of the SUV, listening to Wolfgang's labored breathing, the way he fought for air. With each moment that passed, she fell deeper and deeper into a sense of regret. Wisely, she made sure to keep her thoughts private. She didn't need Prissy or Daniel knowing her misery. She was sure they had enough to worry about.

But if anything happens to my sweet Wolfgang, I don't think I'll ever forgive myself for how I've been acting.

She wasn't able to read minds, but she had been blessed or cursed with some gifts herself. She could literally feel Wolfgang losing ground. He was drifting away from her again. His condition provided a sharp contrast to his normally strong, steady presence. She had challenged that strength and steadiness repeatedly in the past few months.

She frequently argued with her husband, badgered him with her wants and desires. She wanted to try some experimental drugs and procedures that could enhance her abilities. But why? Why had she felt so compelled to convince him that she needed to change?

The answer is simple. I want to be more like him.

It was true. She wanted to know and feel what his kind knew and felt.

But he likes me just as I am.

Sitting in a stranger's car, running from maniacs who might kill them all, she wanted to laugh at the absurdity of her wants and demands. She should have been grateful to Wolfgang. How lucky could she be to have a husband who adored her, who accepted her and constantly fought against her desire to change who she was? Why couldn't she share his viewpoint? Why did she have so much trouble accepting herself?

Stop hiding from the answer, Amelie. You have to face the truth.

She knew Daniel had tried to point it out to her earlier. Little by little, as the years rolled by, she'd begun to use an excuse when she felt herself failing. She told herself that she was only human, a norm.

When she thought about it now, it seemed a poor excuse indeed. Couldn't a human be just as capable and responsible in handling and protecting life as a werewolf? Wolfgang thought so. She closed her eyes and remembered something he'd said to her shortly after they met.

"The spirit, the will, and the ability to love and be there for each other, is in all of us. That's what we have to hold onto."

I agreed with him then. But somewhere along the way, I despaired over being human. But why?

Daniel came to mind again, but it wasn't the adult Daniel she envisioned. It was the younger version of him, the boy who came to live with them after his father and stepmother were killed. Amelie's kind, the WKA, had tortured him to the point that left the once bright, beautifully-gifted child unable to cope. Amelie couldn't bear to think about what he'd endured. Neither could she forgive what had been done to him. She began to hate what her fellow humans were capable of doing.

When she tried to make up for what he'd been through, to give Daniel all the love she could give, it seemed weak and useless in comparison to the violence he'd suffered. Maybe that was the beginning of her downfall. Maybe that's when she started to lose faith in herself and her ability to make a difference. Perhaps Daniel had distrusted her because he'd read her mind back then. He knew she didn't trust herself or her kind.

But it wasn't the love itself that was lacking, was it? It's how I thought about love, and how I believed I didn't measure up.

Where she had failed Daniel, Wolfgang stepped in. Her husband was able to inspire the boy again, to give him purpose.

Almost too much purpose.

She smiled, but there was sadness too. As he matured, Daniel began having ideas of his own, ideas that challenged Wolfgang's. Her husband was yielding, but Daniel wasn't. There were arguments. In the end, Daniel decided to strike out on his own.

Did Daniel ever know how much I cared about him? Did he know how much love I wanted to give him?

It seemed too late to worry about it, especially now. Because of her recent judgments and her stupid failure to keep her thoughts to herself, she let him down again. Daniel sat in the front seat, a few feet away, but the true distance between them seemed impossible to bridge.

Chapter Nine

When the car eventually stopped, Theodore felt stiff but attentive. He heard the sound of a garage door closing. He estimated that they'd been traveling for at least a couple of hours. The entire time he'd been hoping and praying that Wolfgang would survive. Even if he'd been angry with the man before he ran off into the woods, Theodore had had a change of heart. Before they started on their journey, Wolfgang had called him aside and spoken to him privately. Again the ailing man had been kind and apologetic.

"I know you don't understand what's going on," Wolfgang explained. "I know we must seem different to you, strange—"

Theodore cut him off. "No, it's not true! You're not strange, you're—" It was hard to put his feelings into words. Vague impressions filled his mind, and the more he was around Wolfgang, the clearer they got. Somehow, he knew Wolfgang was very special. There was a graciousness in the way he looked and acted. Even in his fragile state of health, there was a nobility about him. In Theodore's world of wishful thinking, Wolfgang's face could have belonged to one of his favorite heroes. If Wolfgang clad himself in armor, he could have been another King Arthur. But Wolfgang also wanted to talk about Daniel.

"Daniel may seem harsh," Wolfgang said quietly, "but he's trying to help you. Remember that and try to be patient. But no matter what passes between the two of you, you're not alone anymore. I'm here if you need anything."

Theodore had smiled back mutely. Wolfgang's pale blue eyes were filled with a deep understanding and comfort that mesmerized him, lulled him into a feeling of safety. But maybe the older man was handing out false hope. Wolfgang could easily die, and Theodore would be alone again. He'd just found a friend, but for how long? His question was interrupted by Daniel's voice.

"Hey kid, are you listening to me?"

Theodore jumped. "What did you say?" he asked, coming back to the moment.

"Take the blindfold off and get your butt out of the car," Daniel said in a gruff voice.

Theodore removed the silk scarf and did as he was told. He looked around at the inside of an unfinished garage. "Where are we?"

Without answering his question, Daniel grabbed hold of his wrist and yanked him forward. "Come with me."

Theodore resented the rough treatment and tried to pull away, but resisting Daniel was like struggling with a guy who threw around tree stumps for a living. "Where are you taking me?"

"I need to lock you up for a while."

"What do you mean?" Digging in his heels, Theodore continued to fight as he was dragged towards a door in the corner of the garage.

"What are you doing, Daniel?" Prissy asked as she watched what was happening.

Daniel's reply was quick and to the point. "Your friend could be programmed to betray us. I can't take any chances."

"Programmed?" she asked.

Theodore pulled harder. "Betray you? Why would I do that?"

"Because you probably wouldn't be able to help it," Daniel said as he clasped Theodore's wrist more securely and led him into a small room. When Daniel flipped on the light, it cast a shadowy glow on the dull, beige walls and scant furnishings. There was a twin bed, a night table and a chair.

As Theodore glanced around, trying to acquaint himself with the small space, Daniel pushed him towards the bed.

"I don't understand any of this," Theodore protested.

Daniel moved back to the door. His orders were simple. "Go to sleep. I'll check on you in the morning."

Theodore stared back with growing anxiety. Daniel seemed bent on being a total jerk, but there was something else about the man that was frightening. Daniel was hiding something, something that felt very threatening.

Daniel seemed to notice Theodore's fear. His hard eyes softened for a brief instant. "You'll be fine," he said almost apologetically. He quickly walked over to the closet and grabbed a blanket off the shelf. When he came back to the bed, he held it out like a soft, woolly, peace offering.

Theodore reached for the blanket. He began to shake, like an animal shakes when someone tries to act all casual and nice just before they pull out a gun and shoot it in the head.

* * *

While Daniel showed Theodore his sleeping arrangements, he succeeded in keeping his emotions in check. Then he saw Theodore's eyes. They were dark, brown pools of innocence that stared back at him with distrust and alarm. For an instant, he almost lost his grip on his uncompromising control.

Oh hell, don't be such a brute. The boy has already suffered enough. Don't add to his trauma.

When he handed the boy a blanket, he got another jolt. He saw Theodore's slightly crooked fourth finger. They had both inherited the same genetic, family defect. It was a horrible reminder. Daniel could put any definition he wanted on the boy, but his brother was standing a few feet away from him.

"I'll be back later," he said as he went to the door to leave. It was everything he could do to reestablish his icy indifference, but he had no choice. Like he explained to Prissy, Theodore was a danger to them all. As if to prove it to himself, he gave the boy the most callous, parting gaze he could manage.

* * *

Wolfgang opened his eyes and glanced around the unfamiliar bedroom. The sound of someone throwing up in the adjoining bathroom had roused him out of a deep sleep. He immediately thought of Amelie. Did she have the flu? A moment later, he knew it wasn't her. No, this was a man being sick.

He glanced over at the chair next to the bed and noticed a laptop resting on the seat. The screen was facing him. Squinting, he could make out the bolder print at the top of the document that was displayed on the screen.

"My results and conclusions after experiments on subject, S114 by Dr. N. Brady."

"Oh no," he groaned with understanding. He knew at once what the file contained. His thoughts instantly went out to the wretched sounds in the bathroom. "Daniel, are you alright?"

There was a soft moan and a pause. "Yes, I'll be out soon."

He listened to the water running from the tap, to the splashing sounds. Finally Daniel emerged from the bathroom.

Wolfgang sighed. "You're not alright. You're white as chalk."

Daniel remained in the doorway, taking short breaths. After a moment, he swallowed hard as if he had to push back another urge to vomit. Finally, he walked unsteadily to the window and stared out. His shoulders drooped as he held his stomach.

"Talk to me," Wolfgang urged.

Daniel gave him a quick glance and went back to staring out at the darkness. "A while back, the group I worked with managed to get their hands on some of the old WKA files that we weren't aware of. I didn't have the guts to look at some of them before. Now I had no choice. If possible, I had to find out what they did to the boy, if we have to worry about him."

Wolfgang gave the laptop another glance and braced himself. He had to know what Daniel had learned. He had to tune into Daniel's mind and ferret out the details of the experiments performed on subject S114. Daniel didn't put up any barriers to Wolfgang's endeavor. His mind was wide open, like that of a child who had just witnessed a gruesome murder.

It didn't take long for Wolfgang to check out the facts, to know more than he wanted to know. "Oh lord," he cried as he tried to process the horror that flashed between them. Now, he was sick and gagging with revulsion too. "You should have let me read the file. You shouldn't have tried to take it all on yourself."

Daniel moved to a chair and sat down, staring at the floor. "Those cruel bastards . . . what they did to him . . . how is he still alive?"

"But he is," Wolfgang said, still fighting his stomach. "That's what's important."

Daniel's head shot up. "I'm going to kill them all someday," he said in a seething whisper.

Wolfgang was still tuned in to Daniel's mind as it filled with memories of his baby brother. Images of a curly-haired cherub with bright, shiny eyes and rosy cheeks gave way to flashes of a child screaming in pain.

Daniel's next words came out in a rush. "My little brother was so happy. He never cried as a baby, not until he became the object of the WKA's experiments. They're worse than monsters! How can anything so vile be allowed to walk this earth?"

Wolfgang watched as the younger man's body stiffened, as his color deepened. He didn't need to tune into Daniel's mind to feel his consuming wrath growing with each intake of breath. If that wrath wasn't contained, it would soon replace Daniel's ability to reason.

"Daniel, don't go there," he ordered in a steady, hard voice. "It's not going to help. You have to hold it together if we're going to get through this. Theodore's already proven he's stronger than they are."

His entreaties had no effect. In fact, Daniel's eyes took on an overly-bright, blazing quality that made Wolfgang brace himself for what was coming next. He was sure Daniel was going over the edge.

* * *

Daniel couldn't stop what was happening to him. Knowing what his brother had been subjected to triggered something lethal in his gut. His hatred was so intense, he was suddenly afraid of what he was becoming. He was turning into a killing machine, a monster of revenge that wanted to obliterate those who'd hurt him and his brother so grievously. Gritting his teeth, his only recourse was to remain frozen in place as the blinding rage ravaged his mind and body. In the background, Wolfgang was pleading with him.

"Listen to me, Daniel, please. Theodore made it, but if you don't rein in your feelings, you won't. You'll be so filled with hate it'll destroy the person that you are. Don't let them do that to you."

Daniel tried to hold on to the admonition. It became a small line of defense as he fought the living firestorm in his gut. Wolfgang was right. If Daniel let his feelings have their way, he'd be worthless to those depending on him. The WKA would win.

Wolfgang grabbed on to the side table and tried to sit up. "We'll help the boy come back to himself. We'll do whatever we need to do."

"You didn't see him in the woods, the way he moves like some clumsy animal!" Daniel shrieked out the words as his breath heaved in and out. "He's pathetic!"

"I understand," Wolfgang argued. "But we have to see more than that in him! He has your father's blood, your blood!"

"Don't you think I know that?" Daniel stumbled over to the wall opposite and fell against it heavily. Bent over, he held himself as the rage was joined by a despairing grief over what Theodore could have been. His brother would have been extraordinary. He would have been handsome and generous and amazingly capable just like their father.

Wolfgang gave him a weak smile. "Your dad was my best friend. You remind me so much of him, Daniel."

A brief memory of his father washed over Daniel. He could almost feel the powerful man's hand on his shoulder, shoring him up, reminding him to be strong no matter what. Concentrating on the memory, he regained a little of his control. "I just need a few minutes," he said finally, trying to assure himself as much as Wolfgang that he was capable of directing the powerful forces inside of him.

But his mind wouldn't stop going back to what he'd read. When the WKA abducted Theodore, they had the perfect specimen to study and test. Daniel's baby brother became their lab animal, enduring endless experiments that involved pain tolerance, his reactions to various toxic and bacterial substances, surgeries, and genetic tampering. The list went on and on.

As Daniel went over it all, he knew his fears about the boy were right all along. He was more certain of it than ever.

Theodore didn't survive because he was strong. Nobody's that strong. He survived because the WKA wanted him to. They wanted to use him.

He was certain of that now. Theodore was placed back into society, into an adoptive family where he was close to the pack's headquarters. He was programmed to infiltrate their world, to lead the WKA to his own kind. And he'd done just that in a roundabout way. Prissy sought him out, didn't she? And it was because Theodore still retained something familiar that pulled her in. Theodore was like poisoned meat that baited the WKA's trap.

Slowly, the fire inside Daniel died away, replaced by the cold hard facts of what they were dealing with. It wasn't a question anymore. He knew what had to be done. Theodore had to go.

He looked at Wolfgang with a calm but unwavering resolve that replaced all of his heated dialog. "Hear me out. No matter how good your intentions are concerning the boy, we have to dispose of him."

Wolfgang blinked back with complete disbelief. "If that's what you think, the WKA has won."

Daniel's eyes ignited once again. "He's better off dead than living like some crippled pawn of those heartless villains!"

"No, he's not! Theodore is still your brother! But you won't let yourself see that!" Wolfgang's passionate outburst was followed by a physical reaction. He fell back against the head board and grabbed for his chest.

"Wolfgang!" Daniel forgot everything as he realized what was happening. The pain in Wolfgang's heart was escalating, seizing the vessel in a crippling attack. Daniel put his emotional angst on hold as he rushed over to the bed. He put a hand on the older man's chest. "You're killing yourself worrying about all of this!"

"It'll pass." Wolfgang shut his eyes. After a minute, he began to breathe easier. Finally, he looked up at Daniel and smiled encouragingly. "I'm going to make it, Daniel, because of you. You were there for me. You gave me a chance. Now give your brother a chance."

Daniel stood motionless, staring back at the man who'd taken his father's place. When Daniel was scared as a child, Wolfgang was always there. Sometimes, when Daniel screamed and kicked and went wild with grief, Wolfgang wouldn't let him go. He held him close, using his embrace as a shelter, a place where Daniel could feel a measure of safety.

"Please, do this for me," Wolfgang asked in a barely audible whisper.

Daniel couldn't fight Wolfgang's pleading eyes or his request. Taking the icepack off of the nightstand, he put it on his own forehead and sat down on the bed. He moaned as he felt its cooling surface sooth the pounding that jarred his brain. As the moments passed, the fire in his gut also began to recede. If only for a little while, he had to give in to Wolfgang's appeal.

He finally broke the silence with a last concern. "The WKA put a tracking device in the boy about six years ago when he supposedly had his appendix out. I'm hoping it's not functioning anymore or that they're not monitoring him that closely. But I think even you would agree we have to remove it, and soon."

"Remove what?" Prissy asked as she and Amelie came in from the hallway. "What are you talking about?"

Daniel looked at Wolfgang for direction.

"Better fill her in," Wolfgang said as he closed his eyes.

Daniel knew that Wolfgang didn't like involving his wife or daughter, but there wasn't much choice. With the events that were unfolding, the two women needed to know more of the facts.

Chapter Ten

Locked in a windowless room, Theodore fell asleep after he realized it was useless to try to escape. When he woke up he had no idea about what time it was. He only knew he was scared. Earlier, when Daniel had turned to lock him in, the intimidating man had a certain cold, unfeeling look in his eyes. Movie hit men had that look when they were ready to take someone out. Too tired to worry about it then, he woke up with an instant replay of those eyes in his mind. Did Daniel's scary gaze have something to do with his mention of Theodore betraying them?

"Why would I betray them?" He sat up and hugged his knees. It was his favorite pose whenever he got anxious as a child. It was easy to revert back to the behavior considering his situation. Daniel couldn't be trusted. Theodore could sense it so deeply, his body began to shake.

"You're always making everything seem like it's a life and death situation," his mother sometimes taunted. "Why can't you relax like a normal child?"

He rocked gently as he thought about her words. Was she right in this case? Was he seeing things in Daniel that were the truth or just an illusion brought on by his imagination?

He released his knees, sat up straighter and tried taking deep, slow breaths. "She's right. I do make everything a thousand times worse than it really is. How many times have I panicked and nothing came of it?"

Instead of Daniel's eyes, he thought about Wolfgang's heartening statement.

He said I'm not alone. If only I could believe him.

For the second time in the past few hours, Theodore's thoughts about the older man were interrupted. The lock in the door turned. As it slipped into place, it made a snapping sound. Theodore's breath was cut short as the door swung open. Daniel stepped into view. Theodore squinted at him, bracing himself for the worst. Fortunately, Daniel no longer looked like a hit-man. This time the man studied Theodore with unconcealed regret.

Theodore tried to ignore Daniel's attitude. He tried to remind himself that Daniel was simply a jerk. But in the end, all he could feel was a deep and bitter anger. He was so tired of being branded a loser, but that's how Daniel regarded him. It was etched on the man's face. The feeling was so shaming Theodore would almost have preferred it if Daniel was a hit man. A bullet through his brain might be easier in the long run. At least it would be fast and lethal. It would put an end to always being seen as someone to be pitied. The label was fast becoming intolerable. So was the fear Theodore carried inside, the fear of not knowing what was going to happen to him. He'd had it tormenting him as long as he could remember. When he spoke, his voice was tinged with fresh anger when he thought about more of the same. "What now?" he asked with a glaring scowl.

Daniel remained in the doorway, but he didn't answer. Instead, Prissy came into view. She was small and pretty as she slipped by Daniel and entered the room.

"Hi Theo," she said sweetly, walking over to the bed. "How are you?"

Prissy's cheerful, sugar-coated tone was definitely worse than a bullet through the brain. She had to have an agenda to be so nice. Would he be sent out a second time? Would he be used by Daniel for some new and dangerous mission?

Theodore pulled up his knees and began to rock again. When he caught Prissy's eyes staring at him, his order was short and curt. "Go away," he ordered.

Prissy acted as if she hadn't heard him. Instead, she offered a smile and issued her own order to Daniel. "Let me talk to Theodore alone."

* * *

Daniel closed the door and waited outside of Theodore's room. He needed to give Prissy some time to accomplish her goal. After she heard some of the less graphic details about Theodore's past, she wanted to help. She insisted that she would be able to comfort him, to gain his trust. Afterwards, with Theodore's cooperation, Daniel would take care of the tracking device problem.

His plan was simple. He'd give the boy an injection to put him under. When Theodore was asleep, Daniel would remove the tracking device. It was probably located close to the surface, so it wouldn't be a big deal.

* * *

Theodore sat on the bed with Prissy sitting next to him. He was trapped in a small room with someone he didn't trust. He kept his eyes leveled on the opposite wall. Earlier, Prissy had been nice in the car, but he didn't think she was really concerned about what happened to him. His anger was expressed in a volley of questions. "What do you people want from me? I already helped you. Why couldn't you leave me at my house? Why did I have to come with you and get locked up like a prisoner?"

"We aren't 'you people,'" Prissy objected. "We care about you."

"Liar! You're just like Daniel!"

Prissy bristled. "What do you mean?"

He tried to control the quivering response in his muscles. His body was shaking like it had so many times. Yet, his mind seemed capable of breaking out of its normal pattern. For once in his life, Theodore felt like he could stand up for himself. "People who care about others don't act like you two. They don't make a person feel small and worthless."

Prissy clamped her jaws shut. When she finally spoke, she was frowning, but apologetic. "If I've made you feel that way, I'm sorry."

"I've heard your apologies before. Afterwards, you came uninvited into my home, threw me aside like I'm nobody and bossed me around. Your apologies aren't worth much." If this group of strangers was going to sacrifice him, at least he'd have the courage to let them know he hated them for it.

"Well, thanks a lot," Prissy said in a sulky voice. "I thought you liked me, that you'd be happy to help when I needed you."

"I did want to help. That's why I got that stuff from Daniel's house. But what good did it do me? You let your ignorant friend lock me up."

Prissy blushed. "I guess I have been a little rude."

He let go of his knees and stared at her. "Rude? You've been horrible," he said as he rubbed the painful bruise on his ribs. He'd got it when Prissy slammed him against the wall the evening before.

Prissy crossed her arms. "You have no idea about how much I'm going through."

"What?" All the countless slams he'd received from bullies throughout his life all began to converge on the moment. "Whatever you are going through is no excuse for meanness!" he shouted.

"Listen you," Prissy argued, "I came in here trying to be your friend, but it's clear you're only interested in being a self-righteous pain!"

Theodore glared back and was about to reply when the door opened.

Daniel stepped inside the room. "What's going on in here?" he asked.

Prissy shot Theodore a hateful look and stood up. As she started for the door, she gave Daniel a seething explanation. "Theodore is a dumb, stupid idiot! That's what's going on!"

Theodore watched Prissy stomp out of the room and followed up with his own explanation. "Prissy is a brat who has no idea about how to treat people!"

Daniel smiled back at him. "Finally, we have something we agree on."

"Like I care what you think," Theodore grunted back. He dared to meet Daniel's eyes briefly. That's when he noted Daniel's reaction, how rigid he became, like he was actually affected by Theodore's rejection. The moment didn't last. An instant later, Daniel's flickering eyes steadied into their usual stoniness as he walked over to where Theodore sat.

"I want to talk to you about something," Daniel said as he was about to sit down. He hesitated long enough to reveal a medical kit from behind his back.

Theodore immediately pulled away. "What's that for?" He'd always been on guard, always afraid of something jumping out and grabbing him. Suddenly, there was an added element in his reaction. He was becoming more and more aware of what was under the fear. He felt his muscles clenching and unclenching, as if his body was preparing itself. The feeling began when he connected with Prissy's father. Wolfgang's penetrating gaze and encouraging words had infected Theodore just as the virus had infected the older man. The effect was spreading, invading Theodore's cells, flooding his tissues with a sense of readiness. "What's going on?"

"It's nothing, relax," Daniel replied. "Did Prissy say anything about your connection to us?"

Theodore shrugged. "Am I connected?"

"No, of course not," Daniel said with a smile. At the same time, he pulled out a syringe from his pocket and began to remove the protective cap. "Just take it easy. This will be over in a second."

Theodore didn't hear Daniel's soothing tone. He was fixated on the needle. Terror coursed through his physical vessel. Normally, that terror would have frozen him to the spot. This time his body came alive. Something inside broke through the icy spell that usually kept him cocooned and immobile. He didn't feel sick or want to throw up. His body shifted out of the deep lethargy he'd always known. It became fully engaged and aligned with its power. He didn't have time to question what was happening. With a quick internal shove, a forceful bodily presence pushed aside his mind and intentional thought. In an instant, he was a new kind of consciousness, keenly alert, leaping out of his seat with legs that went from wobbly to powerful and lithe.

His quick response took Daniel totally by surprise. As the man's eyes went wide and his hand shot out to grab Theodore, his fingers missed their mark. He didn't get a second chance. Theodore dashed across the room, threw open the door and raced through it before Daniel had time to get up.

* * *

Prissy was walking towards the bedroom to check on her dad when she heard footsteps. They came from behind her. Someone was racing up the stairs from the lower level, garage area where she had visited Theodore. She turned around in time to see a person explode into the room and rush towards the window. There was no hesitation. The person crashed through the glass and disappeared from view. The drop was a good eight feet.

"Oh my gosh!" Prissy cried as she ran to the broken pane.

A moment later, Daniel burst into the room and rushed over to stand next to her.

"You've got to be kidding!" he yelled. "The kid's gone completely feral!"

Prissy stared out the open expanse where the glass had been a minute earlier. She saw someone running. They were moving very fast. They soon disappeared into a dense thicket of bush and rock that bordered the property. She glanced at Daniel. "Was that Theo?"

"Yes!" Daniel shouted as he turned and ran for the front door. "Stay here and keep an eye on everything. I'll be back as soon as I can."

Daniel had barely exited the room when Amelie came running down the hall from the bedroom. She called out as she ran. "Are you alright, Prissy? I heard a crash."

Prissy didn't know what to say or how to interpret what she'd seen. She was usually able to weather whatever came her way as long as it didn't involve her family. Now her body shuddered with alarm. All the werewolves she knew became a more gifted and attractive version of a human being when they changed. The person who jumped out the window looked wild and primitive.

She tried to steady her voice as Amelie hurried to her side and hugged her. "Mom, I think I just saw Theodore, but I didn't even recognize him."

* * *

After Amelie propped Wolfgang up on a couple of pillows, he signaled for her to sit down next to Prissy on the bed. "Let me explain some things," he began. "You know how I said Theodore and Daniel were taken by the WKA. Well, there was a reason why they were targeted. Their great-grandfather was a different kind of werewolf. He was what we call 'one of the old ones,' a kind of throwback to what we were long ago. Most of his kind were killed in a massacre in the late eighteen hundreds."

"What is Theo, some kind of animal?" Prissy asked with concern. "I only got a glimpse of his face, but it was almost inhuman. I never saw any of us look like that."

"I've never seen any of his kind either," Wolfgang said with a sigh. "But I suspect Theodore's transformation was so fast that he had no chance to control what he became. Even our brand of werewolf could look inhuman if we didn't teach our children how to manage and direct their gifts."

"Daniel said he's gone feral. What's that mean?" Prissy asked.

Wolfgang rubbed his forehead, trying to explain what it did mean. He'd never had to deal with someone like Theodore, but he'd heard stories. He was sure Daniel had heard the same descriptions. "I can only guess he's lost touch with who he is. You thought he looked like an animal because that's kind of what he's become. His physical nature has temporarily overcome his normal reasoning abilities."

Amelie put her hand on Wolfgang's. "Will he try to hurt Daniel?"

"I don't know. The old ones were supposed to be extremely capable warriors, but they were brought up in a pack. They knew how to handle and integrate both the human and animal parts, just like us. They were simply more connected to their instinctive origins. Theodore never had a pack to teach him anything. He's also been genetically altered. I don't know what he's capable of or how rational he'll be considering the state he's in."

"Maybe I should help Daniel," Prissy said with concern.

"No!" Amelie and Wolfgang shouted out the word in unison.

"You stay here with your mother and take care of her," Wolfgang ordered. "Is that clear?"

"It's clear." Prissy's voice was obedient, but her face contorted into a determined grimace. "But if Theodore hurts Daniel or tries anything around either of you, I'll show him what a wild animal is really like."

Amelie returned a thoughtful look. "I understand that you want to protect the people you care about, but that doesn't mean you want to hurt anyone, right?"

Prissy let her shoulders relax a little. "No, not really."

Wolfgang gave Prissy an encouraging smile. "No matter what happened, I'm sure Theodore is frightened. More than anything, he needs to feel safe. He needs to know that we're his family, and that we want to support him."

* * *

Prissy left the bedroom and her parents with a lot to think about. It was hard to know how to feel, especially about Theodore. In spite of his rudeness when they talked earlier, she knew she still liked him. Of course, she'd never seen his other side before. But the more she thought about it, the more she realized that anyone could look scary when they were out of control.

Theodore's never had anyone explain things to him. He doesn't even know who he is. That has to be tough.

Prissy knew exactly who she was, and she still had a hard time controlling her emotional swings. Supposedly, things would even out once she got through the change she was going through.

Theodore must be going through the change too, a much more intense change.

Her stomach tightened as she contemplated running wild through the woods with him.

The dope might even be fun if he learns to be civilized and stops jumping through windows.

She frowned when she remembered how her father said they were all family. She knew she didn't want that. She had other ideas about what he should be. Of course if Daniel couldn't catch him, Theodore might disappear forever.

Chapter Eleven

The sun was still rising in the early morning sky as Daniel made his way into the stony landscape. It wasn't as easy tracking Theodore this time. He was having trouble catching up with the boy. Sparse, stunted trees and hilly terrain surrounded the house, and Theodore had instinctively taken an escape route through some of its wilder, rockier parts.

Daniel wasn't prepared for hiking or a full-out run. He was wearing his leather-soled, Brunori loafers. He kept losing his footing on slippery slopes and dry brush. He cursed Theodore as he found himself constantly fighting to stay upright. He almost forgot how he'd gotten himself into the mess he was in. When he thought about it, he felt responsible. Theodore must have been very frightened when he saw Daniel with the medical supplies. But one thing impressed Daniel. Theodore's transformation was amazing. The WKA hadn't taken the werewolf out of him after all, at least not all of it.

"The kid is strong and fast," he complained aloud as he stopped to check the trail next to a small creek bed. With a brisk, southerly wind, Theodore's scent was being carried away from Daniel. After five minutes, he finally picked up the trail again, but he knew he'd lost a lot of valuable time. "Great, he's smart too."

Once more, Daniel started running. He also sent Theodore telepathic messages. He was confident the boy would hear him now that he was in touch with his true werewolf nature. Hopefully, Theodore would believe Daniel's assurance that he meant no harm. Of course that was asking a lot since Theodore obviously saw Daniel as a threat.

He crested a steep, open area and became preoccupied with his failure to gauge Theodore and the situation correctly. He chastised himself for his mistakes, upset that he wasn't behaving like he normally did. He wasn't thinking as clearly as he should. With his mind on what he'd been doing wrong, he forgot to focus. He didn't see the deep crevice on the other side of the rock face until it was too late. Jumping over it blindly, he landed with one foot in a narrow crack. It remained lodged in the crevice as his body followed through. An incredible pain shot through his ankle as he fell.

* * *

Theodore stopped running as soon as his body tuned into the one following him. There was good news. His pursuer was hurt and disabled. After sniffing the air as an extra precaution, he knew he could rest and take stock of his own condition. His breathing began to slow, but his jaws remained open. Drool dripped freely down his shirt as he climbed to the top of the highest boulder in the area.

He surveyed a wooded area below and breathed out a low snarl of warning. His brown eyes, now nearly black and glowing with an intense wild glare, scanned the entire landscape around him. He noted its features in great detail. Once he was satisfied that he was safe from any intrusions, he sat down. He began to pick out bits of glass from his hands. In general he hadn't suffered any significant cuts. After the glass was removed, he began to lick his wounds.

While he tended to himself, he remained on alert. His hearing was so acute that a squirrel, leaping onto a branch twenty feet away, made him jump to his feet without a second's hesitation. When he was satisfied there was no threat, he lowered his head and voiced a deep growl of displeasure. His warning made the small creature scurry to a higher branch.

"Theodore, where are you?"

Strange sounds startled him. They made him pause as he started to sit down. He checked the landscape again, but the noise wasn't coming from the environment. It was in his head. He listened more closely, but nothing he heard made any sense. His bodily response was a violent shake of his head as if the noise was from an insect buzzing too close to him.

"Theodore! Listen to me, please. It's Daniel."

This time the words pinged a different part of his brain. Instead of shaking his head, he shut his eyes in confusion. When he opened them, he blinked, trying to understand what was happening. He was in touch with the natural world around him, but the gibberish in his head was different. It made him anxious. How did something so foreign get inside of him?

Just the idea of an alien presence made his body go rigid. It also made him start to itch uncontrollably, especially around his abdomen. He pulled up his shirt and stared at the scar on his gut. He began to growl again, instinctively aware of something beneath the surface of his skin. Whatever it was, it belonged to those who'd hurt him long ago. He had to get it out.

He leaped off the rock and began to search around in the dirt. Where had he tossed the sharp slivers of glass? The sun, coming out from behind a cloud, shone down on a shiny piece a couple of feet away. Snorting, he picked it up, knowing what he had to do.

He sat back on his hunches and began his tedious procedure. He used the glass to slice his way through the skin and surface flesh, breaching the old scar tissue. He growled with determination in spite of the pain. After probing and repeatedly fingering the opening, he eventually found what he was looking for. When he finally got it out, he stared at the small metal object in his bloody hand. Just the sight of it made his lips go back, exposing his teeth as a savage snarl rose in his throat. His next actions were automatic. He set the hated thing down and grabbed a large stone. He needed to rid himself of the thing completely. He beat the metal object, pounding it repeatedly. As he did, a rage began to surge through his body. He used it to continue slamming the object over and over until it was reduced to small fragments that disappeared into the surrounding dirt and brush.

Spent but satisfied that he was free of the thing he hated, he climbed back to the top of the boulder. He sat down and let out a heavy sigh. He was tired and hurting. His wounded side throbbed and his arms and hands were sending out their own signals of pain.

He started licking his arms and hands once more, trying to comfort himself with slow, deliberate strokes of his tongue over the many abrasions. His blood tasted salty and pleasing. After a few minutes, he lay down. The sun's warmth was comforting too. It helped to sooth his tense muscles. After a few minutes, he fell asleep.

* * *

Daniel sat on a large rock, trying to grasp the extent of his injuries. After a few probes and squeezes, he threw up his hands in disgust. "Stupid, stupid, stupid!" He'd been careless, and now he was in trouble. He probably had a hairline fracture plus a possible torn ligament. Even with his amazing healing abilities, he couldn't possibly expect to catch Theodore. It would be hours before his body repaired itself enough to really walk normally. In the meantime, he was stuck.

"Listen, Theo. I have to tell you something important. I need you to come back now. Help me, and I promise not to hurt you . . . ever. I give you my word." As he replayed the message over and over, he realized that he meant what he was saying. Wolfgang was right about Theodore. Damaged or not, the boy was a survivor. He'd proven he was also capable and smart.

He's my little brother, and I'll never do anything to add to his pain again.

It was a nice thought, but would Theodore believe it? Daniel had behaved very badly around the boy. There was another consideration. Theodore wasn't a normal werewolf. He'd gone feral. Daniel wasn't sure about what that meant, but he had a bad feeling in his gut. He suspected that his message wasn't getting through to Theodore.

* * *

Theodore woke up so abruptly he nearly rolled off of the rock where he'd been sleeping. He had to hug the hard surface to keep from slipping further. When he checked out his position, his fear of heights kicked in. He let out a startled cry that shattered the tranquil scene. If he wasn't careful, he'd fall a good ten feet unto the smaller boulders below him. He had to claw his way back from the rocky edge. Once he was safe, his mental processes took over. Where was he? He felt like he'd been cast out into the wilderness. But who put him there? He was also in pain.

Look at my hands and arms! I'm covered with cuts. And my side hurts really bad.

He was tempted to pull up his shirt, but it was bloodied and stuck to his body. He decided it was better not to know what he'd find if he ripped it off.

Think, think about what you did last.

The last thing he remembered was talking to Daniel. Had the guy done something to him? Nothing came to mind, but maybe he'd been hypnotized. But why would Daniel go to all the trouble to deposit him on a rock? And where did the cuts come from?

"Theodore, for the umpteenth time, can you hear me?"

"What?" He sat up straighter and listened to a voice coming through his own jumbled thoughts. It was Daniel's voice. Without even thinking about it, he answered the man telepathically.

"Daniel? Is that you?"

"Finally! Yes, it's me! Where are you?"

"I'm sitting on a rock, but I don't know where."

"That's okay. I can guide you back to me."

"Why would I want to come to you? You'll probably lock me up again. And you had a needle. What was that for?"

"I promise not to lock you up. And I'm sorry if I frightened you."

"Why should I believe you?"

"Because you are my brother, Theo, and I care about you."

The announcement was so unexpected. Theodore nearly pitched off the boulder again.

"It's another lie, isn't it? You're just telling me more lies!"

"I know you don't trust me, but it's true. If you let yourself, you'll know it too."

Theodore shut his eyes. He wanted to believe Daniel. He'd always dreamed he had a brother. But it was just a story he'd made up when he was a lonely kid. Now, Daniel could read his thoughts and was trying to use that story. But Daniel couldn't be trusted.

Who can I trust?

Wolfgang came to mind. In a world filled with liars and people who hurt him, Wolfgang was different. Theodore believed in what the older man had told him. Maybe he had to trust Daniel too, especially since he was in the middle of nowhere.

Daniel! Tell me how I can find you.

* * *

If Daniel felt frustrated with his injuries, he felt like he'd go mad trying to get Theodore to understand his directions. The boy was definitely challenged when he was in his normal, rational state. After an hour and a half of trying to get him to traverse a scant three quarters of a mile, Daniel didn't think he could go on much longer.

"Theodore, for the love of all that's good, are you feeling anything yet?"

"I feel how angry you are with me! But I can't feel which direction to go in."

Daniel counted to ten before he answered. He knew it didn't help, but he had to do something to vent his frustration.

"Theodore, my idiot brother! I can feel you, and you're going in the exact opposite direction. You took a wrong turn. But you're very close, I know that."

"Hey! I'm getting something."

"You are?"

"Yes! I see you! You're sitting on a rock looking very upset."

Glancing up, Daniel realized Theodore was only seventy feet away. The sight of the boy lumbering along like an old man was too much. He wanted to cry, but not because his brother was an idiot. He wanted to cry because his nerves were in shreds. Theodore's behavior acted like a dull instrument of pain, sawing away tediously on every sensitive fiber in Daniel's body. Still, he had to hide his misery around the boy. Theodore was confused enough already. He held up a hand and waved in Theodore's direction.

Theodore waved back and called out verbally. "Are you okay? You look so pale!"

Daniel tightened his jaw, reminding himself that patience was a virtue. "Just get over here, please!"

Theodore responded and picked up his pace. As he got closer, he called out again. "Thanks for not giving up on me."

Daniel could feel Theodore's desire. He truly wanted to be Daniel's brother. Daniel tried to smile back. His reserves were gone, but he forced himself to look happy.

His simple gesture made the boy move faster. Theodore was only ten feet away when his face broadened into a wide grin. "I made it," he cried out. His triumph was cut short when he tripped. He wasn't looking at where he was going, and he went flying forward, landing heavily on the stony ground.

"Ow, ow!" Theodore's cries carried through the still air.

Daniel did feel a tear now. He couldn't help it. He was cursed. The kid was a complete moron when he was sane, and he was like a crazed animal when he transformed. Yet he found himself caring about Theodore anyway. His brother hadn't only affected his nerves. As he guided him back, as he tapped into the boy on a deeper level, Daniel knew Theodore's heart and intentions had a purity that Daniel would never have believed possible after what had been done to him.

"Are you alright?" he called out with real concern.

Slowly, holding the bright red stain on his shirt, Theodore began to get up. "Yeah, I guess so."

"What happened to you?" Daniel demanded when he saw the blood.

Theodore slowly walked over to where he was waiting. "I don't know. I was afraid to look, but my side really hurts."

"Come here, let me check it out."

Theodore froze. "No!"

"Don't be a baby. I just want to see what's wrong."

"You promised not to hurt me, remember?"

Daniel saw the fear in Theodore's eyes and swallowed his anger as he thought about the origins of that fear. "I keep my promises, Theodore. I won't hurt you."

Theodore knelt down next to him and moved his hand aside. As Daniel lifted up his shirt, Theodore looked away.

"Sorry, I can't stand the sight of blood," the boy said with a flush of embarrassment.

Daniel examined the ragged flesh wound. It was deep and dirty. He didn't know what caused the mess he was looking at, but he realized it was where the WKA's transmitter must have been located. Something told him that it was gone. "How did this happen?"

Theodore grimaced. "I told you, I don't know. I woke up on a rock, and I had these cuts and my shirt was stuck to my side."

"Okay, don't get upset about it. If you don't want to tell me what happened, we'll talk later."

Theodore stared back warily. "Did you leave me there, on that rock?" His tone was defiant and confused.

Daniel had to take a moment to understand what the boy was saying. He finally realized Theodore had no idea about what he'd done or what had happened to him. "No, I was looking for you."

"Then how did I get out there?"

"You ran away again."

Theodore sat down next to Daniel. For a long moment he studied Daniel as if he was trying to decide something very important. "I think you're telling the truth this time," he said as he turned his gaze skyward. "I guess that means I'm an alien after all, probably a schizophrenic one. That's why I don't remember."

"Maybe you're something a lot cooler than an alien," Daniel laughed. "What if you're a werewolf?"

Theodore shrugged. "I don't think I'd like that at all. Think about all the shaving I'd have to do."

Daniel smiled back. "Not that kind of werewolf. You've been watching too many movies."

* * *

Using Theodore as a crutch, Daniel was careful as they made their way back to the house. His ankle was healing, but he wanted to give it time to really mend before he put any demands on it. If the WKA or the splinter group tracked them down, he wanted to be in good form to fight them off. "How's your side holding up?" he asked as they neared their destination.

Theodore was slumping under his burden. "The same. Thanks for tearing up your shirt and using it as a bandage. It looked expensive."

Daniel sighed. "I guess you're worth a couple hundred dollars. Besides, there are some clothes back at the cabin I can wear."

Theodore paused. "Really, your shirt cost that much? My mom complains when she has to spend forty bucks on me."

"She's not your real mom."

"I know. She told me I was adopted long time ago."

"Didn't you wonder who your real parents were?"

"Why? Look at me. If my real parents are anything like I am, I don't want to find them."

Daniel jerked his head around and pulled away. "Don't ever think that way about your parents!"

"Sorry." Theodore looked down as his face filled with color. "I know you said that you're my brother, but I still can't believe it. In case you didn't notice, we're nothing alike. I think you made a mistake."

Daniel looked away too. If only Theodore could have known his real mother and father, how much they loved him, how would he have turned out? Would the two of them be more alike if Theodore had never been taken from his parents, from Daniel? Putting his arm around Theodore's shoulder again, he decided that it didn't matter. "I didn't make a mistake."

Chapter Twelve

As Amelie carefully dressed the last of Theodore's wounds, she tried not to let him see her distress. She'd nursed injured werewolves, but none of their wounds looked like Theodore's. His were red and swollen. The one in his side was starting to ooze. He didn't appear to be healing.

"You've been very brave, dearest," she said with a smile. "You hardly flinched."

Theodore let out a gasp of relief, but he didn't reply. Instead, he glanced over at Prissy who was sitting close by.

Amelie realized Theodore had been putting up a brave front for her daughter. He'd held it together in spite of the blood and cleaning and other unpleasantries he'd endured. A couple of times, he'd looked like he was going to faint, especially when he saw the bloody pieces of gauze or when she had to forcefully remove the dirt and grime from his deeper wounds. Still, he hung in there with gritted teeth and a determination that impressed her even if Prissy looked unfazed.

"I appreciate your help," Theodore said as he eased off the kitchen table. "Now I think I'll lie down for a while."

Amelie reached out and put her arms around him. She hugged him tight against her. "Yes, rest is a good idea," she said as she held him for a long moment more.

Theodore smiled when she let go of him. "What was that for?" he asked as if he been given a prize he didn't deserve.

She looked back with affection, seeing the surprise in his eyes. He wasn't used to anyone really caring about him. "You're very sweet, Theo."

"Thanks," he said shyly, turning away quickly as if he was afraid she'd see him blush. After a moment, he glanced at Daniel. "Do you want me to use the room by the garage?"

Daniel was sitting in one of the other kitchen chairs, acting as if he didn't see Theodore's embarrassment. He shook his head. "No, use one of the back bedrooms."

"Right, thanks," Theodore said as he started to walk slowly and with obvious pain down the hallway. "If you need me for anything, wake me up."

Amelie heard him close the door to a bedroom and motioned for Daniel and Prissy to follow her into the living room. "I need to talk to you. Something isn't right with Theodore's wounds."

"I wondered about that," Prissy said as she flopped down into a recliner. "Why aren't his injuries healing? Look at Daniel. It's been about the same amount of time, and he's already much better."

Daniel sat down on the sofa, crossed his leg and massaged his ankle with a frown. "They did a lot of testing on his immune system and his other defenses. His abilities are probably compromised."

"What about traditional medicines? You know, antibiotics? Maybe they'd work," Amelie offered.

Daniel shrugged. "When we were talking on the way back here, Theodore told me he's allergic to most medications. I guess he was a sickly kid as long as he could remember and has tried everything."

Prissy sat up and smiled. "What if he changes again? His body chemistry would change too, wouldn't it?"

Amelie gave Prissy a positive nod. "That could be a possible answer."

"There's a little problem," Daniel said curtly. "You know he can't remember changing. He doesn't know how to change."

"What made him change before?" Prissy asked.

Daniel looked away. "I scared the hell out of him. His body went into autopilot."

"Well, let's scare him again!" Prissy insisted in a sharp tone. "Otherwise, knowing Theodore, he'll probably end up dying on us."

"Prissy, what a thing to say!" Amelie corrected.

"Sorry." Prissy's cheeks turned crimson. "I mean we have to do something, don't we?"

"I don't want to scare him," Daniel replied. "I promised him that I'd protect him from now on."

Prissy stood her ground. "Yes, but he's in trouble. Besides, I didn't make any promises."

Amelie shot Prissy a glance of motherly caution. "You have to be careful. Theodore went through a window the last time. Besides, he hasn't any control. He might even be dangerous."

"Yes, especially to himself," Daniel said. "I'm sure he sliced open his side when he sensed he had a device implanted there. Who knows what else he might do with the memories he has stored in his subconscious."

Prissy smiled again. "What if I give him a little demonstration? I could show him how it's done."

"Honey, he doesn't know what he is, what you are," Amelie said. "You could frighten him."

Prissy's brows narrowed. "I'm not some kind of monster, Mother. I don't change into something primitive like Theodore."

Daniel stopped massaging his ankle and sat up attentively. "You're right, Amelie, but Prissy has a point. If we could give him a crash course, so to speak—"

"What kind of crash course?" Wolfgang asked as he crept into the living room.

Prissy jumped up from the recliner and ran over to him. "Dad, you're up."

"You have a little more color," Amelie said as she helped Wolfgang into a second recliner.

Daniel smiled. "You look like you're feeling stronger."

Wolfgang settled back in his seat. "The bouts come and go."

"It's a good thing you're better," Prissy said as she kissed her father's cheek. "We have Theodore to worry about now."

"Why? Isn't he okay?"

"No, he's not," Prissy announced. "He needs to be scared out of his wits so his body can heal itself."

Wolfgang stared at her for a long moment. "Scare him out of his wits?"

Daniel leaned forward. "What she's trying to say is that Theodore is so disassociated from his gifts, he's unable to heal like us. Prissy came up with the idea of getting him to change—"

"Which he can't do on his own," Prissy interrupted. "So we have to make him change."

Amelie noted that Daniel groaned as Prissy chatted on. The formidable bachelor wasn't used to being around the younger set. "Are you alright, Daniel?"

"I think I need some rest too. Excuse me, everyone," Daniel said as he got up and started out of the room. "I'm going to get a quick power nap before we tackle Theodore's feral side."

"That's a good idea," Wolfgang agreed. "We'll take it one step at a time. When you wake up, we'll get a plan together."

Prissy eyed Daniel as he limped out of the room. "What's his problem? Why is he rubbing his forehead like that?"

Amelie exchanged a look with Wolfgang. Her husband's barely visible smile let her know they were both thinking the same thing.

She'd never seen Daniel look so fatigued and drawn before. Maybe, it wasn't just Prissy and Theodore that were getting to him. Perhaps the young man was also learning that leadership entailed much more than he bargained for.

Chapter Thirteen

Theodore lay in his bed, tossing and turning for over an hour. He needed sleep, but his side was killing him. He also felt incredibly hot. He was sure he had a fever. He always got fevers. He'd had them so often in his childhood that he'd spent half of the time in a tub of ice water. It was the only way his mother could cool him down. That's what he needed now, ice. He forced himself out of bed and made his way to the kitchen. He passed an adjoining bedroom on the way. Its door was half open, and he noted that his brother was stretched out on the bed. Daniel looked as worn as a limp, rag doll. Obviously even tough guys had to take a break.

On the other side of the hall, the door to another bedroom was closed, but he could hear Prissy's laugh coming from the room. Her father and mother's voices soon joined Prissy's.

"Good, they're all occupied. That means they won't even know I'm up," he mumbled as he went to the refrigerator. He grabbed the container below the icemaker to see if he was in luck.

"I'm saved," he whispered. There was also a bag of ice that Daniel had picked up on the way to the house. It was a double blessing for Theodore. In his condition, he needed all the ice he could get. He collected the supplies as quietly as possible and went back to his room. With his own private bath, he didn't have to bother anyone. He'd cool down and maybe even fall asleep in the cold water.

Finally, my luck must be changing.

He had a brother. And while Amelie was cleaning his wounds, she told him he was family. It was a heady thought that made him smile as he put his supplies down on the vanity in the bathroom.

Now, if I can get my temperature back to normal, maybe I can enjoy this new turn of events.

He turned and locked the door. He wasn't a prude, but he did like his privacy. It had always been hard to relax in a bath when he knew people were around. Within minutes the tub was filling with cold water and ice cubes.

"Oh crap, I'm going to get my bandages wet," he sighed as he undressed. He didn't have the strength to care about that now. When he saw himself in the mirror, he realized his entire body was a deep pink. He needed to soak, and fast. If the fever went much higher, he might start to hallucinate. On a number of occasions when it had happened in the past, he'd sent his mother into a panic.

But I'm too old for panicky moms.

He climbed into the tub determined that he could take care of himself.

Maybe I can start acting more confident like Daniel.

As he sat in a foot of water, he hoped to feel instant relief. Instead the water felt tepid at best even though ice still floated on the surface.

What is going on?

He had a moment of panic as he swished the water back and forth with his hand. That's when a wave of heat hit him. It spread out from his gut like he'd swallowed a blast furnace. He'd never felt so hot. Looking at his hand, he saw it go from deep pink to red. He'd never had that happen before either, not that fast. Something was wrong, very wrong. Suddenly, he was burning up. He didn't want to act like a kid, but maybe it was an emergency. He tried to get up, but he was too dizzy to stand.

"Daniel!" he screamed. "Daniel! Help me!"

* * *

Daniel wasn't only dreaming, he was having a wonderful dream. He was taking that vacation he'd been planning for years. He was staying at a five star hotel in Paris. His room was plush, decked out in beautiful antiques and marble floors. He was luxuriating in a scented bath, in a huge, garden tub with ornate, golden bath fixtures. Everything was perfect. At last, he could let all his worries go as he floated in bath salts that gave off the fragrance of balsam pine. The scent reminded him of ancient woods with towering trees.

He was sinking deeper into the warm waters when the dream shifted. A fire alarm went off. He heard people screaming in the halls of the hotel. They were calling his name. He opened his eyes and knew the voices were part of the dream, yet as he came awake, someone was still calling him. He looked up and saw Prissy in the doorway. Her face was flush with alarm.

"Daniel, quick! Get up! It's Theodore! Something's really wrong!"

He was on his feet and pushing Prissy aside the next instant. He ran the short distance to Theodore's room feeling his own panic taking hold. When he burst into the room, he saw Amelie standing outside the bathroom door. Her eyes lit up with relief when she saw him.

"Theodore was calling for you. He sounded very frightened. Now, he's not answering me."

Wolfgang, sitting on the bed, was also trying to be helpful. His face was pale, and he looked sick again as he gave Daniel directions. "The boy has locked himself in, but I'm too weak to break down the door. You'll have to do it."

Daniel didn't hesitate. "Stand back, Amelie!" he ordered. Luckily he still had one good foot to do what was needed. With a hard slam to the lock area, he succeeded in opening the door. He quickly rushed into the bathroom and looked around. He didn't know what to expect, but when he saw Theodore, he pulled back immediately. "Oh hell," he gasped.

Theodore was sitting in the tub, staring at Daniel with hard, black, menacing eyes. They were the eyes one saw in nature films. Theodore reminded Daniel of a bear sitting in its den, awake and cranky after its winter nap. Daniel knew better than irritate him. Instead he backed out of the bathroom as quickly as possible and closed the door behind him.

Amelie, Prissy and Wolfgang all looked at him expectantly.

Amelie was the first to speak. "What's going on, Daniel?"

Daniel held up a hand. "Everybody, listen to me," he whispered. "Be very quiet. We have another situation. Theodore has changed again."

* * *

A half hour had gone by and Daniel was still waiting for Theodore to make a move. So far, the boy had been quiet and hadn't attempted to leave the bathroom. Prissy was waiting with him. She sat in a chair across the room, tapping her foot impatiently. When she looked at Daniel, her face was twisted into a scowl.

"This is ridiculous," she protested. "Thank goodness Mom made my dad go back to bed. We're wasting time. Theo's not going to do anything. He's as quiet as a kept cat. All that we've heard is a little water splashing around."

"Keep your voice down, please," Daniel ordered. "If you can't do that, you need to leave."

Prissy got up from her chair, put her hands on her hips and started towards the bathroom door. "I think you're afraid of him," she whispered loudly.

Daniel glowered back. "What do you think you're doing?"

"I'm going to take a peek, a quick look to see what's going on, that's all."

Daniel was fast enough to beat her to the door and bar the entrance. "You'll do no such thing! I'm in charge here. I'm responsible for you. Now sit down."

"Coward," she taunted, but she did as she was told.

Once Prissy was seated, Daniel let out a weary exhalation. He wasn't afraid of Theodore. But if his brother was combative, Daniel couldn't make any more mistakes. He'd have to handle the situation as carefully as possible. Yet he had to admit, he was tired of waiting too. He gave Prissy a warning look to stay put. "I'll check things out."

"Fine," Prissy pouted, "as long as somebody does something."

Daniel took a final calming breath and reached for the door knob. He never got a chance to turn the handle before the door was jerked open from the other side. Theodore stood in front of him, wearing only briefs. The boy's eyes went wide as soon as he saw Daniel.

"What are you doing here?" Theodore asked with surprise.

Daniel let out a sigh of relief. Theodore looked himself again. "I . . . uh . . . you called for me, remember?"

Theodore scratched his head and paused. "Oh, I did, didn't I? But I'm fine now. I took a cold bath, and I'm good." He held out his hand. "See, I'm back to my normal color." He began to smile as he looked at his arms. "Wow, my cuts are almost healed."

Daniel agreed. "Yes, you look much better."

When Theodore fingered his gut, his smile turned into a grin. "I don't understand. I've always been a slow healer."

Daniel stared at the place where the deep wound in Theodore's side had been. In less than thirty minutes, the area looked almost normal. That was fast, even for his kind. "That's great, but I have a question. Did you have any unusual experiences while you were in the bath?"

Theodore's face went flush. "Oh yeah, I did. It was really bizarre, something about a weird creature. I think I was hallucinating. I guess my fever got too high."

"Theo?" Prissy stepped into view. She'd been in the corner of the bedroom, obeying orders. Now her curiosity seemed to get the better of her. "You're okay?"

Theodore retreated a couple of feet and grabbed a towel to put in front of him. "What are you doing here?" he asked with annoyance.

Prissy pushed her way in front of Daniel. "Don't be so shy, silly boy."

Theodore frowned. "Don't call me a boy!"

Prissy moved towards him. "Then don't be so uptight. You had some ugly looking wounds earlier. Let me see how you're doing."

Theodore's hand tightened on the towel. "Get back! You shouldn't be here."

Daniel could see and feel how uncomfortable Theodore was with Prissy around. "Prissy, stop it! Leave Theodore alone."

Prissy didn't pay him any attention. Instead, she rushed forward and grabbed Theodore's towel. "Don't be such a prude, Theo," she said as she tried to yank away the towel.

Daniel watched as Theodore's face instantly went from a flush of embarrassment to a much deeper shade of anger. "Prissy, leave him alone," he ordered. But the warning came too late.

* * *

At first, Theodore tried to get Prissy to back off because he didn't like her looking at his exposed body. He wasn't in very good shape, and he didn't feel like having her check out his extra pounds. But she wasn't listening to him. Instead, she taunted him, called him names. Next, she tried to bully him by grabbing his towel. That's when his anger escalated. He was tired of people messing with him, pushing him around.

As the words, silly boy, replayed in his brain, he knew he hated being the object of Prissy's ridicule. The hate part started to fill him with a deep seated rage. He knew the volatile feeling was there, but he had always kept it hidden. He didn't want anyone to know about his emotional extremes or the crazy thoughts he sometimes had. At times, when the feelings got too intense, he felt like he could explode.

As Prissy continued to play her tug of war, he backed up against the sink. He was trapped. He'd never get away from her or from all the people who forced themselves on him.

At the same time, he felt his body jerk back, but there was no place to go. As he tried to hold on to his towel, his body jerked again, but this time, he didn't move externally. Something inside of him took over. Again, a powerful hand had hold of him, shoving away the part of him that he knew as himself. It was the creature's hand, the one from his hallucination. It hit him with so much force, his mind blacked out.

* * *

Prissy never saw her kind change so fast. One minute she was playing around with Theodore. The next minute, he was snarling at her.

Daniel was almost as fast to react. He pulled her away from Theodore and threw her into the bedroom so quickly she hardly felt his hand on her arm. She landed across the room, dazed by everything that was happening. She grew up in a world of control and order. The scene in front of her was primitive and violent.

Theodore looked hideous. His handsome, boyish face was gone. All his features were hardened, sculpted into those of a wild brute who belonged in some Neanderthal world. He was hunkered down, baring his teeth and holding his head at a strange angle that accentuated his narrowed, black eyes. They were worse then his menacing teeth. They glowed with a malevolent, vengeful rage that was accompanied by low, vicious growls.

"Get your dad, Prissy," Daniel whispered to her. "Hurry!"

* * *

Daniel stood very still as Theodore warned him to back off. He took the opportunity to tune into his brother's altered mind set. Theodore was frightened and feeling claustrophobic. He wanted to escape the closed quarters of the bathroom. It was Daniel's job to calm Theodore before the situation escalated. That meant no loud noises or quick movements.

When Theodore changed, he was like a wild animal in some respects. Daniel had to avoid anything that could trigger Theodore's survival instincts. And that's what Theodore was experiencing, the need to survive. When he was outside in nature, Theodore's feral side was in sync with his surroundings. Trapped in close quarters, he could easily become upset when anything overrode his sense of safety.

"Theodore, it's okay," Daniel said in barely a whisper.

But Theodore wasn't appeased. He responded with more threatening, guttural noises. He made it clear that he was prepared to fight for his freedom, to flee the scene. Daniel couldn't let that happen. If Theodore ran again, he'd keep running. Daniel didn't know if he'd catch him this time.

"Do you know who I am? Do you know what I'm saying to you?" Daniel had read about cases of feral werewolves, about old ones who were so split their rational mind and their body's instinctive processes were completely unaware of each other. Their body self could revert to a more primitive state that didn't recognize the world of speech. He prayed it wasn't that way for his brother. "Theodore, let me know that you understand."

Theodore tilted his head. He blinked back at Daniel with softer, but confused, questioning eyes. He growled a couple of times, then whined as if he was trying to tell Daniel that he meant him no harm, that he only wanted his freedom.

Daniel's head dropped to his chest.

Oh damn! The kid doesn't have a clue. I'll never be able to reach him.

As he contemplated what he was up against, he heard the door knob clicking open. He glanced over his shoulder and saw Wolfgang letting himself into the room. "Shh, stay back. We've got a problem here. Theodore doesn't understand me. I can't communicate with him."

Wolfgang nodded. "Just relax. He might not know what we're saying, but he can feel us. He's tuned into our bodies. If we remain calm, he might stay that way too."

"I'm trying, but I can feel his mood. He's scared as hell. He wants to get away from all of us. I think we've lost him."

"No, don't go there, Daniel, please," Wolfgang urged.

* * *

Theodore listened to the soft noises the man in front of him made. It was the same gibberish that he'd heard before in the woods. But it was more soothing this time. He liked the way it made him feel. He continued to study the man and noted his eyes. They weren't like those of the hateful, insistent girl. They were kind and gentle. He started to relax a little, but a sound interrupted the moment. The sharp, clicking noise made his muscles tighten instantly. His head came up in a jerk, seeking out the source of the sound. A low rumble started in his chest as soon as he realized another man had entered the room. The odds had changed. It was two against one.

Still, he paused to listen to the sounds the men made to each other, trying to figure out what they meant. As they continued back and forth, Theodore felt his chance to escape. The one in front of him was weakening, he knew it. If he could get past him, there was a window in the room beyond. After he went through it, he'd keep running forever.

With a rush, he tried to throw the man aside, but the man wasn't as weak as he thought. The man grabbed hold of his wrists and fought back. As he struggled against the man's iron grip, a feeling of bondage surged through him, igniting distant memories. Bondage meant terror and indescribable pain. The past experiences were so vivid, he forgot about the soothing sounds the man made, his soft eyes. He had to escape no matter what. It was his life or the man's life. Never again would he let himself be captured and tormented.

His body chemistry responded as he went into a lethal rage. His body was flooded with the need to kill rather than be subdued. As the powerful forces took hold, he felt something go off in his chest. There was a sharp, stabbing pain that shot through his heart. It was followed by a horrible crushing sensation. He tried to breathe, but his lungs wouldn't take in any air. His heart's contraction was so extreme, it disabled him completely. As the man continued to hold on to his wrists, he began to fall. He was helpless to stop the continuous spasm of pain in his chest.

* * *

Daniel didn't understand what happened as he slowly lowered Theodore's limp body to the floor. Theodore had rushed at him, growling and snarling like a vicious animal. It took all of Daniel's strength to hold on to the enraged teenager. Then he felt a dramatic shift in Theodore's physical vessel just before he collapsed. As Daniel tried to calm himself and assess what happened, a hopeless feeling took hold. He was going to lose his brother. He was just getting used to the idea that life could hold good surprises when life proved unforgiving. He shouted for help as he pulled Theodore's body into the bedroom. "Prissy, get my medical case!"

"What happened?" Wolfgang demanded as he crept over. He crouched down next to Daniel and put his hand on Theodore's chest. When he looked up, his face was drawn and pale. "His heart has stopped."

Daniel remembered more details about the WKA's procedures. "Those bastards! Sometimes they implant a device next to the heart. If the subject ever goes into a killing mode, it's set up to shut them down permanently."

"Theodore didn't want to kill you, Daniel, you have to believe that."

Daniel nodded as he prepared to begin CPR on his brother. "I know, I know. He was desperate to get away. He was so afraid of being hurt again."

"Prissy, hurry up!" Wolfgang urged.

"I'm here," she said as she came running. She set the case on the floor and opened it. When she looked at Theodore, tears filled her eyes. "He looks himself again. He's changed back. He's not going to die, is he?"

"He already has," Daniel gasped.

Chapter Fourteen

Theodore was himself again, but he knew with a deep certainty that he was dead. But being dead was a relief. It was even blissful as he floated in the depths of a kind of heavenly body of water. He could breathe in the liquid as if he were a fish. There were no sounds, only a beautiful fluid light that surrounded him. It was so calming, so peaceful. After all his years of being in a world that scared him, he was safe now.

He wanted to stay in the paradise forever. He was alone, but he wasn't lonely anymore. As he relaxed more deeply, he realized the glowing light around him was alive and nurturing. It began to sing to him. A choir of soothing voices filled him with an expansive joy that dwarfed anything he'd ever experienced before. As he floated, he felt like he could dissolve into the water.

Finally, I can let go of everything.

He didn't know how long he stayed in that dreamy existence. It could have been an eternity or a second. There was no sense of time, just a pleasing, tranquil state that was being voiced by the choir.

"Theodore . . . don't leave me again . . . please!"

The choir turned into one voice. It was Daniel's voice. It wasn't as sweet or melodic, but it was enticing, like a lure a fisherman threw in the water. Theodore started to follow it. He opened himself to the feelings that were being directed towards him. Daniel's voice became a hook. It snagged Theodore's heart and started to reel him in.

"Come back, little brother. I'm just getting to know you. You can't leave now."

Theodore knew he had a choice. He didn't have to go back. He didn't want to go back. Why should he? Wouldn't life continue as it always had? Wouldn't he be subjected to more misery?

"You're wanted and needed," another voice chimed in. It was Wolfgang's voice. "You're part of us. Let us help you."

"Yes, my dear child, please come back," Amelie cried softly.

"Theo! Get back here now!" The fourth voice was Prissy's. She was her usual, bossy self, but there was a definite element of wanting in her tone. "Come back or I'll hunt you down on the other side, you big dope!"

Her demand made Theodore smile .

Now who's being silly, Prissy? You think you can tell me what to do, even when I'm dead.

He found himself laughing at how life seemed so serious on the Earth plane. Yet here, in this beautiful, fluid place where he floated, everything was light and carefree. His laughter spread out in waves, a bubble of happiness in an ocean of peaceful serenity. Again, he began to move away from the voices that called to him.

His merriment was interrupted when he felt the line to his physical life tugging again. Prissy was whispering in his ear.

"I like you. I want you back. Please, Theo, don't leave me."

Theodore felt playful, buoyed by her sweetness and her desire. She had that side that always drew him in. His laughter became words of intent. "I guess if Prissy can't live without me, I'll have to go back."

As soon as he made the decision, someone pulled the plug on his pool of repose. As the comforting waters were sucked down a giant drain, he was carried along. As he entered a dark tunnel, he had one thought that he verbalized. "Oh no, not again!" He felt like he was being reborn.

* * *

Prissy's teary face was the first thing Theodore saw when he opened his eyes. She wasn't looking at him. She was crying into a tissue.

"Priss," he said in a croaky voice. The one syllable brought everyone gathered around him to life. Prissy, Amelie, Wolfgang and Daniel all stared at him with a look of disbelief. Obviously, his experience wasn't just a dream. He had actually died.

"Theo!" Prissy cried out. "You're back." She threw herself on top of him, hugging him so hard he felt like her teddy bear, and his stuffing was going to burst.

"Stop it," Daniel ordered. "Don't kill him again. Give him air."

"Theodore, dearest!" Amelie gasped. "I prayed you'd come back to us."

Wolfgang was the only one who remained silent, but his reassuring smile and the way he reached out and held Theodore's hand was all that was needed. If he was being reborn, he felt like he had the perfect family this time around. Only his brother's face, looking worried and strained, made him frown. "I'd never betray you, Daniel," he promised as his voice returned.

Daniel smiled as he leaned in close. His voice was a whisper when he relayed his message. "I believe you, but don't scare us like that again, or Prissy and I will both come after you."

Chapter Fifteen

Wolfgang sat across from Theodore. They were both relaxing in matching, forest green recliners. The house was quiet. Daniel and the women had gone into town to get some supplies. "Just us invalids left at home," Wolfgang said with a grin. After almost losing Theodore again, he was grateful for some time alone. He'd been searching for the boy for so long. He wanted to get to know him. "Are you doing okay?"

Theodore answered with a frown. "I don't understand why Daniel thinks I have to lay around."

"Theo, a few hours ago, you were dead. I think he has a point."

"I know I've never been the healthiest person around, but I always had a strong heart. It's crazy. Are you sure I was actually, like, really deceased?"

Wolfgang let out a deep sigh and paused. "We need to talk about some things."

Theodore sat up straighter. "Talk about what? Daniel told me that the WKA abducted me as a baby, but he wouldn't go into details."

"Yes, well I think he'll want to discuss all of that later when you're feeling better. I wanted to talk about more positive things."

Theodore's expression went blank, and he shrugged.

Wolfgang looked at him with concern. "Don't you believe in good things?"

"I guess. I'm with you guys now."

"Well there are other good things in the world. Take my word for it."

"Is that why someone shot you, because you believe in good things?"

Wolfgang shut his eyes. "Okay, so there are also some bad elements around."

"Who are these bad elements, and why do they want you dead?"

"I guess it comes with my job."

"What do you do?"

Wolfgang paused and fingered the smooth fabric on the arm of the recliner. "Theo, do you believe there are some human beings who are different, maybe special? That there are those who have gifts that most don't have?"

Theodore smiled. "You mean like Daniel being able to talk to me telepathically? Yes, I believe in those things. I've read lots of books about ESP and the paranormal."

"What about you being able to hear him? Have you thought about that?"

Theodore shrugged again. "I guess I thought he made it possible somehow."

Wolfgang shook his head. "No, you made it possible."

"Maybe it's because we're brothers, like he told me. Maybe it has something to do with our genes being similar."

"You're right. I couldn't have explained it better."

Before Wolfgang could say more, his cell phone began to play Beethoven's Moonlight Sonata. "It's Daniel," he explained as he grabbed the phone from the side table. He pressed it close to his ear. "What?" As he listened to Daniel's message, he could feel the color draining from his face. "You're sure? Right . . . yes . . . I understand. Be careful."

When Daniel disconnected, Wolfgang snapped the phone shut and paused. The house felt peaceful just a moment before the phone call. Now, his heart was racing and his mind was scrambling for a plan. But he couldn't let Theodore see the chaotic thoughts he was having. He had to keep his voice calm and even. "Theodore, I know this is sudden, but we have to leave, right now."

Theodore didn't seem to notice Wolfgang's tone. He sat up and scowled back. "What is it? You don't look well. Are you having another attack?"

"Daniel has a friend who's helping us. He thinks the bad elements might have found us. We have to get out of here."

"What do you want me to do? What should we take with us?"

Wolfgang shook his head. "We don't have time for any of that. Since we don't have a car, we'll have to go on foot. We have to split up. You go in one direction, and I'll go in another. We'll have a better chance that way."

"No!" Theodore pulled back. "We have to stay together."

Wolfgang slowly pushed himself out of the recliner and stood up. He was having one of his bad moments. His body was slow and weak. Still, he'd been a leader for a long time. "Go now!" he said in his sternest voice. "That's an order."

Theodore folded his arms across his chest and shook his head. His answer was quiet, but clear. "No way."

"Please, I can hardly walk around the house without falling apart. Can't you understand that?"

"I understand that I'm not leaving you," Theodore said with total conviction.

Wolfgang understood where the boy's defiance was coming from. Theodore had been on the other side of life recently. His fear of dying wasn't as great as his fear of losing his new friends, his family.

"Please, Theo, be reasonable. It won't work. I just can't do it."

"You have to." It was Theodore's turn to issue orders. "We're going together, or I don't move from this spot. So let's go!"

* * *

The hill behind the cabin where the group had been hiding out wasn't that steep, but it felt like Mount Everest to Theodore. He

109

only paused long enough to catch his breath before he continued on. He kept an eye on Wolfgang who was walking beside him. The older man's condition wasn't good. He was using every ounce of strength he had to keep up. Theodore offered some words of encouragement that came out in a gasp. "You're doing great."

Wolfgang let out a wheezy sigh. "I'm like an escapee from a nursing home. Go ahead of me, please. I'll catch up in a bit."

Theodore paused. For an instant, the offer was tempting, not to save himself, but to just give up. Wolfgang wasn't the only one who was ready for a wheelchair. His body was fighting just to put one foot in front of another. But the instant passed. "Forget it. We're in this together."

Wolfgang remained where he was, trying to get his breath. After a moment, he was able to speak again. "Then you have to change."

"Change what?"

"No, I mean you have to activate that part of yourself that jumped through the window."

"I don't remember doing that. Like I told Daniel, I woke up on a rock. I thought someone dumped me there."

"You still don't understand what you are, what we are."

Theodore blinked back at him. "No, I don't. So tell me."

"Some refer to us as creatures, but that's because they're ignorant."

Theodore laughed. "Creatures? That's a good one. Daniel even said something about werewolves."

"He's right." Wolfgang's eyes brightened. "We don't change into animals like in the movies, but the term does have some validity."

"What?" Startled, Theodore staggered back a couple of feet. "That's why Prissy said something about a pack, isn't it?"

Wolfgang crept over to a nearby tree for support. "Yes, that's right."

"Werewolves?" Theodore let the concept bounce around in his brain. After a moment, he found some clarity. He thought about

Prissy being so strong and about Daniel's abilities. "Holy crap! Suddenly, it all makes crazy sense."

"It's not so crazy," Wolfgang said softly. "We're not really that different. Think of us as very gifted humans. We don't turn into hairy monsters."

Theodore swallowed hard. "But it is different than normal, right?"

Wolfgang sighed. "I know it's all very new, but if we don't get going, we'll soon be dead anyway."

The statement hit home. It was harsh enough to bring Theodore back to the rocky hillside. "Well that makes me feel better," he said with a scowl.

"I never wanted this for you or Prissy or any of us. I hoped we could all live our lives in peace. It just didn't work out that way."

Theodore stared hard at the older man, at the steady, pale blueness in his eyes. If there was one thing that never changed in Wolfgang, it was the kindness that was always there. That one fact took precedence over everything. "You're the one person who's always tried to help me. Now let me help you," he said offering his shoulder.

As they started to move forward, Theodore felt a small measure of hopefulness. "So I'm one of you?"

"That's right."

"Tell me about the change I went through."

"At times, it happens on its own, like when you ran off earlier. But for most of us, the change is gradual. It happens when we're in our teen years. Eventually we're always aware of our gifts you might say. They're always there. We integrate them into a sense of who we are."

"But Daniel says I'm different than most. I know he's right. I don't remember changing."

"Yes, and I'm not sure why that is. Your rational mind could be resisting the process. But it would be great if you could embrace it. You'd be so much stronger, and your heart would have a better chance of healing quickly."

"What do you suggest I do?"

Wolfgang shrugged. "I wish I knew."

* * *

They had only gone halfway up the hill when Theodore had to stop. Wolfgang was tugging on his arm. "What is it?"

"They're here," Wolfgang said as he pointed anxiously.

"What?" Theodore tried to get his breath as he stared down the hillside. A car was pulling into the driveway below. The bad elements had arrived.

Wolfgang gestured to a large boulder. "Over there," he said as he hobbled over to an imposing rock. He slumped against it heavily. "You have to go on without me." His tone was harsh and insistent. "I'm too exhausted to keep going."

Theodore paid him no attention. His wounded heart raced as he watched four men pile out of the vehicle. They were armed with what looked like automatic weapons. As Theodore thought about putting distance between them and the bad guys, he realized how exhausted he was too. He decided Daniel was right. Dying took a lot out of him. "Let me think," he whispered more to himself than Wolfgang.

The facts were grim. Wolfgang was in worse shape than he was. The ailing man had used all his reserves to get as far as he had. But Theodore knew he couldn't abandon his friend. The thought triggered memories of old war movies he'd seen. Brave soldiers who were wounded themselves were the heroes who saved their buddies. That was what true friendship was all about. Now, he'd have to pretend he was in a war movie. Glancing back at the house, he changed his mind. He didn't have to pretend. The men below were armed and lethal.

Without a word, he grabbed hold of Wolfgang. "Trust me!" His voice was stronger than his muscles. It took all his strength to heave Wolfgang over his shoulder. Thankfully, the man was more wiry than stocky. Theodore knew he weighed more and had a heavier bone structure.

"Theodore, no!" Wolfgang protested.

"Be quiet, do you want them to hear us?" Theodore's tone took on a harshness he didn't usually express. But he was a soldier now. He was resolved to do whatever it took to get them to safety. His determination helped. A deep down, courageous part of him rallied. Unfortunately, his other parts remained wanting. His body felt like it belonged in a hospital.

Wolfgang struggled to free himself. "You're crazy!"

"Quiet," Theodore gasped as he took his first faltering steps up the hill. He was sure that only God understood where he got the might to carry another man when he could barely keep going himself. Moving one foot in front of the other was almost impossible. After a dozen steps, he was grateful his heart was still beating. How did those heroic warriors perform such valiant acts?

As the incline got steeper, Wolfgang seemed to be gaining weight along the way. The thought didn't help. Theodore had to get his mind off of his task. He had to think about something else. Prissy's pretty face became his focus. If he could save her dad, wouldn't she be impressed? That lofty idea took him about twenty feet.

Wolfgang tried to help him. "Think about letting your body do its thing. Let it take charge, Theodore."

"Don't you think I'm trying? My body isn't listening."

"Just do it! Now!" Wolfgang growled out weakly.

Theodore had never heard Wolfgang sound angry, but reading Wolfgang's mind, he felt another glimmer of hope. He understood what was going on. "Do you think that your anger can provoke me into changing?"

"It was worth a try. Those men are going to know we're missing from the house and start tracking us very soon. You have to do something and fast."

"What if I get angry at myself? That might do it, right?" Theodore had never had much of a rapport with his body. In fact, his physical vessel always seemed to be fighting him. It often got sick or was intolerant of a lot of foods. When he'd tried to work out, he came down with colds. But if Wolfgang was correct, he had to try to reach it if they were going to stay alive. He began to scold himself. "Come on, stop being a weakling! Do your thing! Be your werewolf self! Change, now!"

As he ordered, cajoled, and pleaded with his body, he felt more and more fatigued. Finally, he had to stop. When he glanced back and checked the area around the cabin, he knew Wolfgang had called it. The men were coming out of the dwelling. They were scanning the hillside. He and Wolfgang were going to lose the war.

Chapter Sixteen

The SUV almost went over the edge as Daniel took a curve too fast. Braking, fighting for control, he was able to get back on the highway. As soon as he was on solid pavement, he slammed down on the gas petal again. His driving was reckless, but he had to get back to the cabin.

Besides, he was only putting his own life in jeopardy. He'd left Amelie and Prissy behind at the store. He gripped the wheel and tried to navigate the narrow, winding road as he went over the situation. The location of the safe house he'd chosen was only known to a few of the pack. One of those few must have been part of the splinter faction. Luckily he still had a number of loyal friends. One of them had learned about the attack that was under way. Her warning had come late, but he had to forget about the negatives. Thankfully, there was a secret stash of weapons hidden not far from the house.

There're even boots too, not that I'll have time to put them on.

Daniel did have a couple of positives on his side. He was somewhat familiar with the surrounding terrain after chasing after Theodore. Secondly, he was a much tougher member of the pack than a lot of the others. Most were soft and too indulgent in their lifestyle. Daniel had studied guerilla warfare in his spare time.

He laughed at himself, at his 'be prepared' way of living.

I knew this day might come with the WKA, but it's not the WKA that I'm fighting. Why didn't I know what my supposed friends were up to? Why wasn't I able to read them?

That fact bothered him. It was hard to tell a lie around his own kind, but obviously some of the splinter faction had learned a way to be collectively devious.

But the group can't be that big, can it? There were only nine members, including me, who were privy to the WKA projects. I'm sure four of them are loyal.

That left four. Could he handle that many alone? The four in question were hardcore types like himself. It wouldn't be easy to take on all of them. He was tough, maybe even a bit of a James Bond in the human world, but as a werewolf, the name wouldn't fit. He managed investments for a living. His pursuit of martial arts and related subjects had been a pastime.

He took deep breaths as he neared his destination, trying to clear his head and prepare for battle. He parked along the roadside a couple hundred feet from the house. The sun was setting when he got out of the SUV. That was a plus. Darkness would help Theodore and Wolfgang. Maybe they could stay hidden long enough for him to take action.

If they're not already dead.

It was too painful to contemplate their fate. Yet, he didn't dare try to reach out to them telepathically. The enemy might pick up on his thoughts and discover his presence.

Forget everything but being the toughest bastard you can be!

The WKA might have made it impossible for Theodore to go into killer mode, but Daniel felt himself quite capable.

* * *

Amelie tried to be patient as she stood in the grocery store parking lot. Prissy was clearly out of touch with the virtue. She was stomping back and forth with deep frown lines in her brow. "Sweetie, try not to upset yourself."

Prissy paused and glared at the cars going by. "You have to face facts. Daniel's gone off and left us, and he's not coming back."

"He wouldn't just leave us. He's proven himself over and over."

Prissy paused and scuffed at the black asphalt before she replied. "I saw him on his cell phone just before he disappeared out of the store." As she relayed the information, she looked up at Amelie. Her face went from annoyance to alarm. "Oh no, Mom, what if that means—"

Amelie felt a shock of panic grab hold too. "You think the splinter group found the house, and he's gone back?"

Prissy nodded.

Amelie's knees begin to shake as her mind skipped forward. Wolfgang and Theodore were alone at the cabin. They would both be completely vulnerable if they came under any kind of attack.

"Mom, what should we do?" Prissy cried out.

The fear in Prissy's voice was enough to snap Amelie out of her own angst. She had to think about her daughter's well-being. She had to give her something encouraging to hold on to. "Let's not project the worst. We don't have any real facts yet."

"Maybe I can help," Prissy said as her brow furrowed in concentration. For a long moment, she was mute and focused. When she finally looked up, her eyes were full of tears. "I think Daniel is shielding his thoughts, but I'm getting a sense of his overall energy. He's scared, Mom! He's really freaked out!"

The statement hit Amelie so hard she wanted to cry too.

Stop it! Don't cave in. It's not going to help!

Yet facts were facts. Wolfgang was still very weak. And Theodore, the dear boy who had dimples when he was really happy, was recovering from a fatal heart attack. Neither of them was capable of standing up to the people who were attacking them. A few tears escaped just thinking about them. Did they have any chance at all?

Prissy pulled a tissue out of her pocket. "Don't cry Mom, please."

As they both sniffled and wiped their faces, Amelie straightened her shoulders and took a deep breath. "You're right. We have to stay optimistic."

Prissy sucked in some air too. "We have to get back to the cabin as fast as we can, but how?"

Amelie looked around and saw a young man coming out of the store. "Wait here. I might be able to find a way."

Chapter Seventeen

It was twilight, with just enough light for Theodore to see what was going on below. He stood on unsteady feet as he balanced his load and watched the men fanning out. They were moving swiftly up the hill. In contrast, he was barely moving. It was hopeless to continue what he was doing. Buddy or not, he wasn't physically able to get Wolfgang and himself to safety. He stumbled past a few large boulders, and put Wolfgang down next to the largest one, not gently, but more like a sack of lead weights.

"I'm glad you're coming to your senses," the older man said as he sat up against the rock.

Theodore crouched down in front of him. "Do you think these guys are special? Can they tell what we're thinking?"

Wolfgang nodded, then he looked up with piercing, angry eyes. In a flash, he'd read Theodore's mind. "Don't even think about it," he protested.

"I'm so sorry," Theodore said as he brought a fist-sized rock down on Wolfgang's head. He got the result he was hoping for. Wolfgang slumped over unconscious. Theodore took hold of his wrist, hoping he hadn't delivered too hard a blow. He was relieved to feel a steady pulse. "I didn't want to hurt you, but it's the only way I know how to keep you safe."

Theodore's plan had come to him in a moment of inspiration. First, he'd knock out Wolfgang so that the men below couldn't pick up on Wolfgang's thoughts and thus, his location. Next, Theodore would take off in the opposite direction, flooding the airways with his own thoughts. At least Wolfgang might survive long enough for Daniel to get back. Now he was happy that things were going as he planned. He started up the hill again, pleased with himself and what he'd done.

Oh no! What if they're picking up on my thoughts right now? I have to forget about Wolfgang and only think about what I'm doing.

He switched gears fast and went back to contemplating how to change himself. He had to find a way to become the werewolf that he was supposed to be. Hollywood was great for providing visuals. Wolfgang said they didn't turn into animals, but it was kind of fun imagining being a furry wolf man. He'd seen lots of them in horror films. As he moved away from Wolfgang's position, he used what breath he had to encourage himself. "Be the wolfman! Be the wolf man!" His shouts served double duty. He needed to get the attention of the men coming up the hill. He knew he succeeded when they fired off a couple of rounds in his direction. Luckily, the men were either lousy shots, or they couldn't see very well. Darkness was slowly descending on the rocky landscape.

Theodore also had another advantage. Without the extra weight of Wolfgang on his shoulders, he was able to move a lot faster. He gained ground and felt more confident about his situation until he heard bullets splinter the edge of a tree three feet away.

That could have been me!

It was a hard, ugly thought. It made him change his mantra. "Oh god, I'm going to die again!"

This time he didn't feel comfortable about crossing over. He figured it would probably be a painful death. The men might even take him alive and torture him. In the middle of his gruesome ensemble of ways to exit, a worse scenario crossed his mind. What if the thugs got Wolfgang, Daniel, Amelie or Prissy? He couldn't bear the thought that they'd suffer or die. "You bastards!" He screamed out the words as he struggled upwards.

As the emotions and the adrenaline kicked in, so did his body. He didn't become a creature covered in hair. He became a true werewolf, the kind that didn't look like an animal, the kind that lived in the world and blended in with normal humans. Only

Theodore didn't know he'd changed. Somehow, when the two parts of him came together this time, it was a beautiful, seamless process. His personality and his special physical nature became a whole unit. The transformation that fused his mind with a gifted physical presence was exactly what was needed. He was suddenly moving very fast. Survival techniques seemed to come naturally. He forgot about his heart problem as he ran for his life. Zigzagging, finding the best trails for speed, using rocks for cover, his body was a wonderful, powerful ally. His only job was to let it do its thing.

My gosh! I never knew you could be so amazing!

Praising his body, he began to smile with a joy he'd never known before.

* * *

As soon as Daniel heard the gun shots, he froze. Standing in the weapons cache, arming himself, he nearly dropped the handgun he was loading.

"Theo? Wolfgang? I'm here!"

His mental shout out hit the telepathic airways before he could catch himself. "No!" He couldn't believe he had panicked and compromised his position and possibly theirs. As he reprimanded himself, he heard Theodore's reply.

"I'm okay! Now shut up, please!"

Daniel smiled with relief and pride. His little brother was not only still breathing, he was already better in field tactics than Daniel was. Next, he got a second surprise. He picked up one of the defector's messages. He recognized the sender. It was a sullen guy named Saxon.

"Listen up! I just heard Daniel. He's behind us."

Daniel grabbed more ammo and a second automatic. The group knew his approximate position. He could only hope it might give Theodore a better chance, or at least it might make the team split up. A glimmer of hope filled his mind and heart as he crept out into the darkness. He'd do his best to take out a couple of the traitors before they found him.

* * *

When Wolfgang regained consciousness, his head felt like a melon that had been split open. Touching the place where Theodore hit him, he flinched. There was an egg size bump on his head, but at least his head was intact. The sound of gunfire made him forget his pain. The sound came from down below. Had Daniel come back?

More shots were fired up the ridge and much further away. A sense of elation flowed through his throbbing head. "Theodore must still be alive too."

He tried to stand up and knew he couldn't manage it. Even if he didn't have a fractured skull, the toxins in his system and his earlier exertion were damning him to the status of a feeble, old man.

* * *

Daniel wiped the blood off his face, not feeling the pain of the bullet that grazed his forehead. All he felt was more anger when his vision was affected by the bleeding. Ducking down, he hastily searched his pocket and retrieved a handkerchief. He held it tight against the wound and silently begged his body to heal a little, at least enough to stop the flow of blood. Fortunately, he was successful at cloaking his thoughts. As far as the enemy knew, all was silent where he stood.

After a moment, he crept over to the other side of the rock he was stationed behind. He did a quick scan to see if his opponent was on the move. When he'd been hit, he let out a cry. There was a possibility his attackers thought he was down. When he noted a movement a short distance away, he dropped the cloth pressed against his wound. Taking a slow, quiet breath, he took aim with his automatic.

"Stupid idiot, I'm not dead," he whispered as his finger closed on the trigger. His aim was true when the gun fired. He took out one of the men who scurried towards him. He didn't feel anything but hope as he watched the bullet slam into the guy's chest. When he realized he'd killed the man, he could only pray that his luck would hold. There were three more to go and only one of him.

* * *

Theodore heard the sound of the bullet before it hit him. It tore through the fleshy part of his shoulder, exited and kept on going. If he had been just the human Theodore, he would have been felled by the shot, brought down like a deer in hunting season. But the new, improved version of Theodore made a leap for cover, hiding behind a rock large enough to give him sanctuary.

When he peeked out, he saw that the man who fired on him was still a long way down the hill. He got off the shot just before Theodore reached the crest.

"I've got a little time," he whispered to himself. "Better try to stop the bleeding." As he pressed his hand down on his torn flesh, Theodore's brain picked up on the last thing in the world he wanted to tune into. "Prissy, no! Why did you come back?"

"Stupid girl! Stupid girl!"

He couldn't repeat the phrase often enough. They were in the middle of a gun fight, and she could get herself killed. But what could he do? He was too far away to save Prissy from herself. As he tried to think of a solution, he heard another round of rapid fire shots. This time the sounds came from far below, closer to the house, closer to Prissy.

"Two down, two to go!"

It was Daniel's voice! While Theodore was getting himself shot, Daniel was taking out the killers.

"Prissy! Take care of Prissy!"

Theodore took a chance and sent back the message. Why shouldn't he? The bad guys knew where he was. He wasn't giving away his position. And as for Prissy, she was broadcasting her whereabouts as surely as if she had access to a bullhorn.

"Pull back and regroup!"

Theodore didn't recognize the voice he heard this time. It had to be one of the two villains who were left standing.

"I think I got one of them up on the ridge! Shouldn't I finish him off?"

The man who'd shot Theodore was broadcasting back.

A couple of more shots rang out before there was an answer. After a short pause, Theodore heard the reply.

"Get down here now. We're leaving!"

In the next few minutes, he heard more gunfire. He knew it was coming from both sides. A short time later, as a heavy layer of more firing sounded, he heard a car pulling away. He didn't actually hear it. Daniel heard it and passed the news on to him. After that, he realized his acute and even his ordinary senses of hearing and vision were fading.

"Thank goodness for you, Daniel. Just like you told me you would, you've saved us all!"

After he sent the message, everything went quiet. Theodore went quiet. He slipped back into human mode so smoothly, he didn't realize it. Finally, the world went black.

* * *

Once Prissy arrived at the cabin, she stood immobile, feeling like an idiot. She and Amelie had gotten a ride back to within a couple of blocks of the house. They told the guy who gave them a lift that they wanted to walk the rest of the way. But he was no sooner out of sight when Prissy left Amelie behind.

The plan was to stay together, to see if they could help if one of theirs was injured. Prissy ignored the plan. In spite of her mother's protests, she refused to listen to reason. Like a brave heroine, she gloried in the feeling that she would prove herself. She left her mother behind and ran all the way up to the cabin. Every breath was filled with a need to save her dad or Theodore or even Daniel.

She couldn't accept the thought that she was untrained and incapable. She was fifteen. She could change herself at will most of the time. She could help.

Her idea of being a savior faded quickly once she arrived on the scene. She knew she'd made a mistake. This wasn't some kind of make-believe fantasy. This was a real-life gun fight, and Prissy had never even fired a gun. She stood staring at the hillside. It had turned into a war zone that assaulted all her senses. Her mind and body were wide open to the deafening sound of the weapons. Feelings of chaos and violence came at her in waves so extreme she shook with fear.

But that wasn't the worst of it. Her father, Daniel, and Theodore were all sending her the same message. It was worded three different ways, but it all boiled down to one thing. She was really stupid for getting involved. She was making it doubly hard on all of them because they had to worry about her too.

Thankfully the battle was over shortly after she arrived at the scene. When the enemy drove off and quiet was restored, Daniel came out from behind some rocks. His face was smeared with blood as he ran towards her. When he reached her, his eyes were full of concern.

"Are you okay?" he asked in a breathless voice.

Prissy could only nod back at him. That's when he hugged her. His embrace carried her back to childhood. She was a little girl, and Daniel was like a big brother again. It felt so wonderful to have his strong arms around her. She was safe.

"Where's your mom?" he asked as he pulled back.

"What?" The question cut into her reverie. She immediately thought about Amelie. Her mother was walking up the hill on her own, and the goons who tried to kill them were on their way down.

"You left her? Oh hell, Prissy," Daniel reprimanded.

Daniel had tuned into her thoughts. As she watched him turn and sprint down the drive, he wasn't bothering to shield his own. His feelings were loud and clear in her head.

"How can you be so dense? You could be our leader someday, yet you're acting like a child! Why don't you think about somebody besides yourself?"

When Daniel got to his vehicle and jumped in, his harangue stopped. Now she could hear him worrying about Amelie.

"I'm worried too!" Prissy mumbled back.

She couldn't help the hateful emotions she wanted to level at him in that moment. But Daniel's opinion was justified. She wasn't thinking things out in a way that made sense. But how could she? She was in a nightmare. Nothing seemed real anymore. But even worse, she was failing everyone around her.

Tears of frustration and self-pity wet her face as she turned to run up the hill. She needed to get away from it all. As she ran, her mind blanked out, refusing to think about anything but putting distance between herself and her dismal performance. Theodore had the right idea about escaping. She was going to save all of them the trouble of worrying about her ever again. She'd keep running forever.

Chapter Eighteen

Amelie chastised herself as she started running towards the house. She'd been so focused on what might be happening to the men, she hadn't been taking care of the business at hand. She should have been watching Prissy more closely. Now Prissy had taken off and was already out of sight.

"Oh lord! My shoe!" Her cry of alarm went out as one of her loose fitting flats went flying off her foot. Its arc was impressive, so impressive it managed to travel to the edge of the road and disappear over the steep drop-off. She took a couple of steps and winced. Her feet were extremely tender, and the road was covered in sharp gravel. She had no choice but to recover her shoe. She made her way down the embankment, trying to move quickly, but there were stickers and sharp cinders in the area. Her bare foot was soon protesting with pain. Luckily, her shoe was lemon yellow like her pants. In spite of the lack of light, she was able to see it at the bottom of the gully.

"Daniel and I can commiserate over this one," she complained. "Neither of us is dressed for the kind of craziness we're involved in."

After she got her shoe back on, she started up the incline. Fighting her way to the road again, she slipped a lot, but managed to win out over the steep grade. Once topside again, she knew she couldn't run properly in the flats. Her only recourse was to walk back as fast as possible.

Stay calm. You'll get there.

She repeated the words over and over as she got closer to the cabin. It was the only way she could keep herself from panicking. The sound of gunfire terrified her. It was new and foreign in her world. How could Wolfgang survive a battle with his own kind when he could hardly walk? And Prissy? She couldn't let herself think about what might happen to her little girl if she rushed into the middle of the battle.

With her nerves at a breaking point, she came to an abrupt halt when the gunfire stopped. She paused and listened to the silence, not knowing if it was a good thing or bad. Was her family still alive? Her fear and renewed urgency made her take off her shoes. She began running again. Her feet were painful and unwilling participants, but she didn't pay attention to anything but her need to get back to her loved ones.

A black sedan, flying over the hill in front of her, interrupted her resolve. The angle of the road made her a perfect target for its headlights. Whoever was driving kept the vehicle heading in her direction. He aimed the car towards the shoulder, towards her. She barely had time to jump backwards, falling down the drop off, tumbling through the thistles and brush. When she reached the bottom, she lay dazed. She could hear the screeching of brakes from above. The car was stopping, and she thought she knew why. The vehicle probably belonged to one of the suspected traitors. They must have recognized her.

Her first instinct was to move to safety. She clawed at the ground and found the strength to pull herself around to the other side of a nearby boulder. Lying as still as possible, barely breathing, she realized how many places on her body hurt. It made her angry again. Even if she accepted herself as a human, she was no match for the guys looking for her. She couldn't even read their thoughts.

"Oh no! They can read mine!" She reprimanded herself at once. "You better start praying, Amelie." If she had a guardian angel, she needed his help.

* * *

Daniel didn't have to go very far down the road before he saw a car pulled over and a couple of people on the other side of the road searching for something. When they saw his headlights and saw him pulling over too, they quickly started running back to their car. They were cowards now, cowards who had lost half of their group. They knew they better get the hell out and fast.

Daniel didn't have time to stop them. Before he could get his gun out and fire on them, they were back in their vehicle, speeding away. Besides, his only thought now was Amelie. He could feel her close by. He quickly exited the SUV and ran to the spot where the men had been exploring.

"Amelie! It's Daniel! Where are you?" As he called, he half slid down the embankment, letting his senses lead him to her.

"I'm here," she called back. "I'm behind the big rock."

Daniel closed the distance between them in moments. When he saw Amelie up close, he noted that her clothes were torn and her face was dirty, but she smiled at him anyway.

"Oh Daniel, you're an answer to my prayers!" she said in a trembling voice.

He'd barely crouched down next to her, when she reached out for him and pulled him into her arms. He responded in turn, holding her in a protective embrace. "I was so afraid they might hurt you," he said.

After a moment, she pulled back. "Prissy? Wolfgang? Theodore?" she asked anxiously.

He sat with his eyes shut, trying to send out a message to any of the three.

Amelie tugged on his sleeve. "What is it? Are they okay?"

"Prissy's okay, but I can't tune into Wolfgang or Theo. We have to get back."

* * *

Prissy ran up the hill behind the cabin with only a partial moon to light her way. But her mind wasn't on the moon. She smelled blood.

Its scent activated something primal in her body. Her brain began working again, making her take note of her surroundings. She inhaled deeply and was relieved. She didn't recognize the smell. That meant it belonged to one of the bad guys. The wind was carrying it from off to her right. At least the source of the blood wasn't in her path.

Thank goodness, I don't think I could stand seeing any dead bodies.

The thought sickened her. "Daniel's right. I am a foolish child." Fresh tears made it hard for her to see as she half stumbled over the rough terrain. Earlier, she'd had fantasies about being some kind of amazing, super heroine. She thought it would be great to be like one of the tough women in an action thriller. But the aftermath of the gunfight, with mutilated bodies lying around, wasn't thrilling.

It's all so horrible!

She stopped and sniffed at the air again. The wind had shifted and carried a new scent from further up the hill. She cringed. It was Theodore's blood. In her panic, she'd forgotten about him. She opened her mind, trying to tune into his whereabouts and drew a blank. "Where are you, Theodore?" She called out in a loud, clear voice, but she didn't get an answer. She started climbing the hill as fast as she could. "Theodore, can you hear me!"

She was nearly at the top of the ridge when she slowed down. Her body shook as she made her way over the rocky ground. Had the villains killed Theodore? Her acute sense of smell was her guide. It helped her to keep moving towards Theodore's location. She cringed when she saw a dark form a few yards away. The night felt suddenly cold. She had to wrap her arms around herself as she continued forward. She found Theodore lying next to a boulder. "The big dope probably tripped and knocked himself out."

Her explanation, meant to console her frazzled nerves, was abandoned when she got closer. There was enough light to see that Theodore's shirt was soaked in blood. The ground beneath him was dark and damp. She tightened her grip on her arms as she got close. A couple of days ago, her biggest problem was dealing with her emotional ups and downs. How was she supposed to suddenly face bullets, bodies, and a bleeding Theodore? She dropped to her knees and tried to remember her first aid classes.

But I didn't pay attention. I didn't think I had to.

Daniel came to mind. Years before, he had told her how a person could use their body as an instrument that revealed the health of another person. It was an art among her kind, but not an art that Prissy had cared to learn. As her list of inadequacies grew, her body temperature and her confidence continued to plummet. "I don't know how to help you, Theo," she whispered.

She'd nearly lost her father. Then Theodore actually died. Now, she was facing the aftermath of a brutal battle. It was too much. She felt herself pulling back, wanting to shut out all the horror around her. As her feelings started to go numb, Theodore groaned. It was a reminder that she had no choice. She had to do something. Mechanically, she bent over him. Perhaps she could help Theodore by using the method Daniel had described.

"You're too heavy," she complained as she tried to lift Theodore. Her strength was gone. She felt small and helpless, but she knew she couldn't give up. It took all of her willpower and muscle to get Theodore off the ground, to gather him close to her body. With a heavy sigh, she shut her eyes and tried to tune in to his physical condition. "Nothing, it's hopeless."

The only thing she felt was a need to get away from the smells of death and the possibility that Theodore might die. If he did, she was sure it would be her fault. That's when she heard her father. He was calling to her, filling her mind with the sound of his voice.

"Dad? Daddy?" she called back. She'd been so traumatized by events and felt so alone she'd totally forgotten about searching for her father. "Is it really you?"

"Yes, sweetheart. I'm over here."

The message was enough to snap her out of the cold, incapacitating spell she was under. All of her feelings flooded back in, reminding her that she wasn't alone. Someone was there for her. Someone would tell her that everything was going to be okay. "I'm coming!" she called back excitedly.

As if she were holding a lifeless mannequin, she let go of Theodore without further thought or concern. He fell from her arms, striking his head on the hard ground and letting out another groan. It never reached her ears. She was already on her feet and running. Without a backward look, she moved as fast as possible through the thicket and the underbrush.

* * *

Daniel held Amelie in his arms, trying to balance her weight, trying to gain some ground in their ascent up the steep grade of the embankment. It didn't work. He couldn't get any traction. No matter how hard he tried to help, they kept slipping back. "I'm sorry," he said as he thought about his options. Amelie couldn't climb the grade on her own. She had a sprained ankle and a couple of bruised ribs. Where did that leave him?

Amelie didn't hesitate to make her wishes known. "Please Daniel, don't worry about me. You're wasting time. The others need you more than me."

Daniel didn't think the men who'd attacked them would return, but he hated leaving Amelie stranded. Finally, he knew he had no choice. He felt everyone was alive back at the property, but he didn't know about injuries. There were no answers when he tried to reach Wolfgang and Theodore. They could be in real trouble. Hopefully, Prissy was doing something helpful, but she wasn't answering him either. "How about this? I'll move you into the woods and leave you my jacket. I'll come back as soon as I can."

Amelie gave him a final squeeze of appreciation. "Thank you, Daniel, for everything. Now, please, go help our family."

* * *

As soon as Wolfgang regained consciousness again, he sensed Prissy was close. He immediately called out to her. He needed information about Theodore. He was very concerned about the courageous boy who had tried to save him. Unfortunately, his hail to Prissy didn't work out the way he intended. Her mind was too scattered to provide what he needed to know. Instead, she was rushing to his aid. "My poor child, you're not prepared for any of this."

If only he'd done more to train her for an emergency situation. Daniel had wanted more than that. He had pushed for military instruction. Wolfgang didn't agree with Daniel's viewpoint. He envisioned peace. He didn't want to introduce more fear into the pack by focusing on an enemy. If they prepared themselves for battle, wouldn't they be more likely to encounter it?

Now, feeling Prissy's blind panic, he didn't know what was best anymore. He tried to stand up, but his body wouldn't cooperate. The fever was back. He was blacking out regularly, and there wasn't anything he could do about it. His immune system was on overload. A possible concussion wasn't helping either. He had a hell of a headache.

"Amelie is going to be alright."

When he heard Daniel's voice in his pounding brain, he felt more upset than happy. He hadn't known that Amelie was involved in what was happening, or that she might be in trouble.

He sent Daniel an urgent request.

"Tell me what happened to her?"

"I'll explain later. Are you okay? What about Theodore?"

"I'll live, but I don't have any information on the boy, except that he tried to save me. He tried to divert the gunfire by running off and making himself the target."

"Oh hell! Listen, I'll be back as quickly as I can. Hold down the fort!"

Wolfgang put his head back. Was Daniel kidding? How could he hold down a fort when he could barely sit up? His only choice was to wait for Prissy. Maybe she could help. He didn't have to wait very long before he heard someone crashing through the brush. "Prissy? Sweetheart?"

"Dad?" As soon as Prissy saw him, she threw herself into his arms.

"My sweet girl," he said. Prissy's state of shock and bewilderment was obvious as he held on to her tense, almost rigid body. She hadn't had time to learn to control the powerful physical and emotional forces that came with the change. Her mind and her physical vessel, filled with so much fear, were like overloaded electrical circuits with no grounding wire. "You're safe now. I have you," he whispered. He tried to use his own energy to balance hers, but he was fighting another blackout.

After a few moments, Prissy let go of him and sat back. "I'm sorry, Dad. I'm doing it again, aren't I? I'm only thinking of myself. I should be thinking about you."

"It's okay. I'll be fine."

Prissy's eyes caught a bit of the moon's light as she stared at him. They went wide with concern. "What happened to your head?" she asked as she reached out and touched the large bump on his forehead.

Wolfgang winced. "It was Theo—"

"What?" Prissy's expression went from fear to anger as she pulled away. She quickly got to her feet. "That little jerk! That horrid boy! He tried to kill you!"

"Honey, let me explain—"

"No!" she screamed, putting her hands over her ears. "You and Daniel are crazy to let that WKA freak stick around! But I got you into this. I'm the one who introduced you to that beast. I'll take care of him!"

Wolfgang tried to say more, but Prissy was already in flight. She quickly disappeared into the darkness.

* * *

Daniel had explained what the WKA had done to Theodore. When Prissy heard the story, she felt sorry for him. Later, she'd seen him change and turn on Daniel. No one in the pack had ever looked so ferocious, so wild and savage.

Now, Theodore had tried to kill her father. The awful picture all came together as she rushed back to where she'd found him. Like Daniel had feared, Theodore wasn't what he appeared to be. He was the WKA's agent, out to kill them all.

Prissy wouldn't let that happen. "I may be a baby. I may have screwed up leaving my mom behind, but now I'll show you all just how valuable I can be!" Her seething words were hissed out as she ran. "Theodore's tough. He even survived a heart attack, but he's run out of luck. I'll take care of him once and for all."

As her wrath poured out, Prissy could feel her body change. The weakness disappeared, replaced by an intoxicating surge of energy. She wanted to be a heroine after all. Now, she had her chance. She streaked along in the darkness, becoming the warrior she envisioned in her dreams.

When she got back to Theodore, he was still unconscious. He lay on the cold ground with his blameless face bathed in shadowy light. But it was all a façade. Underneath, he wasn't the sweet person he pretended to be. He was a monster. Prissy's father was proof of it. Theodore had boldly proclaimed he'd never betray them, but it was a lie.

"You ignorant jerk!" Prissy screamed as she threw herself down beside him. She let her rage course through her limbs as she began to pound Theodore's chest and body. She used all her strength to let him know how much she hated him. She called him every name she could think of, trying to get through to him. He had to be made accountable. As she focused on her anger, Theodore became the representative of all those who had tried to destroy her kind.

Hadn't she been told the stories? Throughout the ages, massacre after massacre had taken their lives. It was still going on. The WKA and zealots like them had made it their duty to seek out her people and murder them. But why? Her pack and other packs simply wanted to be left alone. They wanted to live their lives in peace.

"But we're hated because we're different! It's not right!" The statement made her pause. Her eyes filled with a final blazing desire as she stood up. She knew what she had to do. "I'm ending this now," she mumbled as she scoured the area around her. A large rock lay a few feet away. It was perfect for what she had in mind. It took a lot of strength to pick it up and bring it back to where Theodore lay. It took more strength when she hoisted it above her head. But she was determined to finish what she'd started. Theodore would never hurt anyone again after she completed her task. "This is for all of us, you unholy fiend!" she whispered in a low growl.

The sound of a gun being fired made her freeze. She looked up and saw Daniel. He was coming up the hill at a run, but she'd been so completely occupied with her fierce, emotional eruption, she hadn't noticed his approach. He stopped when he was a few feet away. He was holding a side-arm, and it was pointed at her.

"Put the rock down now!" he shouted. Usually, when Daniel changed form, he was even more handsome and grand, but not this time. His face was almost as hard and brutish as Theodore's had been earlier in the bathroom.

"He tried to kill my father!" she yelled out.

"No! He tried to save him!"

She held her ground. "I don't believe you."

"Tune into your father. He's trying to let you know what happened."

With glaring eyes, she did as she was told, calming herself enough to let her father's mind reach out to her. A moment later, she stumbled back and dropped the rock like she'd dropped Theodore earlier. As she listened to the truth, as she realized her mistake, she was appalled at herself.

"I almost killed him," she whimpered as she stared at Theodore's bloodied body. The worst of all realizations hit her. Theodore wasn't the monster, she was.

* * *

Theodore was suspended between the dream world and the hard, solid stuff of reality. Semiconscious, he felt incapable of moving and yet he could hear Prissy screaming at him, blaming him for endless crimes against her people.

Who were her kind, really? He didn't know much about any of it. He didn't even know if he was guilty of what she accused him of doing. There were places in him, hidden places where secrets were kept. He didn't have access to those places, but he knew the contents were dark. Perhaps Prissy was right. Perhaps he was an ogre and didn't know it.

What he did know was that she hated him, and her hate was punishing his body. Just when he was beginning to love his physical form and what it could do, she was trying to beat the life out of it. He should have hated her back, but he only felt sad. He wanted to find the warm waters of peace again, to leave the Earth once and for all.

This time his body wasn't ready to die, nor was it as forgiving. Suddenly he could see the essence of his body's spirit in the form of a beautiful, black wolf. He'd never imagined that his body could have its own separate identity. Yet, it stood in front of him, growling, wanting to protect itself from Prissy.

Theodore understood its anger, but his mind and heart pulled the wolf back, restrained it with a new sense of compassion for himself and for the beautiful, spirit animal that lived in him.

"We're not wanted on this Earth. But wherever I go, I'll take you with me," he vowed. "We'll go to that place that's waiting for us on the other side."

Later, after Daniel managed to get him back to the house, Theodore wanted nothing more to do with the world. He had tried to be noble. He tried to act the part of the hero, but the bruises on his body and the sound of Prissy's rage, repeating over and over in his mind, were proof he'd failed. And it was no small failure, either. He'd given his best, body and soul. It seemed none of it was enough. He didn't want to try anymore.

Wolfgang was wrong. Theodore wasn't one of them. He was an alien just like he thought. His place was in the heavens, and his spirit longed to return there, to fly upwards and join the stars. There he'd find the beautiful planet where there was liquid light and joy, and no one could hurt him ever again.

Chapter Nineteen

Daniel was burdened with more problems after the violent skirmish with the splinter group. Everyone around him was falling apart. Prissy felt shame and disgrace after the way she'd behaved. She had locked herself in the room by the garage. Amelie was doing well enough, but her spirits were flagging as her loved ones suffered. Then there was Theodore. His brother lay in his bed, refusing to talk or even look at Daniel. With all the exertion and strain, Wolfgang had relapsed to the point of being totally bedridden again. Thankfully, even in his weakened condition, the leader of the pack had the will to continue.

"Talk to me," he insisted as Daniel checked out his vital signs. "First tell me about the practical side of things, about Porter and Saxon. Did you alert the pack about them?"

"Yes, and now that their identities are out, they're on the run. Our people are going after them. Hopefully, we'll soon put an end to their little uprising."

"What's the story on Theodore? He did a great job out there, and his shoulder will heal, right?"

"I don't want to talk about him."

"But Daniel, he's proven himself. He's not what you thought. I told you he was ours."

"Yes, you were right." His tone was matter-of-fact. He wanted to avoid a discussion about Theodore.

"I don't understand. Aren't you happy? You have your brother back."

"Not really." Daniel's face was sullen when he turned away. "He's decided he doesn't want to stick around. He won't even acknowledge me. I guess that's my punishment. He's my own flesh and blood, yet I wouldn't give him a chance. Now the tables are turned."

Wolfgang stared back with a frown. Then he smiled. "He's like you. You're both stubborn. You both give everything you have and then you doubt yourselves when you shouldn't. I haven't had time to tell you this, but I'm so proud of you. You're a leader, Daniel. Like Theodore, you've proven yourself under very difficult circumstances. The pack would do well under your guidance. We'll put it to a vote when this is over."

"Forget it, you can keep the position. After what I've gone through, I'm ready for retirement."

"Oh no you aren't. You worked hard for this. I'm not letting you back out that easily. You have everything it takes to do the job."

"Maybe, but circumstances have changed. It'll be a while before I even think in those terms again."

"This job wasn't what I thought it was either. Dealing with individuals is very challenging at times. But you have to talk to Theodore. Make him understand you won't take 'no' for an answer. If you let him continue to slip, he's the type that might never climb out of the hole he's put himself in."

"I've tried my best—"

"Try again."

Daniel stared at the older man, wanting to get angry, but he took a deep breath instead. "Is that what you did with me?"

"You bet I did. And look at you now. My father would have loved to have a son like you instead of one who wanted to study art."

"He had a better one in you." Daniel thought about how well Wolfgang had shepherded the pack throughout the years. He paused. "What can I say to Theo? He doesn't seem to feel any connection to me."

Wolfgang smiled again. "Remember the truth. Find a way to make him know you need him."

140

Daniel threw his shoulders back defiantly, letting his eyes go cold. "But I don't want to need him."

Chapter Twenty

Amelie had been outside Prissy's room for five minutes, but she couldn't get her daughter to open the door. "Please sweetheart, we have to talk about this. Your father needs us to all be there for him." It was her trump card, and it worked. She heard the lock click.

Prissy peeked out. Her eyes were red-rimmed and moist. "Okay, for Dad's sake, come in."

Amelie limped into the room using a cane Daniel found in the garage. After she sat down on the bed, she and Prissy looked at each other but neither spoke. Finally, Amelie put her cane aside and held her arms open.

Prissy hesitated. "I don't deserve your love. I've been the worst—"

"Nothing you did could keep me from loving you. Now come here and give me a hug."

Prissy shook her head and went to a chair in the corner. She sat down, crossed her arms, and stared down at the floor. "I left you, and then I almost killed Theodore. I can't stop thinking about what a terrible person I am."

Amelie put her hands in her lap and sighed. "You left me because you wanted to help your father and Daniel. And I'm sure you had a reason for . . . for—"

"For beating Theodore half to death?" Prissy raised her eyes and blinked back. "Even if he was one of the bad guys, I shouldn't have done that. He wasn't even conscious!"

"Why did you do it?"

"I don't know. I just have all this hate inside of me. It's not fair that people want to hurt us and even kill us."

Amelie looked at her wedding band and twisted it slowly. When she married Wolfgang, her family disowned her. They didn't know about Wolfgang's true nature. They rejected him because he didn't fit their definition of the person she should marry. He didn't have the same religious beliefs or their codes of behavior. "Some people are ignorant. They fear what they don't understand. But that doesn't mean they're all bad. Besides, there are many understanding people."

"At school, a lot of the kids think I'm weird. They go out of their way to ignore me. What if they found out what I really am?"

"What about Theodore? I think he has a crush on you."

Prissy's eyes filled with fresh tears. "He doesn't have a crush anymore. I tried to talk to him a few minutes ago, and he won't even look at me. I think he knows what I did. I couldn't read his mind exactly. He seems to be able to close it off, but I could feel his fear when I was around him. All the while, Daniel stood over him like a bodyguard. He thinks I'm insane after seeing me out there, ready to kill Theodore."

"Sweetie, you're going through a very critical time. Your body has so much going on. That's why your emotions are so powerful."

"I agree. That's why I've put myself in here. It's not safe for me to be around people. When we get back home, lock me in the basement and throw the key away."

Amelie laughed. "I'll do no such thing. You're not crazy, you're scared. When normal humans or even gifted ones like you, get frightened, they do things they can regret later."

Prissy picked at her tissue. "After I almost bashed Theo's head in, Daniel yelled at me. He told me if I continued to close my mind to the truth, that I'd become like the WKA."

"Sometimes Daniel is very wise. And he's right, isn't he? You hurt Theodore because you made judgments without all the facts. You thought he tried to kill your dad."

"It's true! When I saw that huge bump on Dad's head—" Prissy sniffled, screwed up her face and burst into a sob. "Is Dad going to be alright?"

"I don't know."

Prissy shot Amelie a desperate, frowning appeal. "I'm scared, Mom!"

Amelie held out her arms again. This time Prissy ran over to her and hugged her carefully.

"I'm scared too," Amelie whispered. "But I'm here for you, always. Do you understand that?"

"Yes, and I'm here for you," Prissy said. "And I'll never leave you alone again, ever."

* * *

After examining Theodore's wounded shoulder and his general condition, Daniel turned and walked over to a desk on the other side of the room. He studied the desk blotter before he spoke. His words came out in a clinical monotone. "Your actions were commendable, but your heart's in worse shape than ever. You changed out there, but all your energy went into survival. You didn't stay in that form long enough to heal yourself."

Theodore kept his eyes focused on the wall. "So what's that mean?"

Daniel glanced at him and returned his eyes to the desk's surface. "You're going to get your wish. You have a bullet wound which is no big deal. But with your crappy attitude, with the extra emotional load you're putting on your heart, you'll be dead soon."

"That's a relief."

Daniel's face flushed with resentment, but he kept his eyes to himself. "So you're giving up?"

"Dying is a lot better than living."

"That's a great way of looking at it. I'm glad you're happy. Do you have any last requests? Do you want me to give your adoptive parents any explanations when I drop off your body?"

"They'll be relieved too. I'm nothing but trouble as far as they're concerned, a burden they've been stuck with."

Daniel turned and moved closer to Theodore's bed. "From what you've told me, your mother tries to take care of you. I think you owe her a few lines of gratitude, something."

"Give me a break. She says I'm a thorn in her side."

Daniel noted Theodore's shallow breaths, as if each one was painful after Prissy's beating. "She said that? When? Why?"

"She's always saying it."

"What about your father? Does he do things with you, take you to ball games?"

"No." Theodore let out a curt laugh and pulled back in pain. "But it's not all his fault. I'm no good at sports so I guess there's nothing for us to talk about."

"What do you do with your time?"

"I stay in my room and read. Sometimes I play video games or watch TV. What else is there to do? My parents have a life I can't fit into, just like they can't fit into mine."

Daniel had been around Theodore enough to know he wasn't the difficult type. He was a lot easier than Daniel had been at that age, a lot easier than most teenagers. What the hell did his ignorant parents want? "What about me, Theo, do you think I could understand you?"

"Why would you want to? I know what's in your head, did you forget that? You're ready to get back to your own life. So leave me alone. That way, we'll both have what we want."

Daniel stepped closer. "I want a brother."

"Do you really believe that? If you wanted me, why didn't you try to find me? At least Wolfgang tried." Theodore raised his eyes to the window, staring out at the darkness. "Go away, Daniel. Go back to your life. I was never a real part of it before or now."

"Fine, if that's what you want."

Theodore made a sudden grab for his chest, but he didn't moan or make any sign he was in pain. Instead, he stiffened his jaw and took a couple of shallow breaths.

145

Daniel looked away, clenching his fists. He could feel what was happening to his brother's body. Theodore's heart was sending out short, sharp pains on a regular basis, and Daniel couldn't do anything to stop it.

Theodore let out a sigh of relief and another mocking laugh. "When I left this world, I didn't have to think about my life. It was so easy where I went."

"Good for you," Daniel replied in an equally sarcastic tone. He didn't mean to act like an immature jerk, but he couldn't help himself. Theodore was activating feelings he couldn't ignore. "Everybody I loved has left me. I never expected you to stick around."

Theodore glanced up at him with searching eyes. "Look Daniel, you might think you wanted a brother, but I'm not that person, am I? I'm a disappointment to you just like I am to the people who adopted me."

"I don't know what you're talking about."

"Don't give me that! You feel like your real brother is long gone. I'm simply an inconvenience that was thrown into your life. Admit it."

Daniel's face went crimson with guilt. He'd forgotten to shield his thoughts. Now Theodore was reading them. He was privy to one of Daniel's deep down core beliefs.

Theodore's right. I do feel like my little brother is gone.

He quickly tried to cover up his blunder. "You're a great kid. You've helped us. You really have."

Theodore stared back. His innocent face was spoiled by the truth Daniel had let slip. "It's okay. I know the kind of person you wanted me to be. It's like the person I always imagined you'd be. I'd look at the stars and think about a brother. Maybe deep down, I remembered you. But the person I imagined was always so strong, a person I could count on, no matter what."

"Those were childish dreams!" Daniel spit out the words. "You can't count on me. You were right when you said I didn't look for you." He approached the bed and glared at Theodore. "I wanted you to be dead! Do you understand that?"

Theodore nodded back. His eyes were filled with resignation. He was clearly used to harsh criticism. "I get it."

Daniel's body stiffened with fresh anger. "No, you don't get it! I took the coward's way out. I didn't dare hope there'd be anything left of you. I know what the WKA does to their victims. It scared the hell out of me. Now, seeing you laying here like this, my worst fear is happening all over again."

Theodore sighed. "I'm sorry you have to feel like that."

Daniel grabbed the chair next to the bed and sat down heavily. His limbs were weak as if he'd carried too much for too long. He'd fallen into the fatal trap of caring about a kid who was a wreck, who would die soon. He was going to lose his brother all over again, and he hated being helpless to stop it. "They screwed you up, Theo, and I don't know how to fix you. I wish I did."

Theodore's face brightened a little. "Are you saying you do care about me?"

"What does it matter what I think?"

"I don't know. I guess I just figured there was no reason to stick around, but maybe I was wrong."

Daniel rubbed his hands together slowly, trying to calm himself. "Yes, maybe you were."

Theodore lay very still, staring out the window again. After a few minutes, he turned back to Daniel and let out a little laugh. "Well, I'm not dead yet. And I get the idea that if I can change, my body will heal. Will you teach me how to do it?"

* * *

Theodore tried all the suggestions Daniel offered and threw in a few of his own ideas. He wished, willed, and intended to change, over and over. After a half-hour, his face was lined with disappointment and weariness. But one thing kept him going. It was clear Daniel did want to help him. "Am I hopeless?" he asked, putting his hand on his chest, trying to quiet the irregular, racing beat that came and went like the pain.

Daniel tried to smile as he shook his head, but Theodore could tell his brother was frustrated, like when he injured his ankle and had to guide Theodore back to his location via thought messages.

"What now?" Theodore asked.

Daniel fidgeted in his seat. He crossed his arms over his chest. "There is one thing we haven't tried."

"Tell me."

"What about hypnosis? Would you be willing to try it? I know quite a bit about the procedure. We might be able to bypass the resistant part of you."

Theodore thought about what was being offered and let a mischievous smile slip into place. "Okay, but don't turn me into a pig or a donkey. I'm just getting used to the idea of being a werewolf."

Chapter Twenty-One

After Daniel made the suggestion, he didn't know if he could hypnotize Theodore. The odds weren't in his favor. Theodore had gone through so much at the hands of the WKA. Daniel was sure he would oppose manipulation on all levels. But he'd underestimated Theodore once again. Theodore put his fears aside and trusted his older brother. Now the boy lay on the bed in a deep trance state, the picture of relaxation.

"If only I could be so innocent," Daniel sighed as he pushed a thick lock of hair back from Theodore's forehead. Theodore had inherited his curls from their father, along with their father's generous, kind countenance. The color of Theodore's hair came from his birth mother. Her hair was almost black too. While Daniel was fair, with a lighter frame, Theodore was darker, more filled out and open-faced.

"Be open now, Theo. Help me to help you," Daniel whispered in a soothing voice. As he took a seat by the bedside, he collected his thoughts, sketching out a plan about how to proceed. As he posed his inquiries, things went well. Theodore's answers were given with no hesitation. Within a few minutes, Daniel felt they had reached a point where he could ask Theodore the big question.

"Is Theodore telling the truth when he says he wants to change? Does he want to allow his werewolf nature to come out?"

Theodore's answer was immediate. "He's not allowed."

"He allowed it earlier today."

"When his body was threatened by outside forces, it chose survival. But his rational mind can't make the change happen. It's all part of the way he was programmed."

As soon as Daniel heard the answer, he closed his eyes with fatigue and loathing.

Oh hell, it's just like I thought. The WKA has him totally screwed up.

As he railed against the hated organization, he was forced to unbutton his shirt collar. The room felt too warm, but he didn't want to stop what he was doing. He glanced up and looked at Theodore. His brother's face remained peaceful. "Tell me more about the program you mentioned."

Theodore's lids fluttered a few times. "When he was very young, he was given instructions about what he could do."

Again, Daniel's thoughts flashed to the WKA. Memories started to surface. He instantly tried to block them out, but it was too late. His body was already reacting. Just the briefest glimpse into what he'd endured as a child had his hand shaking. He had to wipe perspiration from his brow.

No, no, no! I have to stop myself from going there if I'm going to help Theodore.

His determination did nothing to change what was happening to him physically. Not only was the room too hot, he couldn't get enough air. The space felt claustrophobic. Some deep breathing helped, but his heart continued to race. Before he asked Theodore his next question, he had to get up and open a window. The cool air helped a little. Thankfully, Theodore didn't seem to be bothered by anything they were talking about.

Daniel began his questions again. "Who programmed Theodore?"

The answer was delivered in a casual tone. "You did."

Daniel's eyes flared with surprise and suspicion. "When? When did I program Theodore?"

"When he was a baby, when the bad ones captured the two of you."

"The WKA?"

"Yes."

"I could never do something like that to my own brother."

"You were there. You followed the instructions that were given to you. Theodore trusted you. You passed those instructions on to him."

The accusation hit Daniel with enough force to make his breath stop. There was no oxygen available when he remembered what it was like to be a prisoner of the WKA. The vision was terrifying, making his heart pound so hard he could hear the blood rushing in his ears. His body was letting him know not to continue what he was doing. If he pursued his line of questioning, he might learn the truth, but at what cost? Did he really want to go back to that place where his nightmares were housed?

Stay in the moment! Learn what you need to know, but don't let yourself slip into the past.

But an inner door had already been thrown open. He felt strong hands holding him down, strapping him to something hard. The feeling was so unbearable he almost passed out. He recovered just in time to look around Theodore's bedroom. With clenched fists, he forced himself to breathe again. He had to know what his part had been in what had happened to Theodore. Had he helped the WKA? Was he the one responsible for what his brother was going through? He glanced at Theodore again. "Do you know why I'm feeling like this, like I can't breathe?"

Theodore's voice remained calm as if he existed outside his emotions. "It's because of your programming. You were never meant to understand these things."

"Then how can we be having this conversation?"

"On one occasion, when the bad people left the room, you added a clause, an escape clause."

"Escape clause?" Daniel whispered the words as if he were remembering a prayer. "Tell me about it."

"I can't. You gave very specific instructions about discussing it."

"Please, tell me there's a way to allow Theodore to change into his true, natural self again."

"There is a way, but I can't tell you about it. You gave very specific instructions."

"Is there any way to keep Theodore from dying?"

"Yes."

"How?"

"The escape clause."

Daniel shut his eyes. He had to stop and regroup. He had to claw his way back from feeling he was helpless and at the mercy of sadistic monsters. "Listen to me. Listen very carefully. Theodore is ordered to stay alive. Do you understand?"

"Yes."

"Are you going to obey my orders?"

"Yes, if you use the escape clause. Until then, there's nothing more to discuss."

Theodore's statement had a finality to it, a grim decree Daniel knew he couldn't change. And yet, he didn't have a clue about what Theodore was talking about. What was an escape clause? He searched desperately to find an answer. Instead, he felt himself slipping back into that place and time when he and Theodore were both captives. He heard Theodore screaming in pain. His baby brother was being tortured, and he couldn't do anything to stop it. He could hear himself screaming too.

"Daniel, talk to me! Daniel, what's wrong?"

Theodore's voice broke into Daniel's trance-like state. When he opened his eyes, his hands were grasping the arms of the chair. He tried to focus, but the room was spinning. He shut them again and took a couple of choking breaths. "Just give me a second," he pleaded.

"Daniel, what's going on?" Theodore asked anxiously.

When Daniel was able to collect himself, he saw Theodore sitting up, watching him. His brother had come out of hypnosis on his own. Daniel tried to give him a reassuring smile. "It's okay. I'll be fine."

Theodore didn't look convinced by Daniel's statement, but he didn't press for details. He asked about the session. "Did you find out anything?"

Daniel shook his head. "No, but we'll try again later."

* * *

When Theodore came back to his normal state, he felt like he'd been in a dreamless sleep. He didn't remember anything, but when he looked at Daniel, he got scared. He'd never seen his brother look so pale, so beaten down, like someone had taken a rod to his back and thrashed him mercilessly.

Whatever was wrong, he knew Daniel didn't want him to know about it. His brother's mind was closed to Theodore. Yet, he felt a kinship with his brother that wasn't there before. He reached out to Daniel, hoping to convey his appreciation. "Thanks for trying to help. I'm sure I'm going to be fine."

Daniel came over and took Theodore's hand in both of his. His grip was tight but shaky.

"Of course you are," Daniel said.

Theodore smiled. "Do you want to tell me about what happened?"

Daniel let go of Theodore's hand and walked to the door. "We'll talk later. I have some things I have to do. I'll be back as soon as I'm done."

"In the meantime, I'll get some sleep," Theodore promised.

After Daniel left, Theodore tried to doze off, but his mind was too busy and his body hurt. He looked around the room he was in, noting a couple of pastoral paintings on the wall, a lamp and dresser, a small desk, and the chair Daniel had sat in. It was a simple setting, but it was all new to him. He'd only been away from his regular life for a little over a day, and yet it seemed like a lifetime ago. His recent experiences didn't seem real. Had he truly been battling men who wanted to kill him? He frowned at the thought. Of course, he had. There was a hole in his shoulder to prove it.

"Hi Theo."

He stiffened at the sound of Prissy's voice. She stood waiting in the doorway, as if she was afraid to breach his space. From a purely rational level, he knew she meant him no harm, but his body disagreed. A nervous tremor made him pull his blanket closer. "Can't sleep either?" he asked.

Prissy shook her head, not moving from the spot.

As he studied her face, he felt sad again. Prissy had changed, just like he had changed. She didn't resemble the girl who came to his house the night before. That person was vibrant and confidant. The Prissy who stood outside his door looked drawn and hopeless. "Come in," he said, trying to put some enthusiasm into his invitation.

His forthright tone seemed to give Prissy the permission she needed. She quickly walked over to his bedside chair and sat down.

"Aren't you tired?" he asked.

"How can I sleep when I know Daniel's out burying the bodies of the two guys who attacked us?"

Theodore's fingers tightened on his cover. He didn't want to think about dead bodies. "Daniel doesn't get much of a break."

Prissy glanced at him and looked away. "How about you, what's going on?"

"I guess I'm a failure when it comes to being hypnotized. Daniel said he didn't learn much. But I know he tried."

"Theo?"

"What?" He noted her furrowed brows. They were clear indicators she was upset. "What is it?"

"I've been thinking about what happened before."

"What do you mean?"

Prissy suddenly jerked upright and glared at him. "I can't believe . . . I can't believe I tried to kill you. How could I be capable of such a thing?"

Prissy's sudden outburst made Theodore jump to attention. His heart skipped a beat or two before he had a chance to calm himself.

"Sorry." Prissy quickly apologized and looked away again.

When his voice steadied, Theodore spoke up. "I know you must really hate me. I know because I heard you screaming at me."

"You did? How could you hear me? You were unconscious."

"I guess a part of me wasn't."

Prissy crossed her arms. "I don't hate you. I don't. I was just so angry. You don't know what it's like to grow up being one of us!" She instantly stopped herself and sat quietly for a few moments. "Sorry, I guess that's a stupid thing to say. Of course you know. The WKA abducted you and—"

"Let's just drop it," Theodore said. He didn't want to dwell on his past or the recent incident with Prissy. If he did, he'd only aggravate all the pain in his body. In the silence that followed, he stole glances at Prissy. Something about her reminded him of Daniel and Wolfgang. All of them had a constant undercurrent going. When he tuned into them, they tried to hide their anxiety, but it was there. They were always on alert as if some ogre was going to jump out at them. He'd always felt that way too. "Prissy, I think I understand why you're mad all the time?"

Prissy blinked back. "Is that how you see me?"

He shrugged. "Yeah, sometimes."

Prissy examined her bright, pink nails, running a finger over all the chips in the polish. "I guess I am short-tempered. Maybe I just didn't want to think about that part of myself."

"I'm not saying you don't have a right to be angry. You thought I tried to kill your dad. You didn't want to take me out just because I'm a big dope, did you?"

Prissy noticed his smile and relaxed a little. "I don't know why I called you a dope. But you were acting like one at the malt shop, admit it. I was having a hard time, and you were—"

"Asking you riddles? That was dopey, especially when I think about everything that's happened."

"I think you kind of freak me out, Theo. You were able to forgive me after I acted like some kind of savage beast. You're so much stronger than I am."

Theodore didn't know how to respond, so he pulled up the covers a little more, hoping she wouldn't see him blush. "Listen, I'm really tired."

Prissy got up, but she didn't move towards the door. She reached out very slowly and touched the edge of the bed. "Is it your heart? Do you want me to call Daniel?"

"No, I think the only thing that'll help is rest. Maybe if I can sleep, I'll feel better."

Prissy hesitated as if she needed time to collect herself. "I want to see your chest. I want to see what I did."

"No, that's not going to do either of us any good."

"Please, I need to know. Please, I won't ever ask anything else."

Theodore hadn't dared to look at his battered body, but he felt like he'd fallen off a two story building. His entire midsection was a massive source of pain. But how could he refuse Prissy's request? She seemed so intent, even desperate to know what she'd done.

"I think this is a mistake," he said as he pushed back the covers. His hand lingered on the white t-shirt Daniel had found for him. His own was beyond ruined after being shot. He slowly pulled up the t-shirt to expose his chest.

Prissy let out an involuntary cry. "Oh, dear Theo! Oh no—" She didn't move, but her wide eyes were glassy as she stared at his injuries. "I can't believe I could do such a thing."

Theodore didn't know what to say or do, except to quickly cover himself again.

"Daniel's right! I am crazy," Prissy screeched as she turned and ran from the room. Her cries were plainly audible as she made her way through the house.

Theodore wished there was something he could do to help. Prissy wasn't in her right mind when she'd hurt him. And he wasn't guilty of the things she accused him of doing. If he really considered the circumstances, he knew they were both innocent. The thought brought him the peace he needed to close his eyes. Like he'd told Prissy, he had to rest if his heart was going to get better.

"I'm going to sleep for a long, long time," he mumbled as he started to drift off.

Chapter Twenty-Two

Amelie went back to bed after she'd calmed Prissy down a second time in one evening. It felt so good to cuddle up close to Wolfgang. In spite of everything, he was still alive. A spark of joy and relief surged through her when she listened to his breathing. It had settled into a nice steady rhythm.

Earlier, when Daniel had briefed Wolfgang on the hypnosis session with Theodore, Wolfgang looked exhausted. Happily, he was able to fall asleep shortly after Daniel left. Amelie couldn't believe she didn't follow his example. She always loved the dream state and usually clocked eight hours a night. But even though her body was medicated with painkillers, a different kind of pain plagued her mind. She kept thinking about Prissy and Theodore.

Why does it have to be so hard for them? They're kids. They shouldn't have the kinds of problems they're facing.

When she thought about the bigger picture, she went into more distress. The pack was lucky to have gone as long as they had without some kind of violence. The tragedy with Daniel's family was the last major incident they'd had. Since then, everyone had been extremely careful. The individuals in the group were scattered throughout the city. They communicated secretly. They did everything they could to stay hidden from the WKA or any would-be fanatic who was out for their blood.

Now all their lives were in jeopardy. The two defectors were outcasts now. They might want revenge. They might give the WKA information about the pack. Wolfgang had already sent word for everyone to be prepared to vacate their homes and jobs if the worst came to pass. Adults having to flee for their lives was bad enough, but the children involved gave Amelie the most heartache. Again, she thought about Theodore and Prissy.

What kind of future are we giving you, my poor babies?

She snuggled closer to Wolfgang. Her future was at risk too. She couldn't imagine being without the man she loved. After so many years of marriage, their bond was stronger than ever. She didn't care if she had to nurse him forever, it would be preferable to losing him.

"Stop thinking like that," Wolfgang said, opening his eyes and touching her cheek. "I'm going to be fine."

She clutched his hand and held it tight. "Go back to sleep. You have to get your rest."

"What about you? Don't you think I worry about you too?"

"I keep going over my neediness since this all started. My attitude has been awful. I've failed you."

"Why? Why would you even think something like that?"

"I'm such a coward. I've watched you suffering, and still, all I want to do is keep you here, no matter what. Even if you had to live your days out in a wheelchair, I don't care. Is that love?"

"What do you mean?"

"Love is selfless, but mine is anything but that. All I do is think about how I could lose you. In the past, I've blamed it on being human. I wanted to be brave like you, but I know now, even if I were like you, I'd feel the same way."

Wolfgang pushed himself up and pulled her into his arms. "Amelie, my precious wife, I'm just as selfish. Why do you think I couldn't let you try the experimental drugs?"

She scowled back. "Selfish? You? I don't think so. You're a totally caring man who wanted to paint, to be an artist. You gave up your desires to serve others, but you never complain."

"Why would I? I wanted to express my love for beauty on a canvas. Then I married beauty itself."

She blushed. "That's not how I see myself."

Wolfgang's eyes glowed as he studied her face. "I read that the word 'beauty' was once defined as 'the promise of happiness.' That's how I feel when I look at you. I'm happy. It's as simple as that."

"But what about the fear we have when we think about losing the person we love? Being so passionate about one another is almost a curse."

"Love is never the curse. If you look at the world—"

"The world is a horrible place!"

"No, it's not! The world is beautiful, like you. The master artist, who keeps it spinning, renews its beauty every day. We have the sunrise to welcome us when we awake. At night, we have the stars to bid us sweet dreams." He paused and stared at the ring on his finger. "Before I took over as pack leader, I loved studying nature. Everything works together so perfectly. Whether you delve into anatomy or astronomy, there's perfection in all of it. No, the world isn't the problem. But you're right about the fear, it can consume you and block out the sun and the stars."

"What if the WKA or some radicals kill you or Prissy? I'll have nothing left but the fear."

"No, that's not true. You'll have the beauty of the world if you choose to see it. It's always there for us."

"How could I choose beauty when my heart would be broken?"

"If you let yourself see beyond the pain, you and I would be together in every flower and every child's smile. That's what love does. It allows us to embrace all of life. Fear makes one's perception very small. Love does the opposite. If we refocus a little, we could know that even a breath is a gift. I've learned that lying here in this bed. And that gift can help to mend our wounds."

She couldn't help but smile. "You should have been a poet or philosopher."

"Perhaps you're right. If I had chosen one of those paths, I'd use what I feel for you to fuel my words and thoughts."

She laid her head on his shoulder. "So you're saying it's not love that's my problem, it's my fear. That's the real curse. Is that right?"

"Yes, my dear Amelie, it is."

* * *

Daniel's face was lined with exhaustion as he pulled the second body towards the shallow grave. The soil was too rocky to dig a proper one. Loose stone piled on top of a layer of dirt would have to do for now. Later, he'd make arrangements to give the bodies a proper burial. But the idea of 'later' seemed like an eternity away.

He dropped the body in its temporary resting place and stepped back. He tried to ignore the sick feeling in his stomach. He hated having to do what he was doing. But he couldn't give the job to anyone else, and he couldn't call for help. He was afraid to give away the location of the safe house to any more people in the pack.

At this point, trust was a major issue. He was also afraid to move Theodore and Wolfgang. They were both in very bad shape, especially Theodore. Any disruption could overtax his heart. If his brother could rest for a few hours, maybe he would improve a little. In the meantime, there were bodies that needed attention.

Bodies.

The word made him think about what he'd had to do. He'd never killed anyone before, much less people he knew. The guy he was burying was Martin Clark. He was a twin of Allen Clark, the man in the other grave. The two look-alike brothers had been his buddies in college. Daniel went to football games with them. Now their bodies were riddled with bullets.

What can I tell their loved ones?

He'd gone into battle thinking he'd be fine with taking out traitors. He didn't think about the 'bad' guys as former friends. He didn't have time to think. It was different now. When he looked at the man he had to bury, a dismal feeling set in. Even though he knew he hadn't had a choice, he had killed someone's husband. Mary, Martin's wife, was the cheerful type, always there when the pack needed a volunteer for something. And Martin wasn't a villain at heart. He was totally misguided.

Daniel was sure Saxon was the leader of the outlaw group. Surely, he was the one who had poisoned the minds of both of the brothers. Saxon believed Wolfgang's leadership was failing. In the end, Saxon thought the pack would be exterminated if there weren't changes. He must have convinced the brothers that Wolfgang needed to be removed by any means. Once they failed to kill Wolfgang outright, the group was intent on not only finishing the job, but killing Wolfgang's family, Daniel included.

I should have seen it coming.

Daniel had argued with Saxon, insisting on peaceful changes. Ironically, their different points of view had once escalated into a confrontation. Saxon backed out at the last minute. As the man stepped away, Daniel remembered his opponent's eyes being hard and cunning. When Saxon smiled, he let Daniel read his thoughts. "Fine, my misguided friend, we'll do it your way, for now."

Three months had passed since their argument.

Why was I so blind to what was coming? Why?

When Daniel had confessed his sins of omission to Wolfgang and told him how careless he'd been, the older man assured him he was being too hard on himself. Daniel didn't agree. When he looked at the man he was about to bury, he knew there was no excuse for his carelessness. Then he thought of Theodore.

Hell, I should have cared that I had a brother out there all these years.

It was no mystery about why he hadn't looked for Theodore. After the hypnosis session, he knew he'd been too afraid to think in terms of a lost brother, too traumatized by what he'd experienced. Now it was too late to care. He rubbed his forehead trying to ease his throbbing headache.

Theodore might be going into a grave soon if I don't come up with an answer!

His mind kept turning over the same question.

What is the escape clause? Think, Daniel, think! Theodore's life is in your hands, again.

No matter how hard he tried to dredge up some secret locked away in his subconscious, he failed. The more he judged himself, the sicker he felt. Finally, his body couldn't take any more stress. He fell to his knees and started vomiting. His stomach twisted and heaved, but even vomiting was useless. He hadn't eaten for almost two days. There was nothing left to purge but bile and regret.

He was lightheaded when he stood up again. He'd never had such a weak stomach before. Nausea came and went quickly if he was sick. So why was it so much worse now? Then it hit him. Theodore also had stomach problems. "Great, I can't help him, so I'm joining him in his misery. What a disaster."

Chapter Twenty-Three

Two wolves ran flat out through the woods. Beautiful and wild, one was almost pure silver, the other white and grey. They ran side-by-side in unison, a large male and a smaller, light-footed female. Both were swift and perfect in form.

Theodore knew he was dreaming as he watched the wolves, but the dream seemed as real as life. He could smell the pines and the deep, satisfying scent of the forest's leafy loam. The sunlight overhead, trickling down through the trees, was warm and made the leaves greener and brighter. A gentle breeze tempered the day with a clarity and freshness. Yet he couldn't take his eyes off of the wolves. It was exhilarating to experience these splendid creatures running free in their natural setting. As he began to merge with the reality of the tranquil scene, he felt himself being drawn into the action. He could almost feel himself running alongside the pair.

The explosive sounds of gunshots brought him up short. He became the watcher again. In alarm and revulsion, he realized two men were pursuing the wolves. They were firing on the fleeing animals. One of the rounds hit the female, tearing into her shoulder, making her convulse in the air as she let out a yelp of pain and shock. A second bullet hit the male who had already slowed his pace as soon as his mate was hit. It blasted a large, bloody hole in his side. He went down with the impact.

As the men ran towards them, both animals tried to regain their footing. They clawed at the ground, struggling to reach each other. More shots rang out. This time the male was hit several more times, in the neck and haunch. The female was hit in the head, and she lay still and unmoving. The male battled on, but he never reached his mate. The next volley of shots made sure there was no breath left in him either.

The dream shifted before Theodore had time to process his shock. Another scene presented itself. It was night, and the same men were running through a house, chasing a boy. The boy's face was streaked with tears as he ran, but he couldn't escape the men. He was cornered in a small bedroom. He immediately turned to confront his pursuers. He swiped at his tears, and cried out in fright. "Why are you doing this? Leave me alone!"

Grunting from the chase, a heavyset man advanced towards him. "Why are we here?" he asked with a laugh. "Your kind are vermin! Worse than rats!"

The boy kept trying to wipe his tears away. "What did you do to my mom and dad?"

The man and his partner both laughed this time. Their faces twisted in grim pleasure. "They're dead, you little piece-of-shit. And it was so much fun watching them die."

The boy was stunned, his blameless eyes blinked back with misery. After a moment, he let out a shriek of grief. He rushed forward, attacking the man nearest him with his fists. He dispatched his fiercest blows as the man tried to grab hold of him. The second man put an end to the boy's attack. He used the blunt end of his gun and delivered a swift thrust to the boy's head, rendering him unconscious.

The heavyset man grimaced at the boy who lay at his feet. "Little shit," he scoffed as he kicked the boy out of his way.

As the room grew quiet, the sound of a child crying came from the closet. The heavyset man smiled and walked over to the closet door. He threw it open and looked in. His smile widened when he glanced at his partner. "It's in here. The older one must have been trying to hide it."

"Grab it and let's leave."

As if he'd been given an unpleasant task, the man sneered as he pulled a curly-haired toddler from behind some boxes. Exposed to the scene, the little boy saw his brother lying bloodied on the floor and began to cry louder.

"Shut up, you little bastard," the man yelled back as he slapped the baby's face.

The child screamed out. His piercing wails filled the air with his wretchedness. All the while he squirmed with all his might, reaching out for his brother.

Ignoring the baby, the second man pointed to the older boy. "And bring that one too. We'll find a use for it."

The battered, older boy was stirring, coming to his senses enough to try to protest one last time. "Kill me if you have to, but please, don't hurt my brother."

The man holding the toddler responded by kicking the boy again. This time it was so hard, he was slammed against the wall.

* * *

The baby was still screaming and so was Theodore as the world started rocking. He tried to escape the dream. When he opened his eyes, he realized Daniel was leaning over him, shaking him awake.

"Theodore, you're having a nightmare," Daniel said anxiously.

Theodore looked up at him and recognized Daniel's eyes from the dream. They were the boy's eyes. Daniel was the boy who tried to save his brother.

I was that baby! That means he tried to save me!

Now, Daniel was staring at him with the same concern. As Theodore gazed back, he felt a powerful connection to the past they shared.

I didn't just have a dream.

He had just seen what had happened to his mother and father. They hadn't actually been wolves. They were gifted beings, but they were hunted and killed liked animals. Afterwards Daniel had tried to protect Theodore, but he couldn't. Both of them had been captured.

He blinked at Daniel. "Those men! What they did to you!" he said as his voice cracked and became a shriek of grief. His body responded with sharp, stabbing pains in his heart. This time they were so deep and convulsive, he was gasping for air. The nightmare wouldn't go away. He was in the powerful arms of the revolting man. He watched as his brother lay bleeding on the floor. Daniel was reaching out, still trying to fight his attackers. Daniel was like the wolves. He wouldn't give up. He was willing to give his life before he'd let them take Theodore.

Now, Theodore could feel his brother reaching out to him again. Daniel was tuning into Theodore's thoughts. As he did, their minds merged, they were both thrust into that place where darkness and pain held them captive.

As soon as Daniel understood what was happening to Theodore, he tried to help. "No, Theo! Please! Your heart can't take it, please. Let go of the past! Don't let it in!"

In spite of his pleas, the pain of all they'd gone through began to flood into Theodore. An inner, forgotten vault had been flung open, revealing all the horror, all the monstrous experiments he'd endured as a baby. It ravaged his mind with a plague of unspeakable atrocities.

Daniel started shaking him. "It doesn't help to remember," he cried out. "Please, Theo. I'm begging you, don't go there!"

Theodore tried to listen to Daniel, but he was stuck in the nightmare, and it was squeezing the life out of him.

* * *

Daniel's breath was heaving and frantic as he watched Theodore battle for life. He remembered being outside earlier, digging graves and thinking about Theodore's fate.

I'm going to be burying my brother next!

His overwhelming panic was intensified by Theodore's labored attempts to breathe. Daniel shook him with more and more desperation, begging him to come back from the darkness that was swallowing him. Finally, he snatched Theodore up in his arms and held him to his breast.

"Please don't die. I did my best to take care of you. I tried, but I couldn't!"

As he held Theodore, he did the only thing left. He tried to take everything they had suffered into himself. It filled his body just like it filled Theodore's. The ghastly burden transported him back in time. He was the twelve-year-old kid again. He was the boy in the bedroom, staring up at the violent man who was laughing at him. The man was taking great pleasure in telling his story.

"You should have seen your parents, begging on their knees, pleading for your lives!" As the man laughed, his small, hateful eyes lit up. "It was fun watching 'em squirm, watching 'em die when I shot 'em."

After that, the same monster got hold of Theodore. The vision was so clear. Daniel could see every fold of flesh in the man's fat, sneering face. When the man glared at the child who dangled in his large fist, he scowled with disgust. The screaming baby was nothing to him, just an unfeeling nuisance. He didn't refer to the baby as a person. He used the word "it." It was an animal that would be useful in laboratory testing. The scene was so real Daniel tried to reach out through the memory and fight back. He saw himself fight to reclaim his brother. But again, he felt the man retaliate. This time, when the man kicked him, it was with so much force Daniel couldn't help but scream in agony.

The pain was almost more unbearable when Daniel relived it. The blow he sustained was so excruciating something inside of him ripped apart. As he held Theodore tight against him, as he cradled his dying brother, a scar from the past was torn open. He felt a gaping hole deep within the depths of his being. It was a hole that held a secret, a lost treasure hidden in the darkness. Now that secret poured out of the wound and filled Daniel with a phrase, a mantra.

"I am my brother's keeper. I am my brother's keeper," he cried out over and over. As he repeated the phrase, as he rocked Theodore, something began to happen. Daniel felt lighter, as if a great burden had been lifted. His mood shifted enough to allow him to witness what was happening to Theodore. His brother's body and mind were experiencing a profound journey back from that dark place they'd visited. The terrible memories that had fired through Theodore's brain and lodged in his chest were loosening their claws. The sharp talons that were buried in his brother's heart were dissolving. Light began to fill the space where Theodore had been a prisoner. As it did, the vessel that had been cloaked in misery for so long was being freed. The chamber full of horrid memories was finally being restored to a state where healing could take place. Theodore's face reflected the changes. It lost its deathly pallor. His cheeks regained a bit of color, and his breathing began to return to normal. The brother that Daniel feared he might have to bury was not only alive, he was looking better by the minute.

As Daniel rejoiced at what was happening, his mind filled with another vision. This one was perfect. He saw a young man, strong and handsome, striding towards him. The person wasn't clumsy or awkward or fearful. He smiled back with confidence as if he was returning from battle, glorious and renewed. As the vision faded, Theodore stirred in Daniel's arms and opened his eyes.

"You did it. You saved me," Theodore whispered.

Just as the pain had filled him, now Daniel felt Theodore's love. It was a powerful force he didn't resist. He'd been alone for a very long time, keeping his heart shielded and safe from harm. Theodore's gratitude and happiness became a sweet, honeyed balm for his ailing vessel.

* * *

When Daniel and Theodore both regained a sense of composure, they sat looking at each other like they were kids again. "Welcome back to the land of the living," Daniel said with a smile.

Theodore grinned back. "The escape clause! You remembered the escape clause."

Daniel nodded, recalling what he'd done when they'd been abducted. As a young boy who couldn't escape the hands of the

WKA, he'd had to come up with a trigger that would bring Theodore back from whatever hell the WKA had visited upon him. "They made me program you, Theo. I had to tell you to reject your true nature, your gifted side. I had no choice."

When Daniel tried to refuse, they tortured Theodore. Later, when he had a moment alone with his baby brother, Daniel devised a plan. In his young mind, it was simple. Someday he swore he'd get his brother back. He promised to restore Theodore's heritage. Even though Theodore was only a toddler, Daniel gave him the words that would make it happen. Afterwards, the WKA had brainwashed Daniel too, and he'd forgotten about the trigger phrase. "They threatened to kill you if I tried to find you. They planted a suggestion that I forget about you completely. But you found me."

Theodore's face was pure joy. "And guess what? You're exactly like the brother I always wanted."

Daniel let out a sigh of relief. It came from years of being guilt-ridden. On some subconscious level, he knew he'd had to hurt Theodore. Even if it wasn't his fault, he couldn't forgive himself in the years that followed. "Maybe, just maybe, now we can both be free again."

Before Theodore could respond or they could celebrate their victory further, Prissy burst into the room.

"Daniel! Come quick! Dad just got a call concerning Saxon! I think he's told the WKA where we are."

The momentary calm of rejoicing came to an abrupt end.

"That bastard! I didn't think he could be so cruel!" Daniel jumped to his feet, switching gears instantly. "Tell your dad I'll be right there."

As Prissy ran back out, he turned to Theodore. "How do you feel? Do you think you're up for round two? We have to get out of here."

Theodore's eyes widened with newfound strength. "After what I just saw, I think I can face anything. Besides, whatever just happened helped my body. My heart feels a little better."

Daniel nodded. "Try to change again when we get in the car. That's your best bet for healing quickly."

Chapter Twenty-Four

Theodore rode shotgun in the big SUV. It was an hour before dawn. Everything was still shrouded in darkness. He was thankful Daniel was in the driver's seat. He trusted his brother's abilities. Daniel had definitely proven himself in the shootout with the rogue pack members.

Daniel gave him an encouraging look, then checked on the back seat passengers. "Is everyone buckled up?"

Wolfgang sat between Amelie and Prissy. He nodded to Daniel. "So it's agreed we don't use the road, right?"

"Right," Daniel said as he started the engine. "The bastards could be here any minute and there's only one road in. It's narrow with steep drop-offs. If we ran into them trying to leave, they could box us in before we got to the highway. We'll have to use the old mining road on the other side of this hill. If we can make it to the top before they get here, I think we have a chance of getting away."

"But the terrain is so rocky and rutted," Theodore added. "Do you think you can get to the top in this car? It's not exactly made for this kind of terrain. My mom slows down to a crawl for speed bumps."

Daniel shot him an 'I don't believe it' look.

Prissy let out a hiss of disapproval. "Theo, we don't have time to hear about your mother's driving habits," she yelled. "We could all be killed if the WKA gets to us."

Theodore glared at her. With the danger they were facing, she sounded more like her old self again. "I'm not worried about the car, I just don't know if it's capable of climbing a hill."

"We'll find out soon enough," Daniel said as he put the SUV in reverse. He gunned it out of the driveway, swerved sharply, and turned in the direction of the hill. "Hold on, everyone," he ordered. He rammed the gear shift into drive and pressed hard on the gas petal.

The fast movement of the car lurching forward made everyone grab for something to brace against. Theodore immediately put a hand on the dash and one on the side of Daniel's seat. His shoulder burned and his body ached, but he had to ignore his physical pain. He wanted to help.

Daniel read his thoughts. "Watch for rocks and gullies," he instructed as he drove off the property and into the brush. They immediately hit a deep rut, but Daniel was going fast enough to navigate over it.

"I think my dad said this car has very good shocks," Theodore offered nervously.

"Please shut up!" Prissy shouted as her head hit the side window.

Theodore didn't blame her for being upset. He knew what was going through her mind. The thought of the WKA and what could happen to them if they were captured was more frightening than being killed.

"It's going to be alright, honey," Wolfgang said as he reached out for Prissy's hand.

"I'm sorry, everyone," Daniel apologized, "but we have to get up this hill, and it's going to get very—"

"Rock!" Theodore yelled, cutting him off.

Daniel swerved just in time to avoid the hazard and hit another rut.

* * *

The SUV was three-fourths of the way up the hill when Daniel saw two vehicles in his side mirror. They had stopped at the property line, but they had powerful searchlights probing the area, including the hill behind the house.

"Oh hell," he groaned. "They're here, and I think they've spotted us. They'll probably start firing soon. Everybody needs to get down as low as possible."

Wolfgang responded instantly. "Prissy, Amelie, take off your seatbelts and see if you can squeeze yourselves down close to the floor."

"What about you?" Amelie cried out.

"Don't worry about me! Just do as I say!"

Daniel glanced at Theodore. "You too, Theo! Slouch down as far as possible."

"I'm helping you navigate," Theodore protested.

"Stay down!" Daniel shouted. "They're coming up after us!"

As he spoke, the first rounds of gunfire sounded from the bottom of the hill. It shattered the quiet, night air and the darkness with a lethal announcement of what was coming.

* * *

Theodore forgot about Daniel's directive to change form. From what he'd been told, Daniel and adult werewolves lived their lives in an elevated state of awareness. When they wanted, they could intensify those states. He had only managed the feat one time when he'd actually been conscious of the change. Afterwards, he reverted back.

That was the way it was for his age group. Both he and Prissy were in an in-between stage. It would take a year or more for their true nature to develop fully enough for them to remain in their gifted state. Girls usually began to change sooner than boys so

Theodore didn't feel so bad about being older and still in the middle of the change. However, in the present situation, he had to be at his best.

I've got to change, and I have to do it fast!

As the car leaped and fell, bouncing them about haphazardly, as the sound of gunfire continued, his body seemed to know what was needed. The physical part of him sent out signs he recognized from before. It was a good feeling, a powerful feeling. His muscles felt stronger and more sinewy. His focus became one-pointed, and his perception went from a feeling of confusion to one of clarity. Most importantly, his intense fear was taking a back seat to a growing sense of boldness.

He smiled at the thought that he could be helpful just as a bullet shattered the back window. It continued forward, grazed his outstretched arm and exited through the windshield. Glass and cries of shock filled the car.

"Is everyone okay?" Daniel shouted.

Theodore didn't hear any answers. The experience was so traumatic, so life threatening, that a part of him was catapulted out of his body. He was in the SUV, and then there was a loud cracking sound as if something broke free.

Suddenly he was floating above the vehicle. When he looked down at the car, he saw that Daniel didn't pause in spite of the gunshot. He was trying to get the SUV behind the cover of a nearby boulder. The two jeeps below were gaining on them. Men were firing out of the side windows. Bright bursts of fire from their gun barrels lit up the darkness as a volley of bullets sought their target.

* * *

After the bullet took out the back window, Daniel's breath hung suspended in dread until he heard Amelie, Prissy, and Wolfgang yell out. They were okay. When he didn't hear Theodore's voice, he glanced over only long enough to see that his brother had passed out. Trying to navigate and tune into him at the same time, Daniel finally knew his worst fears were unfounded. Theodore was alive. Nothing vital had been hit, yet.

Bullets were flying all around them as he searched the area for a place to take cover. "If we can make it to that rock over there, we have a chance," he called out, offering a bit of hope. With the darkness, the deep shadows and the constant bouncing in all directions, it was hard to see ahead. He barely had time to alter his course, dodging one rock only to hit another.

"Hold on!" he yelled. The SUV leaped upwards, and then came down. It landed in a large, cavernous rut and pitched forward at a steep angle. Daniel tried to put the car in reverse, but the front wheels weren't able to get any traction on the loose shale and sand. The back tires were barely touching the ground. The SUV was stuck. It was a perfect situation for the men pursuing them. Bullets began to hit the vehicle. Daniel didn't know if they should try to make a run for it. The rock he'd been going for was fifteen feet away. After a moment's consideration, he decided it might just as well have been a mile away. The gunfire was almost continuous.

He scrambled to come up with a plan. The only option was to lay down enough gunfire for the others to get to safety. There was a problem with his solution. He was almost out of ammunition. The safe-house wasn't set up for war. He'd been lucky to have the weapons and bullets he'd had for the first battle. Now he knew he couldn't outgun the number of men coming after them.

* * *

From Theodore's aerial vantage point, the SUV below looked like a big, white, sitting duck. It had lurched upwards after hitting another rock and slammed down into a deep rut. The wheels began to spin, but they couldn't catch. Bullets continued to punish the area, striking trees and rocks. One hit the SUV's back fender and a spray of more bullets peppered the bumper. Theodore's only thought was that his brother, Prissy and her family were going to die. The WKA would succeed and massacre them all.

Before he had time to worry about their fates, a part of him went into action. Without thinking, he began to dive from his elevated position. He felt like a great eagle plummeting to earth. The term, hell-dive, took on new meaning for him. He moved at an incredible rate of speed, a falling object that would soon collide with the stony landscape below.

But I'm not in my normal body.

His realization was as immediate as the correction he made before he hit the ground. Whatever he was, it was something that felt like a form of sorts, and it managed to make a sharp-angled turn and straighten out. He was now moving towards the two enemy vehicles. The men inside the jeeps were getting out now that the SUV was stranded. They'd be able to attack their target more effectively if they moved forward on foot.

Theodore was on them so fast he didn't know what he was supposed to do. Again, the unfamiliar part of him was in charge. It knew exactly what was wanted. It changed his form again. Landing a few yards behind the five men, he realized he wasn't alone. Two wolves, one all-silver and the other white and grey, were standing on his flanks. They were the wolves from his dream, and both were snarling. Theodore was snarling too. That's when he understood what he was.

I've turned into one of them!

At the same instant Theodore realized he'd become an animal, one of the men turned and saw him.

"Look out!" the man yelled out to the others. "Wolves! Behind us!"

Theodore and his two companions instinctively leapt forward before the men had time to regroup. They were on top of the men almost instantly, throwing three of them backwards. One man hit his head on a large rock and was rendered unconscious. The large, silver wolf that had attacked him was free to go after the fourth man who had already started to flee.

Theodore's wolf-self wasted little time on his target, snapping down hard on the man's gun hand. Bone crushed beneath the force of his powerful jaws. The taste of blood and the sound of the screaming man filled his senses. Theodore knew he had to go after the fifth man. He looked up and saw the man a few feet away. The man turned to face him. He had a weapon, and it was pointed at Theodore's head.

Before Theodore had a chance to think about his fate, the smaller wolf lunged forward and side-swiped the man. He got off a shot, but it missed its mark. It didn't hit Theodore's heart. The bullet slammed into his good shoulder. The impact was so great he was thrown backwards. He landed in a heap and lay still for a second. He heard his own breath. He was panting, hard and fast.

* * *

Daniel and Wolfgang tuned into the skirmish below them at the same time. They were able to see everything through what they knew were Theodore's eyes. But it wasn't the Theodore who lay unconscious in the passenger seat. This was his spirit's vision. It had obviously left his human form behind and transported itself to the battle scene further down the hill.

Daniel had heard of stories from long ago that spoke of such things. As he witnessed what was happening, he found it hard to believe. There was something else to consider. The gunfire in their direction had suddenly stopped.

"Everyone move out while you have a chance!" he yelled.

Wolfgang was bent over in the back seat, pushing down on Amelie and Prissy, trying to keep them as low as possible. Now he sat up. "Prissy, Amelie! When Daniel gives you the order, run for—"

"No!" Daniel shrieked, interrupting him. A single shot rang out as he screamed, as he saw a WKA thug take out one of the wolves. Daniel had seen the man getting ready to fire at the wolf's body. It was the one Theodore's spirit was in. But Daniel was helpless to do anything about it. He'd never experienced anything like what was happening. Yet he knew instinctively that Theodore could be injured. The knowledge simply popped into his head.

Daniel immediately looked over at the passenger seat. His brother remained unconscious, but a bright red stain appeared on his shirt. "Take care of Theo!" he shouted to Wolfgang. He grabbed his gun from the foot well and quickly exited the car. He didn't hesitate for even a moment. He started down the hill. He ran as fast as he could, all the while tuning into the scene below. It played out in his mind, like his own private theatre-showing. The silver and the grey wolves were still fighting. The man who'd gotten off the shot was on the ground. He was battling for his life as the she wolf tried to get to his throat. She'd already savagely bitten the first man she attacked. He was sitting up, holding a bloody hand to his neck, trying to staunch the flow of blood that was bubbling through his fingers.

The silver wolf had disabled his second quarry too. The man lay motionless as the great creature backed away. The third wolf, the one that was Theodore, was trying to stand, but he kept falling back with every attempt. Finally, he stopped trying to get up and lay still. He'd lost consciousness. As soon as he did, all three wolves disappeared as quickly as whispers of smoke on the wind.

Before he could get to the scene, Daniel heard the sound of a helicopter. The flutter of the blades was headed in the direction of the house, in his direction.

Chapter Twenty-Five

Amelie glanced up at the helicopter. It was hovering over the area where the two jeeps had stopped. Its searchlight was focused on the scene below. The area was quiet. The fighting was over. "Thank goodness our people got here when they did," she said. "Poor Theodore!"

She turned her attention back to the boy who lay very still on the ground next to her. She pressed a hand down on his wound.

Prissy stood a few feet away. "Do you want me to do that?" she asked in a quivering voice. "I want to help."

Amelie looked up and nodded. "You're stronger than I am. Maybe you should take over."

Wolfgang was nearby too, leaned heavily against the SUV and breathing hard. "How's he doing?"

"He's losing a lot of blood." Amelie wiped her hand on her flowered blouse, adding splotches of red to its pastel pattern. "He needs medical attention."

"One of our men on the chopper is a doctor. He'll be here in a minute."

"What about the two WKA men who survived? What are you going to do about them?"

Wolfgang hesitated. "I don't know yet."

Before he could say anything more, Daniel and a second man came up the hill on foot, approaching the group at a dead run.

"The boy's over there, doc," Wolfgang said to the man carrying a medical bag.

Before the man got a chance to attend to Theodore, Daniel was already at his brother's side, feeling for his pulse. His face was hard and enraged when he glanced up at Wolfgang. "Why can't we just shoot the bastards who did this?" he yelled.

Wolfgang stared back at him, his eyes compassionate but uncompromising. "They might be cold-blooded killers, but we aren't."

Daniel glared back, his face flushed with outrage. "They deserve to die!"

Chapter Twenty-Six

When Theodore woke up, he felt like he'd been dreaming for a long time. He didn't know what time it was or what day it was, but reality was pulling him to itself slowly, giving him time to feel warm and well. When he opened his eyes, the first thing he saw was Prissy. She was standing close by.

"I thought I felt you coming back," she said, smiling. "You've been unconscious for two days."

He glanced around, noting the light green walls and soft music in the background. Then he noticed the IV in his arm. "Where am I?"

"You're in one of our medical facilities. It's underground, away from the city."

He remembered the wolf he'd been, how it was brought down by a bullet. Did it really happen or was it one of his dreams? He shut his eyes and took stock of how he felt. He wasn't in any pain, but he sure wasn't ready to take on any more of the WKA. The very thought made him flinch. "Where's Daniel?"

Prissy looked towards an open door and raised her finger to her lips. "He's taking a nap. He's been hovering over you constantly. He's ready to collapse himself."

Theodore's brows narrowed in thought, going back to what he and his brother shared before the WKA attack. "He worries too much."

Prissy shrugged. "He's your brother."

"How about you? Are you alright?"

"I'm fine. Just trying to be the obedient cub," she said with a smirk.

He laughed. "I kind of miss the old Prissy."

She frowned. "That Prissy is gone. She was a complete failure and worse."

"Hey, don't say that."

She bit her lip. "I went kind of crazy."

"Everything that's happened is crazy," he said quickly. He realized Prissy's bossy, assertive side didn't scare him anymore, not as long as she didn't get that 'I want to kill you' look in her eyes. But he missed their mischievous sparkle. He reached out for her hand, recalling the time he'd held it in the malt shop. He felt more confident, even hopeful now. "I guess we're all changing."

Prissy looked down nervously and carefully slipped her hand out of his grasp. "I'll get my parents. They'll be very happy you're awake."

It was clear that Prissy didn't trust herself. Theodore changed the subject. "How's your Dad?"

"He's under a lot of stress. He's been busy trying to handle everything that's been happening. He won't get the rest that he needs."

* * *

Wolfgang put the telephone down and sat back heavily in the upholstered chair. Taking care of his duties as pack leader had never been more challenging. He could only hope he was making the right decisions.

"How is everyone doing?" Amelie asked, coming over with a cup of tea.

"Everyone's on alert. We've got Porter, but Saxon is still out there, and who knows what he'll try next. Hopefully his vendetta only extends to Daniel and us. If I didn't have to stay here, it would be easier. I'd be able to meet with people, and—"

Amelie frowned. "Thomas will take care of things until this is over. He's a good man. He's very capable."

"Yes, you're right."

Amelie put the tea down on the table next to him, kissed his cheek and stood back. "Can I get you something else? Are you hungry?"

He smiled as he studied her eyes. They were bright and filled with a look he recognized. He hadn't had time to tell her how much he loved her since the attack at the cabin. "Come here," he said in a whisper.

It seemed to be the invitation she was waiting for. She quickly came forward. "Yes?"

"I miss our privacy," he said as he pulled her into his lap.

"I know. I can hardly wait to get back home."

"I hoped you and Prissy would never have to go through this kind of thing."

"What about you?"

He sighed. "My kind has been going through it forever. It's the way it is. If you hadn't met me, you wouldn't know about any of this. You wouldn't be sitting here, frightened."

She put her arms around him and hugged him tight. "As long as you and Prissy are safe, I can face the rest of it."

He coughed when she continued to squeeze him.

She let go and pulled back. "I'm sorry. I didn't know I was that strong."

After he got his breath, he laughed. "I did. You've always been my rock."

She gave him a playful look. "So I'm your reason for happiness and your rock? I like that."

"And what am I for you?" he asked with a flicker of desire in his eyes.

She hugged him again, this time much more carefully. "I don't know," she giggled. "What if I decided you're just my plaything?"

His eyes sparked. "I could live with that."

"Hi, am I interrupting something?" Prissy stood in the doorway, giving them an impish grin.

183

Wolfgang looked back at her with embarrassment.

Amelie sat up hurriedly. "What is it, sweetie?"

"I came to tell you Theodore is awake."

"Did you tell Daniel?" Wolfgang asked.

"No, I didn't want to disturb him. He looked so tired."

"Get him anyway. If he finds out we let him sleep, he'll be furious."

* * *

Daniel awoke with a start when he heard a soft, knocking sound. He was still exhausted, but he pushed the feeling away and opened his eyes. Prissy was standing in the doorway.

"Theo's awake," Prissy announced.

"What?" He tried to rouse himself, but his brain felt fuzzy. After days of worry, he'd finally fallen into a deep sleep.

Prissy came forward a couple of steps. "I didn't want to bother you, but Dad said you'd want to know."

Prissy's message finally got through. "Of course I want to know," he blurted out too loudly, then paused. "I'm sorry. I didn't mean to yell at you."

"It's okay."

He glanced at her with softer eyes. "Tell Theodore I'll be right there."

After Prissy shut the door, he stared up at the ceiling, trying to calm himself, trying to be grateful Theodore was awake. During the long hours Theodore was unconscious, he'd been so quiet and unmoving in the hospital bed. He looked more like an overgrown child than a maturing sixteen-year-old. All the time, Daniel couldn't help thinking Theodore wouldn't survive very long in the cruel world they inhabited. He'd already had a fatal heart attack and been shot twice. Daniel feared what would happen next. Whatever it was, he could feel it coming. Something, some terrible fate, seemed ready to deliver a final blow.

When he got out of bed, he didn't know if he could go on. Sometimes, he wanted to leave it all behind. If the WKA had finished him off, he wouldn't have had to carry around all the pain. He'd only survived because he learned to use what had happened to him. The pain became a constant reminder not to get too attached. It became a barrier that protected him. Now that barrier had been breached. He'd connected to Theodore on the night of the WKA attack. Daniel knew love was possible again, but at what cost?

Look what happened afterwards. I ended up sitting in a hospital room, in complete agony, wondering if Theodore would recover, if I'd ever be able to protect him if he did make it.

That was the problem. Daniel's track record was a joke. He'd tried his best and failed Theodore repeatedly. How was he supposed to go forward if he knew he could fail again?

I'm no good for him. It's not going to work.

Startled by a movement in the corner, he jerked back. Two wolves were staring at him with dark, searching eyes. They were the two wolves from the battlefield. They'd been haunting him. They kept popping up out of nowhere ever since that night when he'd first seen them. When he looked into their eyes, he knew they were trying to convey something, but he couldn't grasp what it was.

"What do you want from me?" he whispered. Was he losing his sanity in the middle of the mess they were in? "What the hell is going on?"

The question went unanswered. The wolves disappeared as quickly as they came.

Great, one more thing to try to figure out.

He shut his eyes and ran a shaky hand through his hair.

Calm yourself. You have to get Theodore through this, and then you can disappear.

Maybe he'd leave the pack and go somewhere far from everything he knew. It was his only comforting thought with all his other concerns. Saxon was still loose. Would the man betray the entire pack? Then there was the WKA. The local chapter was up in arms after some of their members were killed and two were

185

missing. Those two were very lucky Wolfgang was in charge. They'd be dead and buried if Daniel could have made the decision.

Chapter Twenty-Seven

Theodore thought about the night when he and Daniel remembered their shared past and connected as true brothers. On that amazing night, life changed completely. Everything went from darkness to light. He was filled with a joy he didn't know was possible in the real world. Presently, he was happy again. He was sitting in a hospital bed surrounded by smiling faces. Amelie, Wolfgang and Prissy were all gathered around him. Even Prissy looked sweet as she reached out and let go of her usual reserve.

"Your hair is getting longer," she said, picking at one of his curls. "Maybe you can let it grow out a little."

Theodore shrugged. "My adoptive mother would hate that. She can't stand it when it gets over my ears. She says I look like a shaggy dog."

Prissy laughed. "Or perhaps with a bit of gel and styling, you'd look like a cute werewolf."

"I'm just happy to see you awake and feeling better," Amelie added.

Wolfgang stepped closer, putting his arm around Amelie. "The doctors say your wounds are healing well, and that your heart is doing much better."

"I feel good," Theodore said with a grin. It slipped away when he saw Daniel coming out of the adjoining room. His face was gaunt and thinner than ever. While they stared at each other, Theodore could feel Daniel probing his mind and tuning into his body.

"I'm glad one of us feels good," Daniel finally said as he took his place at the bedside.

"Are you okay?" Theodore asked. Not only did Daniel look exhausted, but Theodore felt a swirling eddy of dark emotions just below the surface. He didn't have time to go deeper.

"Hey, stay out of my mind," Daniel insisted, trying to sound playful. "I'll be fine now that you've decided to stick around."

Theodore ignored his tone, wondering why Daniel seemed so unhappy.

Daniel picked up on it at once. "I said I'm fine."

"Will you two lighten up?" Prissy said. She frowned. "I want to know about a few things, like how Theodore turned into a wolf."

Prissy's question grabbed the attention of the group. They all turned to Theodore and stared at him expectantly.

Theodore shrugged at first, then he caught Prissy's excitement. He remembered the feelings he'd experienced as he soared through the night air. "Not just a wolf! Why didn't anyone tell me I could fly? I've never felt anything so exciting. After that, when I became a wolf, it was incredible. The idea of biting people is sort of weird."

Theodore stopped his commentary when he realized the group looked confused. He noticed that Prissy in particular had an irritated expression. "What is it? Why are you looking at me that way?"

Prissy crossed her arms. "It's not fair. You're one of us for five minutes, and you turn into a real animal. You're totally strange. You should know that."

Theodore's excitement quickly faded. "What are you saying? Why am I strange?"

Daniel gave Prissy a sample of how disapproving his eyes could be as he sat down on the bed. "You're not strange. You're very special."

"Of course you are," Amelie said as if the statement needed reinforcement. "From what Wolfgang told me, you were incredible."

Wolfgang moved to where Prissy was standing and put his hands on her shoulders. "She didn't mean to offend you, did you Prissy?"

Prissy moaned unhappily. "Why's Theodore get to do all the cool stuff?"

Theodore's smile returned. "You think I'm cool?"

Prissy finally smiled back. "Yes, you big showoff, but don't let it go to your head."

Theodore frowned. "I don't even know what happened. Why am I special?"

Daniel looked at Wolfgang. "Maybe you can tell him a little about us. You know the stories better than I do."

"Are you sure?" Wolfgang asked. "Your father was the pack's record keeper, the one who carefully preserved our history. You're better equipped to inform Theodore—"

"Please, I'm tired," Daniel replied.

Wolfgang nodded and looked at Theodore. "I don't know what your beliefs are, and I don't want to upset you by telling you things that might make you uncomfortable."

Theodore let out a small laugh. "After all that's happened? Besides, I used to think I was an alien."

Wolfgang's smile widened. "Perfect. In some ways you are."

Theodore's stomach tightened. He was just getting used to the idea that he belonged to the group around him. "Am I?"

Daniel's face finally relaxed a little. "It's okay. Let Wolfgang explain."

* * *

Wolfgang sat back in a hospital style chair next to Theodore's bed. His face was thoughtful. He wanted his information to be as accurate as possible. "Our type of being's creation story goes back to a time when man was in his infancy. Most people assume that human development was a natural evolution, just like that of all the other animals and life on Earth. I can't comment on that, but I know that our type of human developed differently."

He stopped and looked at Theodore, allowing his eyes to go bright, almost glowing. "The universe is vast and even though humans don't think there is life out there, they're wrong. There are many forms of life, many beings that populate other star systems. Some are very advanced. Some of them visited Earth long ago."

Theodore spoke up. "I bet they were from Sirius, weren't they? Astronomy's been one of my hobbies. I've always been fascinated by Sirius for as long as I can remember."

Daniel shook his head and smiled. "Do you want to tell us the story?"

Theodore blushed. "Sorry."

Wolfgang continued. "You're right. The visitors were from Sirius, and they were very interested in how Earth and mankind were progressing. They studied this world and its creatures. They wanted to help mankind along, but in our case, their work was more of a sideline."

Wolfgang crossed his arms and laughed. "Our ancestors were a very 'limited edition,' so to speak. The Sirians saw that men, beings of free will, were struggling as they fell deeper and deeper into the heaviness of matter. On the other hand, they observed the wolves. The creatures were somewhat individualistic, but they weren't too caught up in themselves. They were also completely loyal to family. They had a nobility and sense of honor the Sirians admired. They were pure and beautiful."

Theodore sat up straighter, looking more excited than ever. "We have some of their DNA, don't we?"

Daniel sighed. "Yes, but that's not all. Along with the wolf DNA, it's been told that the Sirians gave us more than that. They gave us part of their DNA too, a more evolved DNA. That gift is what has enabled us to use aspects of our human DNA that normal people haven't learned how to use. It's there in everyone, but it's dormant."

Wolfgang stared at Theodore. "In the early days, we lived in harmony with the normal humans. Because we had the Sirian DNA in us, we were more connected to knowledge and wisdom and even tried to teach what we knew. We were also more in tune with nature because of the wolfen influence. Even now we remind ourselves of that fact by using terms like 'the pack' and 'cubs.' Because of those two influences, we were able to feel more a part of the greater universe and also this world. We didn't feel quite as separate from each other as most humans. When we looked at the world around us, we felt at home. When we looked at the stars, we knew there was something out there that cared for us."

Theodore sighed. "I guess that's why I love astronomy."

Wolfgang nodded. "Unfortunately, as time went by, our relationship with normal humans began to change. They began to see us as different."

"And they were afraid of us, right?" Theodore asked with a frown.

Daniel's dark eyes flickered. "Yes, and you know what people do when they're afraid."

Wolfgang nodded. "We were hunted and most of our kind were killed. Part of the reason so many perished was that many of us didn't want to fight back. In tune with more wisdom, we knew killing was wrong. There's one Source of creation for all things, for all beings, in all the galaxies. It loves all of us. So how do we go against that fact, how do we kill another of the Creator's beloved beings?"

* * *

Daniel sat quietly, listening to Wolfgang's narrative. He already knew the stories of his ancestors. He'd heard them many times. His father often recited an oral history to him as a child to make sure it would survive. However, when Wolfgang spoke about the pacifist nature of his kind, he felt like he was hearing the idea for the first time. Perhaps, he was. He was hearing the story with the ears of a murderer, not with those of an innocent boy. The person who sat in the hospital chair killed two of his brethren only days before.

Daniel resisted the thought. He tried to deny his wrong doing, but in an instant of crystal clarity, Wolfgang's account delivered a blow of insight that wouldn't be silenced. He couldn't swallow the hard lump of damning evidence stuck in his throat. And yet, another part of him was screaming, demanding to be heard. In a sudden outburst of rage, he leapt off the bed. He was in fighting mode again, but this time he was battling for his soul.

"Yes! Our ancestors died, didn't they? They didn't stick around, oh no! They took the easy way out! Not like me. I stayed! I fought!"

In a rush, he rounded the bed and glared at Wolfgang. His eyes were stony and accusing. "You were ready to leave the world too, weren't you? If it hadn't been for me, you'd have died on that driveway. You would have let your soul be driven from this accursed world. But what would have happened to Prissy and Amelie when Saxon came after them?" He clenched his fists. "Do you remember what you said to me? 'Take care of them.' That was your last order before you passed out. Yes, that's always the way. Let Daniel take care of everything. And if that means getting out there on the battlefield, he does it. He takes a gun, and he kills."

As Daniel let the words come out, he was barely able to control his body. Battered by a treacherous, inner storm, he stumbled over to a dresser. He braced himself against it as he continued. "And Daniel keeps killing if he has to because it's his job. When the quote, 'enlightened' ones, the Wolfgangs, leave this world, it's Daniel who stays and protects what's good and true. It's Daniel who bloodies his hands. It's his soul that has to carry the sins. My father died on his knees, begging! Is that what I was supposed to do when Saxon came after my family with an automatic?"

As Daniel posed the question, he turned and stared at the people in front of him. His outburst had stunned all of them into silence. Amelie had hold of Prissy, as if she needed to protect her. Theodore looked back blankly. Wolfgang was the first to respond. He got up and walked over to where Daniel was standing.

"Daniel, I would have fought for my family too, if I'd have had the strength. I promise you, I'm not one of those ancient ones. I would have done what you did, under the circumstances."

Daniel swayed back and forth as his eyes became pools of desolation. "Even so, we're not the same. I hear myself saying all these things, and yet there's more underneath. I'm making excuses for the truth." His face hardened, trying to stay the tempest that was driving him into a despairing prison. "You would have killed to protect, but I have a hate inside of me, a hate that goes to my core. When I saw the WKA men after the battle, all I wanted to do was kill them." His voice broke and became a cry of desperation. "Now, listening to you, to myself, I know that I'm lost!"

Wolfgang grabbed Daniel's shoulders. "No, you're not, Daniel. What you're feeling is a result of the torture you and Theodore were subjected to. Hate is a response we use to stay alive when we feel everything's been taken from us. The important thing is that we got you back."

Daniel shook his head. "Maybe that's why they let me go. I feel like I brought part of them back with me, the part that hates and wants to destroy." His eyes flitted back and forth. His mind was racing, trying to escape from what was coming. "I thought Theodore was the poison, but now I realize, it's me! I've been fighting for leadership, trying to teach the younger ones to be ready to fight back." He glanced at Prissy. "But all I'm teaching is fear and hate. The WKA wanted me to split the pack and bring it to ruin." He tried to pull away from Wolfgang's steadying hands, but the older man held on to him.

"Many of your ideas are good, Daniel," Wolfgang insisted. "And I believe we can work together."

Daniel slumped in despair. It was the kind of despair he'd felt in that dark cell where the WKA had imprisoned him, and he didn't know how to escape his fate. "I'm tired of it all. I'm tired of who I am."

"Stop taking it all on yourself," Amelie said forcefully. "You're not the only one who gets afraid and angry. I didn't know what I was capable of when I thought about Prissy getting hurt or

Wolfgang dying. But even before all of this started, I was afraid of just being me, like I wasn't enough. So maybe when you came back to us, I made your fear worse. Then I passed it on to Prissy."

Wolfgang started laughing quietly as he let go of Daniel. He moved slowly over to a chair and sat down again in a heavy slump. "I'm sorry, everyone. I'm not laughing at you. I'm laughing at how crazy it all sounds." He looked at Amelie and then at Daniel. "You two are both so selfless in your approach to life. Yet you're both so hard on yourselves. It's insanity."

Amelie turned and smiled at him. "Thank you, my dearest, for always believing in me."

Daniel blinked at him. "Maybe it's insanity from your vantage point, but from where I'm at, I don't have any answers. How do I stop hating the monsters who murder us? How do I find some peace inside of here?" he asked beating at his chest. "I'm out there telling Prissy not to hate, but I'm just saying the words. I don't feel them."

Wolfgang sobered. His eyes were bright with conviction. "That's why we have one another. And the bottom line has never changed. We're all made of the same stuff. We'll find a way for you to understand and feel good again, to have the peace you deserve."

Daniel looked past him, at Theodore. He wanted to believe Wolfgang, but he couldn't let go of the rage coiled around his thoughts. If it meant something might happen to his brother, he'd fight the enemy no matter what.

Another thought slipped in as he tried to get his breath. Maybe he was flawed because of his lineage. His birth mother, overly sensitive and anxious, hadn't wanted children. When she got pregnant, she'd been depressed, scared of bringing a child into their dangerous world. After Daniel was born, she'd been unable to cope. She ran off, deserting him when he was very young. Maybe her fear had infected him from the start. Maybe it was in his blood. Maybe for him, fear was stronger than love.

Wolfgang shook his head knowingly, obviously tuned into Daniel's thoughts. "No, you're strong and true, Daniel. You have to believe that."

* * *

After the others left and a strained silence remained, Theodore sat looking at Daniel. He didn't know what to say. He surprised himself when he blurted out a few words. "I'm sorry about your mom, Daniel."

Daniel's head shot up from the chart he'd been studying. "What are you doing in my mind? Don't you have any idea about respecting my private thoughts?"

Theodore blinked back contritely when he saw the hurt and disappointment in his brother's eyes. "I didn't mean to pry. The information was just there. I'm sorry it's so painful."

Daniel hesitated, but finally replied in a business-like tone. "One night, my mother didn't come home. My father never found out what happened to her. Finally, he received divorce papers he had to sign and send back to a lawyer." He glanced at Theodore. "There, are you satisfied? That's all there is to it."

Theodore stared at his covers and smoothed them out. "Yes, I understand."

Daniel let out a bitter laugh. "Your mother was just the opposite of mine. She was strong, like you." He took out his wallet. He opened it, slipped out a photo and handed it to Theodore.

Theodore examined the four people in the picture. He carefully traced his finger over each of them. "Is this our family? Is this my mom? She was very pretty." He glanced up. "But you're holding me, Daniel, and you look happy."

Daniel nodded as he took out the second photo hidden under the first. "This is my mother."

Theodore studied the tall, blond woman's delicate face. Her pale blue eyes were soft. She looked small compared to their father, fragile. "She's beautiful."

Daniel held out his hand to retrieve the snapshots. "Yes, beautiful, but not dependable. Unlike my mother, yours would never have abandoned either of us."

Theodore put his hand on Daniel's arm. "And neither would you. Wolfgang is right. You're the best brother I could have. No matter how you see yourself, that's what I see."

Daniel gave him the slightest smile as he stepped back, looking spent and empty after his emotional purge. "Maybe I should go to bed for awhile."

Theodore put his head back and shut his eyes. "Maybe I'll play."

"What do you mean?"

"Psychic gifts are nothing new for you. I'm just learning about them. It's great because when I'm the regular me, I still seem to have a few available."

Daniel's brows narrowed. "Just don't go leaving your body again."

"Of course not," Theodore laughed. "I'm going to let my mind wander around this place. It's like I've been blind and deaf my whole life, and now I have my senses back. I can tap into things. I can go beyond this room."

"Theodore, don't invade anyone else's privacy like you did mine. We can use our gifts, but not just for amusement."

"I know."

Daniel started to leave. "We'll go over it later. Let yourself wander a bit, but mind your manners."

"Stop being a big brother for five minutes," Theodore replied as he felt his consciousness fan out. Unhampered by walls and physical barriers, he could begin to feel the presence of others in the building.

This is so amazing. I'm amazing.

As he smiled at himself and what he could do, his mind hit a snag. His sweet ride through space hit a dark, heavy pool of danger. The waters were murky, but it was there.

"Daniel!" He called out as the door to his brother's room was closing.

Daniel turned. "What now?"

"Something's wrong!" Theodore's eyes narrowed as he continued to investigate. When he looked at Daniel, he was scared. "We have to get out of here! We have to leave now."

Daniel's body stiffened. "Oh hell!"

Theodore could feel his brother scanning his mind, then the building. "What's going on?"

"I'm not sure, but thank goodness you're feeling better," Daniel said as he turned in the doorway. He reached up to take hold of a red lever mounted on the side of the doorjamb. He pulled the lever down. An alarm went off. A loud, blaring sound repeated every other second throughout the building.

Daniel was instantly in motion, running to the closet, yanking some clothes off of a hanger. "Quick, put these on," he ordered as he threw a sweat shirt, jeans and shoes on Theodore's bed.

Theodore had already pulled the IV from his arm. The good part was that his mind was in a heightened state of awareness. He hadn't fully changed, but he felt more capable. He fought his way out of his hospital garb, ignoring his wounds and quickly dressing. "Daniel? I'm ready," he called out.

Daniel rushed back to Theodore carrying a few items he'd retrieved from the other room. For a long moment, he studied Theodore from head to toe. He seemed somewhat pleased with his assessment. "Come with me," he said as he moved swiftly out into the hospital hallway.

Chapter Twenty-Eight

Theodore sat in the passenger seat of a ten-year-old Land Rover. From what he observed, evacuation of the facility was going smoothly. Fortunately, there were only a dozen people present. Everything in the world of the pack was done on a volunteer basis. The doctors who attended to Wolfgang and Theodore had regular physicians' jobs. The others who were at the small complex were also volunteers. Most of them were acting as guards.

Theodore looked over at Daniel. His brother was nervously tapping his fingers on the steering wheel. "I don't know how I know it, but it's not the WKA that's doing this. It's one of ours."

Wolfgang leaned forward from the back seat. "Is it Saxon?"

Theodore shrugged. "Maybe."

"Who else would it be?" Daniel asked impatiently.

For Theodore, the situation reminded him of the night when the WKA attacked. The vehicles were different, but Daniel was driving and Wolfgang, Prissy and Amelie sat in the back. Theodore was happy he could ride shotgun again. When he looked at Daniel, his brother's jaw was set and rigid, and his eyes stared fixedly at the aging pickup in front of them. When the doors to the facility finally opened, the battered truck in front of them started to edge out. It slowly climbed up a steep incline, one that led out of the underground building. Daniel followed close behind the pickup, riding its bumper.

Once they cleared the exit, Theodore's keen senses fanned out again. He tuned into the guards stationed outside. He stared out his window, trying to locate them, but he didn't see anyone.

"They're hidden a ways out from the exit," Daniel explained. "They'll leave as soon as we're all clear."

The Land Rover shook and rattled as they drove down a rutted, graveled road. There was evergreen forest on both sides. It was a tranquil setting. When Theodore looked at the side mirror, he saw the doors to the facility closing behind them. They were camouflaged and blended in with the woodsy setting. "Maybe I was wrong," he said, glancing over at Daniel. "Maybe it's a false alarm."

"I'm glad we're leaving," Prissy said insistently. "You and Dad are both better off in the fresh air where you can breathe. That place can be claustrophobic."

"Where are we going?" Amelie asked, looking at Wolfgang.

Wolfgang did a quick head check at their surroundings. "I don't know yet. We'll figure that out later."

After they'd gone a short distance, they reached the main highway. The old pickup in front of them pulled out, but they had to wait for a long line of cars to go by. When the road was clear of traffic, Daniel was about to pull out too. The sound of an explosion made him jerk around instead.

"The facility!" Wolfgang yelled.

Theodore was speechless. He stared back at where he'd been just minutes before. Dust hung in the air and debris littered the ground.

Prissy spoke up. "Was it Saxon?" she asked in a trembling voice.

Wolfgang nodded. "Yes, I think so. He must have slipped in close enough to plant explosives. Somehow, he's shielding his thoughts completely. Our best guys didn't pick up on him."

"Theodore did," Amelie said in a gasp.

As soon as she spoke, Theodore felt like everyone was trying to tune into him.

"Are you getting anything else, Theo?" Daniel asked as he stepped on the gas. He was headed back in the direction of the city. "Am I missing something?"

Theodore shook his head. "I don't know. I'm trying to think, but there's nothing there."

Wolfgang let out a heavy sigh of relief. "Good."

The older man's attitude made Theodore feel better. He knew that if he could relax, his abilities wouldn't be hampered by his fears. He sat back, trying to stay as calm as possible. The scenery helped. They passed wooded areas that soon gave way to small farms. Houses dotted the landscape. He had a thought about all the people who were oblivious to what the pack faced. Most folks were probably at work or planning out an evening with their family. They weren't running for their lives. When he glanced back at Prissy, she looked the opposite of relaxed. She had her legs crossed and was nervously shaking her foot.

"Do you think the pack's in danger, Dad?" she asked.

Wolfgang shook his head. "I think Saxon wants to hurt us, not the pack itself. He might think that he can still get control if Daniel and I are out of the picture."

"Damn, damn, damn!" Daniel shouted, slamming on the brakes.

Everyone in the car was thrown forward. The car zigzagged a couple of times before it came to a stop on the side of the road.

Once the Land Rover was stationary, Theodore immediately scanned the road and the area on either side. He had reflexively braced himself on the dashboard, but he was grateful Wolfgang had insisted they all wear their seatbelts. "What is it, Daniel?"

"Didn't anybody see them?" Daniel asked as he turned to the back seat. "Wolfgang! Did you see them?"

Theodore looked back too. Amelie, Prissy and Wolfgang were all searching the highway.

Wolfgang continued to glance in all directions. "See what? What did you see?"

"The wolves!" Daniel yelled as he white knuckled the steering wheel. "It's the same pair that helped Theodore. They appeared in the middle of the road. I almost hit them."

"I think it's a sign," Wolfgang said. "We must be going in the wrong direction. Turn around."

* * *

Theodore was getting pretty good at tuning into the thoughts around him. With night coming on, there was a heavy gloom of silence in the Land Rover. The vehicle was moving away from the city and away from everyone's home. He felt a strong sense of displacement in the group. It was almost stronger than the danger they might be facing. That's when he realized he was the only one who felt differently. He didn't want to go back home. He didn't want to return to his normal life. The thought of being with his adoptive parents was really tough. Yet, it seemed inevitable.

After Saxon was caught, the pack could return to relative peace. There was no database with their names or addresses anywhere. They never committed any information to pack records. They knew better. They'd return to quiet lives. Daniel would go back to handling investments, and Theodore would return to his original situation. He knew he didn't have much choice. What else could he do? Could he let his mother think he was dead? He was sure she tried to do her best and seemed to care in some strange, detached way.

"Give me a break, Theodore. That's so depressing," Daniel whispered in a quiet tone, one that Amelie, Wolfgang, and Prissy wouldn't hear. "I'm not going to just forget about you when this is over."

"Are you sure?" Theodore asked just as quietly. He'd been sincere when he said Daniel was the best of brothers, but that was in extraordinary times. "You're saying that now because you have to. But once things are sorted out, you'll return to your life, and I'll return to mine. It's that simple."

Daniel frowned. "It's not that way at all. A pack supports one another, like Wolfgang said."

"But I have to go back to my parents, right?"

Daniel let out a weary sigh. "I haven't figured out what's next. I've been a little busy with other things. But the WKA placed you with them, and I promise I won't let them get their hands on you again."

"That's right. I can't go back." For a brief moment, Theodore felt a small spark of hope. It was followed by more clarity. "But I have to, don't I? My mother, I mean my adoptive mother, will go nuts if she thinks I'm dead. What choice do I have?"

Daniel glanced at him. "Do you love her?"

"We've never been close, but I don't want to see her hurt."

"You're a good person. I wish you weren't in this mess."

He gave Daniel a quick glance, then stared at the road. "I'm glad I'm here. Even if something happens, and I never see you again, I'll know you exist. I'll feel like I have real family somewhere." He smiled with a sudden idea. "Maybe I can act like I ran away from home. I can send her notes from all over, saying I'm fine."

Daniel smiled too. "That's not a bad idea."

"And I could live with you, right?"

Daniel didn't reply.

"You'll be great," Theodore encouraged him. "I admire you, don't you realize that?"

Daniel let out a small laugh as if he wanted to lighten the mood. "I'm a wreck. I'm not fit to take care of anybody." He paused. "Except in a shootout, that is. Try to understand my position. You can stay with someone else in the pack."

Theodore swallowed back the bile that burned his throat. "So that's it? Like you said, you're always stuck with the problems, and I'm another burden you'd have to take care of. Well, that's not what I want either." He felt his stomach lurch. "Now pull over fast, I'm going to be sick."

* * *

Daniel sat inside the car, staring at his brother. Theodore was on the side of the road trying to recover from a bout of vomiting. Daniel tried to help, but Theodore refused to let him get near. That's when Amelie stepped in. As Theodore calmed down after his second vomiting spell, she stood next to him, rubbing his back.

"What did you say to Theodore?" Prissy asked from the back seat. "He looked so upset when you tried to talk to him."

"He thinks I don't want him around."

Prissy laughed. "Are you kidding? I've been watching you. How could he think that?"

"Because I don't. When this is over, I want to find a safe place for him."

Wolfgang, who was sitting next to Prissy, leaned forward and put his hand on Daniel's shoulder. "But it won't work that way. You're going to break his heart if you farm him out."

Daniel scowled. "At least he'll be alive. That's all that counts," he said calmly, not letting himself get sick too.

* * *

Theodore tried to get his stomach to settle down. He didn't want to upset Amelie any more than he already had. He could feel her motherly concern and worry. "I'm okay," he insisted.

Amelie didn't move. She stood behind Theodore with her hands on his shoulders. "I don't think so. Tell me what's bothering you."

"Nothing, I just have an upset stomach." What good did it do to tell the truth? Amelie couldn't make Daniel change his mind.

"Is this about Daniel?"

He shrugged back at her.

Amelie gave his shoulder a gentle squeeze. "I understand he's having a hard time, but you still have one another. I thought that was what you both wanted. Is something else wrong?"

"Yes, I'm sick of thinking I belong somewhere and finding out I don't."

Amelie turned him around and looked at him. "Theodore, that's not true. I don't know what's going on exactly, but you always have a home with Wolfgang and me. Prissy might be a bit much at times, but I think you could put up with her, couldn't you?"

"Thanks, you're very nice, but I better go back to my parents."

He found it so easy to lie to her, but he'd have to find a way to keep his true intentions from Daniel and the rest of their kind.

Amelie's brows narrowed. "Don't do that, Theo. I may not be like all of you, but I know when someone isn't telling the truth. And I don't appreciate it."

"I'm sorry, but I don't want to talk about what's going on."

"It's difficult, I know. How do you think I feel? I love my husband and daughter with all my heart, but I'm human. I don't have their gifts. In the past, I felt like they were in a club, and I was always trying to join and didn't know how. But I'm realizing it was me. I was creating a barrier that wasn't there."

Theodore stood looking back at her. Amelie had the most understanding eyes he'd ever seen. They seemed to invite him to go further, to delve into her thoughts. Her frustration was obvious, so was her feeling of being the different one in the family, the different one who didn't measure up.

"I could have hidden that from you," she said. "I do it with my family because humans know how to hide their feelings too. But I wanted you to know you're not alone. Everyone on this planet has the same emotions. They may ignore them or shut them away, but everyone has them. The trick is to learn how to love each other in spite of our feelings. We have to go beyond them."

Theodore studied the ground and scuffed it with his shoe. "How can I love Daniel when I know he doesn't want me around?"

"You have to find a way, a reason. You have to love him when he's not capable of loving you back."

"I don't know if I can, but I guess I could try." He looked up and saw Amelie's smile. It was generous and sweet. It made him feel a little better. He began to consider her offer. Maybe he could live with Amelie's family. If he did, Amelie could teach him so many things he needed to learn. Werewolves were amazing, but right now he'd settle for Amelie's human kindness and compassion. He looked at the ground again. "So you'd take me in?"

Amelie threw her arms around him. "In a heartbeat!" she said with enthusiasm.

Chapter Twenty-Nine

When Theodore got back in the Land Rover, he fastened his seat belt and gave Daniel a quick frown. "I've got good news. You don't have to worry about me." Next, he turned his attention to Wolfgang and Prissy in the back seat. "If it's alright with you guys, Amelie asked me to live with you. First, I'll have to square things with my parents, but afterwards, maybe I could move in for a while. Is that a problem?"

Wolfgang smiled back. "Of course not. You can stay as long as you want."

Prissy crossed her arms. "What about your snoring? A couple of times, when I checked on you at the facility, you were a real buzz saw."

He laughed when he saw Prissy's playful eyes. "I guess I can tape my jaws shut."

Prissy smiled too. "Alright, then it's okay."

Daniel's face was flushed with anger when he shot Theodore a quick glance. He returned his eyes to the road and queried the group in a controlled but edgy voice. "Can I start driving again or does someone else need to throw up?"

Theodore felt his face flush too. He tried to remember what Amelie said, but it was going to take some practice to forgive Daniel for his attitude. "Sorry for the inconvenience. It won't happen again."

* * *

With the Land Rover on the road again, the group discussed their options, where they could stay for the night. In the middle of their discussion, Wolfgang's cell phone rang. He held it close to his ear for a long moment.

"Saxon is dead?" he finally asked. "When? How?" He sighed with relief as he listened to someone on the other end. "Yes, we'll come back to town. Thanks." After disconnecting, he looked at Amelie. "They caught Saxon trying to blow up our house. They weren't able to take him alive."

"Thank goodness it's over," she gasped.

"At least we don't have to worry about our own," Daniel said as he pulled the car over to the side of the two lane highway. With a sharp turn of the wheel and some gas, he got the vehicle turned around.

As everyone celebrated, Theodore stared anxiously ahead. "What now?"

"Can we go home?" Prissy asked.

"Soon," Wolfgang said. "We'll go back to town and stay with friends for a couple of nights until we're sure everything is secure."

"Can we stop at a gas station or convenience store?" Theodore asked. "My parents are probably frantic. They usually call me every day. I better let them know I'm alright."

"Yes, that's a good idea," Wolfgang said. "I'd let you use my cell, but it's better you use a pay phone."

"No problem," Theodore said. "I'll have a few minutes to think about what I can tell them."

* * *

While Theodore talked to his mother, he could see Daniel outside the phone booth. His brother looked tense as he paced back and forth. Happily Prissy and her family gave him more privacy and had waited in the Land Rover. After a few minutes, he hung up the phone and stepped out of the booth.

Daniel immediately came over to confront him. "What did they say?"

Theodore rubbed his palms together anxiously. "My parents flew back early when they couldn't reach me. They have the police out looking for me."

"What did you tell them?"

"I said I decided to take a little trip of my own and lost my phone. They didn't buy it, but Mom was somewhat appeased when I explained I was fine."

"The WKA has people in the police force. I'm sure your name was recognized. They probably have your home phone tapped. They might also have your house under surveillance."

Theodore went very pale. "What am I going to do? My mother sounded like she was ready to go into hysterics. What if the WKA tries to hurt her or Arthur, my dad? I should go back and warn them."

"That's too dangerous." Daniel let out a disgusted sigh. "Oh hell, another mess I have to handle."

"It's my mess, not yours," Theodore said as he pushed Daniel out of the way. He started back to the car. "I'll talk to Amelie and Wolfgang about it. You go back to doing what you do. I'm not your problem any more."

"Don't be so stupid!" Daniel yelled. "I'm responsible for you!"

He turned to face Daniel. "No, you're not! You're officially relieved of being my brother."

Daniel clenched his fists. "That's a childish statement."

"Better to be a child than someone who can turn off his feelings, like you, Daniel. Amelie says I should try to understand you. Well, forget that and forget you!"

As soon as he made his declaration, Theodore felt a sudden rush of tears cloud his vision. Shame was next. He couldn't stand the thought of Daniel seeing him act like a baby. It made him angrier than ever. He needed to get away from his older brother and his bad attitude. As he crossed the road and approached the

Land Rover, his body was its awkward self once again. He even tripped over a raised crack in the road and nearly fell. As embarrassment and his clumsiness joined forces, he had to keep going. No matter what Amelie said, he felt like he didn't belong anywhere. The thought brought on more tears. He started running. He ran past the Land Rover and headed for the treed area that bordered the road. He kept swiping at his eyes, but the tears wouldn't stop. Neither would the feelings of abandonment and anger.

"Forget you, Daniel! Living with you is the last thing I want!"

It wasn't the truth, but his statement, shouted out with as much voice as he could muster, felt good. So did the idea of hiding himself in the woods. He loved nature. It always gave him sanctuary when he was upset. He welcomed the forested area even more after knowing what it felt like to be a wolf.

I wish I could be a wolf again!

Wolves never deserted their own. They never gave up caring for those they loved. They were beautiful, swift animals that were free of all the selfish emotions people had.

Please, please, let me be that kind of creature!

His body jerked internally, coming alive, responding to his desires. He started picking up speed. He didn't become a true wolf, but he did feel free. He changed effortlessly into the gifted person he was.

A voice called after him. "Come back here, Theodore! I'm sorry!"

He glanced back and saw Daniel at the edge of the woods, shouting at him. It brought on another angry outburst. "I don't want your apologies, you loser!" he yelled back.

* * *

Daniel couldn't believe it. Theodore was running off again. How many times would the kid exhibit the same behavior? It was so tiresome, and he was out of patience. He was trying to give

Theodore the best chance possible at a good life, and he was getting nothing but grief in return.

When Prissy jumped out of the car and ran over to him, he knew he was in for more problems.

"Wow, he's so fast!" she said. "You'll never catch him, Daniel, not unless his heart gives out."

He gave her a hateful look, but she only glared back with accusing eyes. "It's your fault. He's your brother. All he wanted was for you to love him," she said as she started running. She headed in the direction Theodore had taken.

"Come back here!" Wolfgang and Amelie yelled in unison as they exited the vehicle.

Prissy didn't seem to hear them as she disappeared into the trees.

Daniel started running too. "Fast, is he? I'll show him who's fast." Daniel knew he might not be the best off-road driver, but he was known for setting track records with his fellow werewolves. Running was as natural as breathing for him. It wouldn't take long for him to catch up to Theodore. When he asked his body for more speed, it responded with ease.

He hadn't gone very far when he realized speed wasn't his real problem. Dry leaves and underbrush littered the forest floor. As he took sharp turns trying to follow Theodore's erratic pattern, he was sliding again. He cursed himself for always wearing the wrong shoes. The next moment, he forgot about footwear as he pushed himself even more. It had been awhile since he felt the exhilaration of expressing his true nature in a real race. Besides, he didn't like being called a loser by his little brother.

To hell with my shoes! I'm going to show Theodore who he's dealing with!

Unfortunately, he was soon to be living proof of the saying, "Pride goeth before a fall." Running in an all-out sprint in wooded conditions and leather soled shoes, he lost his balance going down a steep hill. Flying forward, his body flipped over a number of times. He came down heavily towards the bottom, with his head slamming into the base of a large tree. He felt like he'd taken a hammer blow to the head. Blood spilled down his neck and unto his shirt. Staring up with surprise and wounded dignity, the branches above him faded in and out of darkness.

* * *

Theodore felt Daniel go down. The ungracious tumbling, the shock of losing all control was as clear as if he'd been the one taking the punishment. He stopped running immediately and turned in the direction he'd come from. "Daniel! Are you alright?" he yelled out. As he paused to listen for a response, he felt like a fool.

Daniel's right! I am childish. I've run away again.

"Daniel! Answer me!" He waited to hear a response, but Daniel didn't call back. He did hear Prissy. She was yelling out his name as he started backtracking. He came around a bend at full speed, completely focused on Daniel, and he nearly collided with her.

Prissy screamed out her disapproval when she was almost trampled. "What's wrong with you two? You're both babies!"

He paid her no attention. Grabbing her arm, he turned her around and dragged her behind him as he began to run again. When he reached Daniel, he stopped short. Daniel's head and face were streaked with blood. He looked disoriented when he let out a moan.

"I'm sorry," Theodore cried out as he knelt down and reached out to Daniel. He didn't know what to do.

Prissy stood to the side with crossed arms. When Theodore glanced up, she stared back with a look of disgust. "You two don't need the WKA to take you out. You're doing a great job all by yourselves. They should call you the Trauma Twins, Tripper and Runaway."

Daniel's eyes widened at her remarks, and he moaned again.

Theodore felt his brother's embarrassment. It triggered a quick reply. "Listen, Prissy the Punisher, leave my brother alone."

Prissy's face reddened. "Thanks a lot," she said. "And I actually thought you'd forgiven me."

Theodore glared back. "And I thought you were going to be nicer."

* * *

Theodore stood outside the Land Rover. With the back door opened wide, he could see Amelie taking care of Daniel. His brother was stretched across the back seat of the vehicle with his head in Amelie's lap. She was bandaging the deep gash he'd gotten in his fall. Theodore moved closer and peered in. "He's going to be okay, isn't he?"

Amelie glanced up and let her scolding eyes settle on him briefly, then she looked at Prissy who stood next to Theodore. "Thank goodness your father was well enough to help you two get Daniel back to the Rover."

"I'm really sorry about what happened," Theodore said repentantly.

"I'm sorry too, Mom," Prissy added.

Prissy's tone was one of remorse, but when she looked at Theodore, she didn't look sorry. She frowned back with hooded eyes. They had said some very unkind things to each other.

Theodore avoided her scowl and turned back to Amelie. "What can I do?"

Amelie didn't answer, but Wolfgang was clearly in charge now.

"Get into the car, both of you," he said as he climbed behind the wheel and started the engine. "Prissy, ride up front. And Theodore, you can sit behind the rear seat. You'll be closer to Daniel. He might have a concussion. I want you to use your scanning abilities and let me know if you pick up on any changes in his condition."

"I don't know how to do that," Theodore protested.

"It shouldn't be too difficult. When you tune in, go a little further. You'll understand once you try it."

Theodore got his chance to test Wolfgang's instructions once they were all in the car and on their way. He started by shutting his eyes. In spite of being nervous and doubtful about his abilities, he made himself calm down with a couple of breaths. After he'd cleared his mind, he reached over the seat and put his hand on Daniel's chest. At first, he only felt Daniel's chest wall rising and falling, but he continued to concentrate on tuning in. He smiled when he started getting feedback. "I think I know what you mean. I'm having all these thoughts about what's happening in Daniel's body."

Wolfgang glanced in the rear view mirror. "Good, when we get back you can update one of our doctors."

Prissy looked back at Theodore with disapproval. No matter what they'd said to each other earlier, she seemed intent on pointing out his mistakes. "I thought you and Daniel were happy to find each other. What's wrong with the two of you?"

"Prissy, please be quiet," Amelie corrected. "It's complicated. Let Theodore alone."

Theodore swallowed hard as he took his hand off of Daniel's chest. "No, she's right. I was really mad, and I called Daniel a loser."

* * *

Even though he was only semiconscious, Daniel kept seeing the words, 'Loser,' 'Trauma Twin' and 'Tripper' flash in and out. They made him feel like a complete fool. But he couldn't hold on to the insults very long. He felt too sick to stay focused on the outer world. Instead, he let himself escape his troubles.

As weariness closed in, he slipped into a dreamy state. He was in the lavish Paris hotel suite again. It was wonderful. He saw himself soaking away all his fatigue in the elegant, heated, whirlpool tub. The lights were dim and a dozen elaborate, golden candelabra were placed around the room. Their soft glow complimented the sound system. It streamed in woodland sounds of birds and a waterfall in the distance.

In reality, he could afford such a vacation. He could afford to retire and move to Paris. He'd done very well with his investments. But he chose to keep that part of his life private. He lived in a modest house and only splurged when it came to his wardrobe.

I could have left it all behind and lived a quiet life of leisure.

The thought brought him back to reality. Instead of a stress-free life, he let another need rule his actions. He wanted to change things, even rule the pack. Now he knew why. The WKA planned it that way. It was a difficult concept to contemplate, but it wasn't as difficult as thinking about Theodore. To protect his brother from the WKA and whatever else might come along, seemed like a staggering job, one he'd be saddled with for the rest of his life.

What an optimist I was when I was twelve. I would have taken on the world.

Now as his head lay in Amelie's lap, he didn't have the desire to rule the pack. He didn't have enough desire left to take out the trash. It was clear he'd lost his courage. He was great when it came to fighting and hating, but that was part of survival and what the WKA had done to him. But what about living? What about feeling the all-consuming fear and still going forward in love and strength? He almost laughed at the idea of valor at this point.

Forget living and loving. Move to Paris and leave all the pain behind.

It was tempting, but he knew that the idea had to wait.

You're going to hang in there, coward or not. You're going to get Theodore through this mess. You'll never be able to live with yourself otherwise.

It took all his willpower to pull the broken pieces of himself together. When he opened his eyes, he searched for his little brother. "Theo, where are you?" he whispered, trying to keep his head from exploding.

"Daniel!" Theodore's excited face appeared from behind the seat.

Daniel grabbed his head. "Are you okay?"

Theodore paused for a brief moment, long enough to turn his smile into a penitent frown. "I'm sorry if I'm a pain!" He blurted out the words loudly as if he were delivering an address to a room of the hearing impaired.

Daniel's head was like a steel drum, and Theodore's words were striking it mercilessly. "Fine, whatever, just keep your voice down," he pleaded.

Prissy looked back with a deep frown spoiling her pretty face. "Yeah, Theo, you're with more sensitive people now. Remember that when you want to go yelling at us."

Daniel closed his eyes again and groaned.

Right, sensitive Prissy, I almost forgot you're here to help.

Chapter Thirty

By the time they got back to the city, to the home of a doctor in the pack, Daniel was feeling a little better physically. His natural healing abilities were working. On the emotional front, he wasn't doing nearly as well. After the doctor gave him the usual cautions about taking it easy, Amelie seemed very concerned. She was hovering over him. He had to appease her fears. "I'll be fine," he insisted.

Amelie didn't buy it. "I'm just so grateful you don't have a bad concussion."

"I guess I should be thankful too," he said glumly. The words felt meaningless when he said them.

Amelie gave him a motherly smile. "I'm sorry you're having such a tough time."

"Thanks," he said in a listless tone. He was about to tell Amelie he needed solitude and rest. He hesitated when he realized he found Amelie's company comforting. At least that had changed. However, Amelie's kind ways couldn't help him with the big problems in his life. His stomach felt nauseous every time he pondered his future.

"What is it? What's that face you're making?" Amelie asked.

He glanced up at a mirror across the room and saw himself. Amelie was right to question his appearance. He was sitting in a wing back chair with his head swaddled in a wraparound bandage. Slightly slumped over and washed out, he looked like a veteran returning from a war. "I'm just exhausted," he groaned.

Amelie crouched down in front of him. "I know what you said to us earlier, but no matter what you think about yourself, you did a wonderful job out there at the safe house. You saved us from thugs on both sides. Can't you take a little solace in that?"

He shrugged despondently. "I don't know anymore. Everything is a mess, and I can't figure out what to do about it."

"I think you're worried about Theodore."

Her statement hit the mark, a mark he couldn't face. He turned away without comment.

Amelie's voice was very soft when she spoke. "Dearest Daniel, you can't control the world. Somehow, you have to learn to trust there are happy times ahead."

"I can't!" His protest made his head pound harder, but he didn't care. "I can't go through it again, thinking this world has any mercy. I'm going to help Theodore, get him on track and then—"

"And then, what?"

His eyes grew dark and hard. "I don't want to be here to see him get hurt again. I'll do my best to safeguard him for now, and then he's got to figure things out for himself."

Amelie's face lit up. "That's good, Daniel. It's called 'letting him grow up.'"

"It's not good for me. I know how I am. Theodore will always be my little brother, the person I can't protect." He grabbed the arms of the chair with both hands. He clung to them, hoping they would steady the turmoil in his mind. "So strange, isn't it? I find my brother, then I fall apart."

"It's not strange at all," Amelie said. "You've been doing more than your share for too long. Others would have given up, but you didn't. You've been in the trenches since you were a child yourself. You're right, you're exhausted, that's all."

"I'm an investor," he said with disgust.

"And how do you spend the rest of your day? You're out there learning what you can do to help all of us. You're having nightmares about what happened to you, about what you're afraid will happen to the pack." Amelie's eyes sparkled as she reached out and put her hand over his. "Wolfgang and I both know how hard you try. You've been a real challenge, but it's because you believed it would help the pack."

"I'm the WKA's stooge."

"I don't believe that. You've tried to use what you experienced to safeguard the rest of us."

"I wish you were right."

"I know I am," Amelie insisted as she stood up. "Now I'll let you rest. And don't worry, I'll take care of Theodore."

"Good, I need time to think about his future."

"You need time to let yourself heal."

"I don't have that luxury. That's the point. I know how Theodore thinks. As soon as I'm okay, he's going to be wanting something from me again. I have to be prepared."

* * *

While Daniel was resting, Theodore considered his options. He had to get a plan together, one that was reasonable and best for all concerned. After his running-away fiasco, he had to be very careful in how he approached his future. He didn't want to go back to his old life, and he couldn't burden Daniel or Amelie's family with another responsibility.

The WKA was his first concern. The organization was the major threat in all their lives. He knew he had to destroy any link between himself and the pack. He also needed to protect his adoptive parents. He had to break that link too.

If I were simply gone, but gone in a way that made sure nobody worried about me, everyone would be fine.

The thought spurred him on. He knew Daniel loved him, but his brother wasn't able to handle the extra strain Theodore posed. It didn't matter. Theodore had been handling being alone since he was a child. He'd been okay without a real family. Why did he need one now? On the plus side, he'd discovered he was some kind of gifted being, with powers. He didn't have to be afraid all the time.

After some deliberation, he decided his best bet was a simple one. He'd go to the airport and get on a plane. His destination didn't matter. Once he was out of everyone's lives, he'd contact his parents and Daniel. He'd let them know he was striking out on his own. He'd break his ties to his past.

It wouldn't be easy to survive without anyone's support, but he was sixteen years old. He was almost an adult. The only things he needed to get started were money and identification. His wallet was at his parents' house, and he'd been saving up his allowance and other monies for a long time. If he could slip in, get what he needed and slip out, it would be perfect. The WKA might be watching the house, but he doubted it. His mother had surely called the police off, and the WKA would know he wasn't planning to come home for a while.

With newfound confidence, he laid his head back on his pillow. He'd been given the living room sofa as a place to sleep. It was a large, over-sized piece that accommodated his needs. He'd sleep for a little while before he set out on his new path.

As he settled into the comfort of the couch, he smiled. Someday, after he successfully put his plan into practice, his adoptive father would probably be proud of him. Finally, the person he called his son would be acting like a real man. "I bet he's been waiting for that day for a long time," he said aloud. As he pictured himself as capable and skilled at living independently, he drifted off.

* * *

Daniel opened his eyes and looked at the clock. He'd been asleep for hours. He stretched out, testing his body. Not only did he feel better, but an idea had come to him when he was waking up. The answer to his problem was so obvious, so simple. He'd take Theodore with him to France. He'd retire and find them an apartment in Paris. They could find safety there. His eyes softened with relief. He'd made it all so complicated when it wasn't. "Why didn't I think about it before?"

He got up, went into the bathroom, and looked at himself in the mirror. The first thing he had to do was get rid of the turban of bandages. Once he had the bandage off, he was relieved to see the gash was healing nicely. Trimming his facial hair and getting a hot shower would help to revive the rest of him. He opened the medicine chest and noticed a toothbrush still in its wrapper, a beard trimmer and an electric razor. There were also fresh towels and even a change of clothes on a cabinet. He grabbed the items off a shelf, grateful to his host. The pack was that way. They were always prepared for visitors. If you needed to stay somewhere for a day or a week, you were welcomed into people's homes. Hospitality was an extremely important part of pack life.

After his shower, Daniel felt an excitement as he got dressed. His new plan was buoying up his spirit. He thought about how much fun he could have with Theodore. He wanted to show him not only Paris, but all of Europe. He'd make up for all the years Theodore had spent feeling alone.

As Daniel was leaving the bathroom, clean and looking civilized again, he took another glance in the mirror. "Not bad," he muttered as he examined himself. After days of weariness, he felt renewed. Life didn't look depressing anymore. His only problem now was convincing Theodore that his big brother wasn't a loser. He had bridges to mend, but Theodore had a forgiving heart.

"A lot more forgiving one than mine," he mused.

* * *

After getting a few hours of sleep, Theodore woke up feeling ready to strike out on his own. The thought of taking responsibility for himself seemed more like an adventure than a problem, at least for the moment. As he crept through the quiet house, he felt good about being able to make his own decisions. He smiled to himself. With everyone sleeping, his escape would be easy. Even transportation turned out to be simple. He found the keys to the Land Rover on the kitchen table. He'd borrow the vehicle. Later, he'd tell Wolfgang where he could pick it up.

Once outside the house, Theodore took a deep breath of the night air. It was fresh and invigorating. He'd never felt so excited about being alive. He wasn't just a dumb, ordinary kid. He was a special type of being. He was strong and smart. He had an incredible body, an ally that would help him when needed. His confidence deepened as he walked to the truck and climbed into the driver seat. Everything was going his way, everything but leaving Daniel and his new family. He let himself feel a twinge of sadness, but he didn't allow the feeling to go further. He couldn't think in terms of heartache or let neediness slip into the picture. He had to persevere, for Daniel's sake.

"Go into zombie mode," he ordered aloud. It was a game he used to play. If he could stop thinking about his unhappiness and numb out, his feelings couldn't get a hold and sway his thinking.

* * *

As soon as Daniel saw the empty covers on the couch, his head started throbbing again. He put a hand under the blankets, checking for warmth. The cushion was almost cold. Theodore had a good head start.

"Where are you?" he whispered. His mind was already swimming with scenarios. The WKA would take Theodore prisoner again. Or even worse, they'd kill him outright. Or maybe, Theodore would run away once again and keep running from Daniel. Rejected and alone, he'd become bitter and angry like his older brother. With Theodore's gentle heart, Daniel knew that would be worse than death.

Stop it. Don't go down that road.

If he was going to help his brother, he had to forget everything but connecting with him. With deliberate effort, he made his shoulders relax. He cleared his mind of everything but the moment and tuning into Theodore. When he made the connection, his jaw tightened.

Oh no, he's going to his parents' house.

Daniel hadn't given the residence much thought since the night he'd been trying to save Wolfgang. Impressions flooded in. Heavy, dark furniture and poorly lit, aging lamps filled the rooms with a shadowy gloom. Furniture polish mixed with disinfectant accosted the nose. A grim sense of neatness and absolute order belied the fact that a sixteen-year-old boy lived there. This wasn't a place where a child could play with abandon. But it was the place where Theodore was raised.

When Daniel first saw Theodore, the boy was the only thing that was out of place in that house. His clothes were definitely not in keeping with the house décor. With his parents away, Theodore had clearly given himself permission to wear what he wanted, baggy jeans and a 'Black Holes Suck' t-shirt.

"He must have been happy to have the place to himself," Daniel mused.

Now Theodore was going back to the dismal house where he'd spent the last fourteen years. Daniel had to move fast to catch up with him. The keys to Doc Leonard's car were hanging in the hall that led to the garage. Hopefully, he'd intercept Theodore and have him home before anyone knew he was gone. There had been enough drama the last couple of days. The others didn't need to know about his brother's latest escapade. He wanted to spare Theodore that much.

Daniel sent a single-minded thought out into the ethers.

I can only hope you're listening to this message, Theodore! We're going to Paris, and we're going to have a great time.

Chapter Thirty-One

When Theodore arrived at the neighborhood where he'd been raised, he parked the Land Rover a couple of blocks from his house. He was on guard again and totally focused on the situation at hand. He avoided any thought of what he'd left behind. He had to maintain a new attitude. He was on his own, but he wasn't the same person who visited Daniel's house in search of the vaccine. He'd come a long way since then. He wasn't nearly as frightened. No matter, he had to be extra cautious. He walked in the shadows and covered the distance to his house in a stealthy, careful manner.

There were no strange cars, no people watching him this time. Nothing seemed out of the ordinary. In fact, the neighborhood felt so normal and his house appeared so quiet, it was as if he'd never been away. It wasn't a comforting feeling. It was a disturbing one that threw him back in time. He'd come full circle. He'd gone through an unbelievable adventure, but now he was back where he'd started. A pang of isolation and regret grabbed hold. His gut ached. Everything that had happened felt like a dream. He was just Theodore again, the kid who didn't fit in.

The feeling became even more acute as he searched in the bushes in the back yard, looking for the spare house key. How many times had he been in that same yard searching for a way out of his unhappy life? How many times had he looked to the night sky, hoping to find solace in the stars? But no matter how bright or beautiful they seemed, they remained so far away.

"And in some ways, nothing's changed," he whispered as he stopped and glanced heavenward.

He had to take several, deep breaths as the full impact of his situation settled in. One comforting thought pushed its way through his misery.

No matter what, I have a brother. Maybe we're not together, but Daniel's real, and he cares about me in his own way.

He remembered Daniel's encouraging smile and how his big brother had been there for him on that last night at the cabin. Daniel's words, "I am my brother's keeper," replayed again in his mind. They were a reminder that he and Daniel were united. They might be separated, but that bond would always be there.

Even now, Theodore could feel Daniel's concern. It helped him to keep moving. He lifted a rock and found the key he was searching for. He quickly went to the back door of the house and let himself into the kitchen. The lighting in the room was sparse. A lone, fluorescent tube was located under one of the cabinets. It cast its eerie, artificial glow on twenty-year-old appliances. He only took a couple of steps forward when he had a moment of panic. He'd almost forgotten what a dark and scary place the room could be at night He knew it was a ridiculous thought. How could a kitchen be scary?

Still, he was holding his breath as if some dark and sinister presence was waiting to jump out at him. He had to force himself to take in a breath of air that reeked of disinfectant. He tried to think about the last few days and his new identity, but the smell was too strong. It delivered a message. He wasn't on his own yet. He was standing in the middle of his mother's domain.

The foreboding woman's mark was stamped on every inch of the place. The grey-green, Formica countertops were spotless and dull. They'd lost their shine long ago, testaments to his mother's daily scrubbings and her campaign to keep everything sanitary to the point of being sterile. Theodore was sure no germ would dare to set foot in the hygienic environment. It was an expanse of barren cleanliness.

Keep moving. Forget about the past.

He made his way across the room without taking off his shoes. His mother would never know he'd broken one of her rules. Besides this was his last trek across the floor, and he didn't think he'd introduce anything his mother couldn't handle with her mop, pail and bleach. But nothing could get rid of the melancholy feeling that went with the territory. Happily, he wouldn't be part of his mother's world after that night. He was sure his father wouldn't be as lucky. As soon as the graying executive came home each night, he became a minimum wage flunky who never challenged his wife's sharp tone and unbending rules.

Both of them are so unhappy.

He stood next to the kitchen table, fingering its clean, cold surface. Did his mother realize what she was like? After being around Amelie, the woman who raised him seemed so different.

Amelie is kind and sweet, the perfect mom. Lucky Prissy.

He felt a twinge of envy and a terrible craving, like he'd been living on bread, water and loneliness. Meanwhile, people like Prissy were surrounded by a banquet of love and support. The thought didn't help, and he knew he had to push it aside no matter what. He had to forget what he didn't have. He couldn't completely abandon the idea of family. Daniel suddenly felt so close. He rubbed his temples. He wasn't doing a very good job at being a zombie. He could almost hear his brother calling out to him.

Don't go there. It's just wishful thinking.

His face flushed into a frown. He'd made his decision. He had to act like a man, not give in to some childish longing to be back with his brother. He couldn't cave now. He had to be strong and think about Daniel's wellbeing.

The guy needs a break. He looks like he's going to have a nervous breakdown. I should have listened to Amelie.

He'd had his chance and blown it. He should have given his brother some space and moved in with Amelie and Wolfgang.

Too late for all that.

He gave the grey-green kitchen walls a last once over as he pulled a note from his pocket and placed it on the table. He had composed a short, conciliatory explanation for his parents, telling them about his plans to be on his own.

Nobody will be bothered with me anymore.

He tiptoed his way through the house, not daring to wake his parents, especially his mother. She was already furious with him. He didn't have the courage to face her now. When he got to his bedroom, he breathed a sigh of relief as if he'd achieved some great feat instead of traversing thirty feet through a suburban house. As soon as he let himself into the familiar space, he switched on a small lamp on his dresser. He glanced around at the place he'd used as his retreat. His telescope was posted close to the window, waiting to expand his vision of the night sky. His solar system mobile hung over the desk, slowly moving with the air currents. And on the far wall, his book shelves were crammed and overflowing. The sci-fi novels, astronomy books, and survival guides were all great for escaping from life.

Survival guides? I wonder if I'll need a couple of those where I'm going.

He sat down on the bed. Everything was exactly like he left it a few days before.

So this is where I've spent so much of my life.

Another wave of sadness hit him when he thought about all the years he'd spent in the room. It was the place where he'd hid himself, but he couldn't block out his mother's shrill complaints or his father's empty protests. How many times had he sat on his bed, listening to their arguments, listening to his mother's uncompromising meanness and his father's stifled words of surrender? Their bleak relationship saturated the airways. He couldn't escape it by shutting his door.

I guess I was kind of living in hell and didn't know it.

He'd been aware of his loneliness and his general state of unhappiness, but the full impact of his daily life overwhelmed him now. He had been so alienated, so out of place with the people he called his mother and father. In turn, they were miserable with each other. When he stood up again, he wondered if his future would really be different. He remained still as his mind and his life

228

teetered between his past and what would be. Finally, it seemed like a fruitless effort to figure it all out. He only had the moment and his plan. Hopefully, his plan would work.

He went to his dresser with an encouraging thought. As an accelerated student, he already had enough high school credits to graduate. Perhaps he could work and go to college at the same time. He could become a competent man of the world. Someday, he could make Daniel proud. He smiled as he rummaged through his dresser drawer. He imagined himself to be as tall as his brother and just as accomplished.

When that day comes, there'll be no more neediness. We'll be a happy family again.

After a few sweeps through the contents of the drawer, he found his wallet and some money in an envelope. His savings didn't amount to much, but he figured there was enough to buy a plane ticket. He stuffed the bills in the wallet and was about to shove it in his pocket when the ceiling light came on. Startled by the sudden glare, his body reacted immediately, changing in an instant. He jumped around to face any new threat coming his way.

"Mom!" As he stared at the short woman standing in the doorway, every muscle in his body was taut and ready for action. "What are you doing up?"

His mother, Phyllis, was pale and trembling as she clasped her chest. "My lord, Theodore, you moved so fast! And why do you look like that?"

He knew in that instant he didn't need the survival guides in his bookcase. The new Theodore would be there for him. Still, he didn't mean to frighten anyone. "I'm sorry," he stammered, trying to soften his eyes. He'd seen Daniel's glow too bright when he was confronted. He knew he must look just as strange.

* * *

Backing out of the driveway, Daniel felt a jolt. It came from Theodore. What was happening to him? Daniel's connection to his

229

brother was almost too strong. He'd never been able to tune into anyone so completely. He could feel his brother's alarm as if it were his own. Was it life-threatening, or was Theodore simply reacting to something unexpected?

After a moment, Daniel relaxed a little. The spike was over. Theodore's emotional readout was returning to a less panicked state.

Just stay calm, Theo. Don't let yourself get rattled. I'll be there soon.

While he monitored Theodore's situation, he also tried sending out messages. It was frustrating. He could tell he wasn't getting through to his brother. Theodore's mind was closed to him.

Of course it is, you jerk. You told the kid to take a hike. He's trying to go it alone.

Going it alone had been Daniel's theme. He'd come close to marriage a couple of times, but he'd slipped out of both relationships before the appointed day. He was a very eligible bachelor in the pack and a coveted one. Many of the women, looking for a suitable mate, found him almost irresistible. He was handsome, strong, successful, and sensitive when you got to know him. A charming smile was the final element that helped the fairer sex fall under his spell. But he couldn't commit. He merged onto the highway, determined to break the pattern. He'd be the family Theodore needed. He just had to catch up to the kid.

* * *

Theodore watched his mother move back cautiously, as if she hardly recognized him. Her distrustful eyes were easy to read. She saw him as dangerous. That was understandable. He'd changed drastically since she'd seen him last. His body wasn't soft or docile anymore. He stood straight and tall, with his head erect, not bent down and submissive.

"Hi . . . I . . . uh . . . came back," he said. It was taking time to control his facial features and his speech. He felt very powerful when he transformed into his new self. It wasn't easy to appear meek and dutiful like the old Theodore had always been. When he saw himself in the mirror on the opposite wall, he startled himself. His eyes were dark and intense. He'd never imagined he could look so formidable.

His mother, Phyllis, was different too. Harsh words and intimidating gestures were the weapons she used to control the two men in her life. She gaped back at him mutely. She was contracting into herself instead of advancing towards him. He could feel her growing fear. It was the only expansive part of her. It slammed into his body, like stormy waves crashing in from the sea. He steadied himself, becoming more alert, preparing himself, but for what? He'd read that dogs could sense fear. Maybe he felt what they felt. Maybe animals simply reacted in kind, but he wasn't an animal. He wasn't afraid. He was the new, confident Theodore standing in his old bedroom. He knew it was up to him to change the situation. He had to do something to put his mother at ease. "How was your vacation?" he asked quietly.

Phyllis remained with her arms crossed, holding herself nervously. But her eyes grew harder as her anger flickered in and out and began to grow in strength. "Where have you been all this time? Don't you know how worried I've been?"

Theodore noticed that her voice was returning to normal, taking on the familiar, accusing tone he knew so well. He responded with his most appeasing smile. "I needed to get away for a little while. You know, have a little fun, that's all." His face melted into genuine contrition. "I'm sorry." He didn't have any desire to cause her grief.

Seeing him back off and become more like the Theodore she knew seemed to bolster her courage. She stood straighter too. "Fun? I was nearly out of my mine with worry!"

"I didn't mean to—"

"Don't give me any of your lip!" Her voice rose in volume. "How dare you put me through that kind of pain!"

Her outburst seemed to restore her, to bring her back to herself. Moving towards him, her face reddened with the livid antagonism that was coming to the surface. "You brazen, little heathen. I've dedicated my life to you and your worthless father. And this is what you do?" She started to raise her hand at him.

Theodore could feel her need to hit him, to vent her anger. But he also felt her mind working, wondering how far she could go. He wasn't a little kid anymore. He wasn't helpless to stop her tirades.

For a long moment they studied each other. He knew the woman who stood in front of him still frightened him deep down in that place where he'd once been helpless. Still, his fear wasn't as compelling as it had been in the past. Questions formed and needed answers. This was the person who raised him and supposedly cared about him, so why was her face scarlet with rage?

"Why are you so angry, really? I know you were worried about my running off, but you've always been so angry with me," he said in his softest voice. "Aren't you happy to see me, Mom?"

Her face was strained and hard as she lowered her hand. "Don't give me that 'Mom' crap! You don't care about me! You're selfish! You and your father both!" She snorted with more fury. "Why should I be happy to see you?"

He continued to study her, this woman who was short and stout and dressed in her fluffy, white robe. Her resentment towards him and his father was palpable and mean-spirited. Her small eyes, set in a plump, aging face, glared back at him with a grand consuming passion of unhappiness.

"I'm sorry," he said again in a whisper. He took deep breaths, letting himself absorb this newest bit of information. How had he been so blind to this woman's feelings? Why had he thought he mattered? Hadn't he known the truth all along? "You never really wanted me, did you?" The words trickled out before he had time to censor himself.

"What?" she cried out in surprise. His question seemed to make her replace one outrage with another. "What did you say?"

He moved closer to her now. "You never really loved me, did you?"

Her intent stare narrowed, boring into him with a new viciousness. "Want you? Love you? What choice did I ever have? I took you in and took care of you!"

Theodore stiffened at the idea of being at the mercy of this woman's care. A feeling surfaced from some dark depths and revealed itself. He remembered her hands on him when he was a small child, how he was too weak to escape her grasp. No matter how he cried and fought her, she scrubbed him like one of her dirty pots, leaving his skin red and raw. He'd put away those memories, like so many others. It was easier that way. Now they were all rushing in at once. His hands tightened into fists as he gathered the information he needed. "Then you should have been happy I was gone."

Her eyes bulged, filled with a new fury. "That's how you see it, don't you? You unappreciative, you thankless—" She paused again, looking frustrated when she was unable to find a word that described her abhorrence of who he was. "I've given you and Arthur everything. I've slaved around this place, keeping it spotless! I took care of both of you. I've given and given, and for what? My youth, my life is gone! The two of you have sucked me dry! I have nothing!"

He stood mute and unmoving, not knowing how to answer her lifetime of frustration.

She seemed invigorated by her declaration of ruin. Her face grew hard and malicious. "Well, let me tell you something before you go running off again." She pulled the note he'd left for her out of her pocket and waved it at him. "You are nothing! You were the unwanted reject that was forced on me!"

She stepped closer to him, so close her breath heaved in and out in his ear like a bellows of hate and loathing. In a low, cruel voice, she hissed out her tale of disappointment. "I wanted a child so much, but I couldn't have one of my own. I wanted a baby I could love. I wanted a sweet child, but I got you instead. You were hateful from the start, a screaming brat who did nothing but cry and push me away! As you got older, you became a sullen, self-centered, cold misfit I had to put up with."

Theodore felt suddenly weak as he stepped back. "I tried," he said. His voice choked as the pain of her words pulled him into her world of misery. "I tried to be good, but I could never measure up to your standards."

Her face took on a grim sense of power, enjoying his wretchedness. "You were no good from the start. How could I make something worthwhile out of a miscreant?"

Her vicious attack wasn't based on fact, and Theodore knew it. He stood up straighter. "That's not fair. I did what you told me to do, I know I did." As he spoke, his eyes darkened again. He relaxed the tight hold he had on his body. Given permission to express what he was feeling, his muscles tensed. If needed, that part of him was ready to come to his defense.

His mother reacted immediately to the change and began to back away. "Maybe you did try, maybe you can't help what you are." She took a deep breath, and put a hand to her chest. "I've tried to prepare myself for this day. I really hoped I'd never have to face it."

It was a strange, mystifying statement that engaged Theodore's curiosity. It also made him feel vulnerable and frightened again. "Face what, Mom?"

She shook her head and swallowed hard. "Don't call me that . . . ever again."

"Why? What aren't you telling me? What's the matter?"

"Never mind," she said, using her forced, polite voice, the voice she used for people who mattered or intimidated her. "I think you better go." She stared at him with faded eyes as if she'd lost something, perhaps her dream of a better child or a better life.

Her expression made Theodore regret his earlier outburst. "I'm sorry. I'm sorry I wasn't what you wished for, that you had to put up with me."

She shook her head and bit her lip. "It's too late for your apology. You might think I never wanted you, but you never wanted me either. That's the point."

For the first time, he saw the slightest glimmer of a real person under all the anger and bitterness. "Maybe I didn't know how," he said as he reached out to her.

She pulled back and looked away.

He felt her distancing herself from him, placing him outside her world like he'd never been her child. "After all these years, you can do this to me? Disown me without any feeling at all?"

She remained resolute. Her face became an unyielding façade of determination. "Just go. We have nothing more to say to each other."

He tried one last time to do the right thing. He leaned over to kiss her, like he always made himself do, but she moved away.

"Leave," she said quietly, but with bitterness, like he was hurting her with his presence.

He moved slowly to the bedroom door. He didn't know what else to do. "Goodbye."

She glanced up. "Where will you go?"

He shrugged. "When I get to the airport, maybe I'll just take the first flight out. It doesn't matter, does it?"

"No, I guess it doesn't," she said as her eyes followed him out into the hall.

* * *

Once Theodore was out of the room, Phyllis slumped down on the bed. She grabbed a tissue from a box on the nightstand. She pressed it to her mouth and tried not to cry out, but a short sob escaped her lips. She'd said things to the boy she'd raised, things she'd never admitted to herself. Her declaration left her with the facts. Her life was nothing but a series of disappointments. But it wasn't her fault. She'd been cursed with a situation that was impossible.

"I tried. I tried so hard, but Daddy is right. He's not really human."

She proved her point to herself by resurrecting Theodore's reaction when she'd surprised him. "He is an animal!"

As the thought settled in, she let out a gasp. "Oh Daddy . . . don't blame me. It's not my fault he turned out this way." She put her hand over her mouth and sobbed into her tissue again. She wondered why she didn't feel more about Theodore, how she could have cared for him all those years and not feel something, but she didn't. All that surfaced was more anger. She'd given so much for so little in return.

She stood up and went to the window overlooking the front yard. Peering out and seeing Theodore walk down the driveway, she pulled her cell phone out of her robe pocket. She paused and stared at it, then pressed a number on the touchpad. When a connection was established, she put the phone to her ear and listened to the rings. Tears rolled down her cheeks when she heard a voice on the other end.

"Daddy, it's me . . . yes, he was here. He's like you said he'd be. Oh Daddy, you're not angry with me, are you?"

Chapter Thirty-Two

A sudden chill made Daniel grip the steering wheel with stiff fingers as he steeled himself against Theodore's mood change. The boy's mind was adrift in a sea of heartache and disbelief so profound, it made Daniel shiver.

"What the hell happened to you at that house?" He asked the question aloud as if Theodore could answer him.

He wished he could stop the car and concentrate fully on what was going on with his brother, to really understand his thoughts, but he couldn't spare the time. In the middle of the emotional chaos in Theodore's mind, Daniel sensed locations were shifting. Theodore was on the move again.

"Where are you going now? Theodore, tell me. Let me help you."

There was an exit ahead, and he decided he had no choice. He had to pull over. He had to know where Theodore was headed next without the distraction of driving. Once he took the exit ramp and found a place to stop, he relaxed and shut his eyes. It wasn't hard after that. "Oh hell, he's headed for the airport!"

* * *

Phyllis held her cell phone to her ear with a shaky hand. Her father's harsh voice always did that to her. When she'd made the call, she'd been resolute. But thinking about Theodore reaching out his hand to her, she felt a twinge of guilt. A life was in her hands. Even if she didn't feel much, she wanted to make sure her conscience was clear. She needed that. She was always so much weaker than her father.

"Are you absolutely sure there's no way to reverse what Theodore's become?" she asked in an almost apologetic voice.

Her father's short, angry reply, made her cringe.

"I'm not wasting time," she whimpered back. "I just want to be positive I'm doing the right thing, that this is the only way. I know he's killed people, but maybe you could turn him over to the police."

She leaned against the wall as she listened to him go on. She knew she'd never win with him. "Okay, I'll tell you. He's going to the airport. You're a lot closer than we are, you'll have time. But Daddy, please, just promise me he won't suffer. Even an animal should be put down quickly."

After she heard her father disconnect without even a goodbye, she shut her eyes. He always made her feel like a helpless child. Now he was in charge of the fate of the boy she'd once called her son. There wasn't going to be a happy ending for Theodore. But it wasn't her fault. At least that was a comfort. When she opened her eyes, her husband was standing in the hall, just beyond the doorway.

"What the hell is going on, Phyllis," he asked in a low, guarded tone. "Was that your father?"

She looked at his scowling expression and wiped the tears of resignation from her face. "Go back to bed, Arthur. This is none of your concern."

"What do you mean? I heard you. You were discussing our son with that deranged nutcase you call your father."

"Don't speak about him like that! He's a scientist. He's dedicated to helping—"

"Helping? He's like one of those Nazi doctors. He's obsessed with his own ideas and doesn't give a damn about anyone else."

"He's the head of a very elite group of men, men who have given over their lives so they can watch out for the rest of us."

"Whatever, all I know is what he did to you."

She shuffled over to the bed. "He tried to correct my infertility problems."

"Get real, woman, he used you like a guinea pig. And after all was said and done, what good did it do?"

She looked up at him, her eyes wide and bleak. "He tried. I know he did."

"The only decent thing that ever came from his hands was our boy. Do you remember that day we got him?" he asked in a plaintive voice. "Poor little guy. Do you remember the shape he was in?"

"Daddy explained all that. He was a very sick child. Daddy saved him." She stared at her lap as she twisted the tissue in her hands. "I never told you this, Arthur, because I knew you'd never understand. But there was something very wrong with Theodore."

Arthur walked over to where she was sitting. "What are you talking about?"

She looked up and let out a great sigh. "He's not like us."

Arthur's gaze narrowed. "What the hell do you mean?"

"He has something wrong with his genes. Daddy tried to help him, tried to cure him, but—"

"His genes? There's nothing wrong with Theodore. He's bright and thoughtful. Maybe he's quieter and more sensitive than some boys, but he's fine. His genes are fine."

"I thought so too. I've watched him all these years, and I thought he was going to be okay, but he's not. He's psychotic, just like his parents were. They were murderers. And he has their DNA. Daddy checked it all out. Now, he's insane too. Daddy said he killed some people."

Arthur glared back at her. "Our Theodore? He would never do anything like that. It's your father who's insane to even suggest it! My god, Phyllis! I heard you on the phone. What is your father planning to do?"

She looked down and squeezed the tissue tight in her fist.

Arthur reached out and grabbed her arms. "Answer me!" He shook her as he shouted. "I said 'answer me!'"

"Leave me alone!" she shrieked back. "Daddy has no choice. I tried everything to make Theodore normal. It's better this way."

Arthur let her go and pulled away.

"You drove both Theodore and me crazy with all your obsessive behavior! You and your father, with all your rules and need for control!" He stumbled back, rubbing his forehead. After a moment, he looked up and stared back with disbelieving, hard eyes. "Oh no! Oh no, he's going to kill our boy, isn't he?"

"He has to. The person you think of as your son is . . . is—" She raised her chin defensively. "You didn't see him tonight. He's changed."

Arthur's eyes flared. "Did he hurt you or threaten you?"

"No, but he acted so different! Why can't you understand?"

Arthur began shaking his head. "Understand? I understand it all perfectly. It all makes sense. You're as insane as your father!"

* * *

Arthur knew he didn't have a moment to waste. He rushed out of Theodore's room and into the master suite. He was mumbling words that seemed too horrible to be true. "My boy! That maniac is going to kill my son."

His breath was quick and filled with dread as he yanked his car keys from the bedside table. "I should have known something was wrong all these years! Now I have to stop that madman!"

Still in his pajamas, he ran through the house, through the dark rooms to the garage. When he flung open the door, he felt like he was in a nightmare. His body was shaking and weak as he pressed the garage door opener. How blind he'd let himself be. When his son was growing up and needed him, he'd deferred to his wife to keep peace. He'd kept himself busy at work because he didn't want to face her constant haranguing on how things had to be.

"And Theodore is going to pay for my sins! My god, my god, how could I have let this happen?"

Chapter Thirty-Three

Prissy couldn't sleep. It was becoming a habit that started when her father had been shot. When the bullet struck him, it shattered her world too. Things were supposed to be getting better, but nothing seemed like it was before. She wasn't in her own home, and the pack was on constant alert. The WKA would definitely step up their efforts to retaliate after some of their men were killed. Then there was Theodore. She was worried about him even if his halo was a little tarnished.

That's a new one for me. I've never worried about anyone outside of my family before.

She crept out of the bedroom she was sharing with Doc Leonard's daughter. She had a weird feeling about Theodore's safety, and she wanted to look in on him. She tiptoed into the living room, making sure she wouldn't wake him up. She didn't want him to know he was important to her. When she saw the empty couch, she tried to tune into his whereabouts. After a moment, she knew he wasn't in the house.

Don't tell me he's gone again. And I thought he was more mature than me. That's a laugh.

She went to the window and searched the street. The Land Rover was missing too. Theodore hadn't taken off on foot this time. She frowned, trying to ignore an odd feeling that she might never see him again. She hurried to the library where Daniel was supposed to be bedded down. Daniel was gone too.

It's probably nothing. Why am I getting upset?

After all, what Theodore and Daniel did was none of her business. Still, she couldn't dismiss Theodore too quickly, even though he'd said some very unkind things to her. She paused, knowing she'd been at fault too. The bottom line was that she wanted to do whatever was best.

She quickly walked down the hall to the guest bedroom and rapped on the door. As soon as her mother answered her knock, she blurted out the news. "Mom, Dad, maybe it's not important, but Theo and Daniel have both disappeared."

Amelie was the first to ask questions. "Are you sure they're gone, not just somewhere talking?"

"I don't know," Prissy said, happy to hand over her burden to her parents. "But it's nothing, right?"

"I don't know, honey." Amelie put an arm around Prissy and looked anxiously at Wolfgang. He was already getting dressed.

Prissy pulled away and studied her mother's face. All the color was gone. "What is it, Mom?"

Amelie ignored her question and addressed Wolfgang. "Dearest, I have a very bad feeling about what's happening."

Wolfgang grabbed his phone. "I'll call Charles. He's the best we have when it comes to tracking someone telepathically. Maybe he can tune into one of them."

Prissy watched her father leave the room and turned her attention to her mother again. "Are you getting one of those feelings, the ones you get about the future?"

Amelie hesitated as if she was checking something before answering. When she spoke, her words were measured and forthright. "I don't have your gifts, but yes, I'm afraid I do feel something is very wrong. What about you?"

Prissy backed up and crossed her arms. "I'm angry at Theodore. He was just a nice guy before all this started. He was a little stupid at times, but sweet. Now, he's become very impulsive when he should be more mature. We have enough problems already." She paused and groaned. "But who am I to talk? We all know how I've behaved."

Amelie smiled. "It's been a tough time all around."

"What's happening to us, Mom? Even Daniel is completely out of it."

"Fear has that effect, especially when we go into survival mode."

"I wish we could go back to the way life used to be."

"Me too. The only good thing about what's happened is that we'll get our priorities straight."

Prissy shut her eyes, wondering about her priorities. Again, she wanted to help. But the chaos she'd experienced had taken its toll. She didn't feel like all her circuits were online. She had to make herself calm down and concentrate. A small spark of insight made her light up with surprise.

"Mom, I don't know how, but I tuned into Theodore. He's very upset and wants to leave us. He's driving to the airport!"

* * *

Doc Leonard insisted on going with Wolfgang. The plan was to intercept Theodore. As he drove, he glanced over at the pack leader with concern. "If you need help, I'm here, remember that."

"Thanks," Wolfgang said, keeping his eyes forward.

"Can you tune into Daniel's or Theodore's mind."

"No, and I can't call Daniel. He forgot his cell phone back at the medical facility."

Doc hesitated. As a physician and personal friend of Wolfgang, he didn't want to add to the man's stress by voicing his own misgivings. Daniel was in an unstable emotional state. If things escalated with the WKA, neither Daniel nor Wolfgang was in peak condition to say the least. He was particularly worried about Wolfgang's physical state. Their leader was still weak, still battling the toxins in his body. He gave Wolfgang another glance. "Do you know why Daniel took my hand gun? Did Charles or Prissy get any insight into what this is all about?"

Wolfgang stared out his side window. "The only thing everyone agrees on is that Theodore has run off. I'm sure Daniel is worried about his safety. He thinks Theodore could do something to alert the WKA and get captured again."

Doc swallowed hard. "I don't blame him for being concerned. I remember Daniel as a child, when we got him back from—" He paused. "What a horror story. Did you ever discover how he got away?"

"No. As that traumatized boy, Daniel could barely speak. He even tried to pretend Theodore was dead. I guess that way he didn't have to think about what might have happened to him. Fortunately, they've reconnected, and Daniel has gotten a lot of his memories back. But I don't think he remembers the part about escaping."

"There must have been a reason they let him go. It's always bothered me."

"Daniel's afraid they let him go so he'd betray us."

"You don't believe that, do you?"

"Never."

"You're that sure?"

Wolfgang's gaze shifted to the road, his brows furrowed deep with concern. "I'm one hundred percent positive. The only real danger is what he's capable of doing to himself."

* * *

Speeding along the interstate, Theodore thought about the last time he'd driven to the airport. His parents needed to catch a flight to Florida to board a cruise ship. His father suggested Theodore drive them. The entire time that they were en route his mother complained and criticized his driving while his father stared stoically at the road. By sanctioning the drive and not adding any criticism of his own, his father let Theodore know he was supporting him in his subtle way.

I had a father who wouldn't open his mouth and a mother who never closed it. How did I end up with the two of them? Did the adoption agency even screen people?

The burden of his mother's rejection and her hateful diatribe about who he really was, made Theodore forget all his wonderful plans to excel. None of it seemed fair. Bitterness was seeping into his mind, as if she'd infected him with her thoughts. He countered it with his rising anger. "Life is a joke," he muttered. "Those beings from the stars obviously screwed up big time thinking they were helping us."

But that didn't change what he had to do. He had to get on a plane and fly somewhere.

I'll probably end up working in a convenience store for the rest of my life.

His energy sagged at the prospect, and he felt tired again. He'd only had a few hours of sleep. He wanted to go back to bed and sleep forever. As if the idea was a hypnotic suggestion, his eyes started to close. The loud, drawn out blare of a horn instantly brought him back to driving and the road. He was veering into a neighboring lane. He swerved, jerking the car back into his own lane with reflexes that felt slow and sluggish. Luckily the car alongside had braked just in time to prevent a collision.

His body was back to its old self, the clumsy, blundering Theodore was driving. The change had happened towards the end of his conversation with his mother. No wonder he felt so depressed. Even his gifted-self retreated from the woman's spell of misery and gloom.

When he glanced over at the adjoining lane, he saw the angry face of the passing car's passenger giving him the finger. "Sorry, sorry!" He mouthed the words hoping they helped excuse his actions. He might not have much to live for, but he didn't have the right to endanger someone else. It was a relief to see the airport exit coming up.

* * *

"Theodore! Stay awake!" Daniel felt and even glimpsed Theodore's close call on the highway. His mental shout out was delivered as an urgent directive, but he knew he was wasting his energy trying to connect with his brother. Theodore's emotional state was consuming him, making him withdraw even more.

Daniel could only wonder at what would make Theodore seem so despondent. Sure, the kid was upset with Daniel, but something shifted after Theodore left his parents' house. It was as if a black, airless cloud had settled over his mind.

Daniel stepped on the gas, relieved he was only a few miles from the airport. He continued to target Theodore's mind with urgent messages. Perhaps one would slip through when Theodore let his guard down. "Stay clear and believe in yourself. It's going to be alright."

* * *

Arthur's hands were clutching the steering wheel so hard they ached. As he neared the exit for the airport, he knew he had no choice about what he was doing. He had to save Theodore from Phyllis' lunatic father. Unfortunately, he'd had time to think about what he could do or say to change the situation, and his self-confidence was flagging. He liked to tell himself he was a skilled man in the business world, but in Karl Neumann's world, Arthur knew he was nothing.

I let that madman come to our house and order us all around. I was never able to support my wife and boy.

A blaze of shame and fear brightened his face when he saw the sign announcing his exit two miles ahead. Instead of being the jock he encouraged Theodore to be, that he'd thought he was at one time, he'd found out he was only a pretender. He'd never forget the one time he tried to stand up to his father-in-law. It was etched in his mind, a disgrace he'd always be saddled with.

But he wasn't the only one who was deeply affected by Karl Neumann. When he'd dated Phyllis so many years ago, it was easy to see she was afraid of her father. As her fiancé, he'd had the puffed-up idea he could change the situation. He'd believed marrying her would change everything. He soon found out the truth. During the wedding reception, Neumann had taken him aside, asked to speak to him outside in the back alley. Arthur was still cocky and sure of himself when he agreed. His boldness didn't go very far.

Neumann had a brutal gleam in his eyes when he informed Arthur about what the marriage really meant. Neumann was still in charge of his daughter. Arthur's only function was to support her and make sure she had what she wanted. When Arthur objected to being ordered around, Neumann went into a rage and threw him up against a dumpster.

Arthur had never seen anyone look like they wanted to kill before. But he knew his new father-in-law was totally prepared to end his life then and there. And Karl Neumann didn't want to do it swiftly. Cruel, pitiless eyes glared back at his new son-in-law. This was a man who enjoyed making others suffer, enjoyed his power and domination over his victims.

Arthur felt a numbing cold grab hold when he relived the scene. Then he imagined Theodore in Neumann's clutches and something shifted inside of him. He hadn't stood up for himself, but a blind courage coursed through his veins when he thought about his son being threatened.

You insane gorilla! Whatever it takes, I'll stop you from hurting him.

The words echoed in his mind as he let another thought surface. It was one he'd never allowed before. He couldn't. It was too unbearable.

What did Neumann do to our child before he gave him to us?

Arthur's breath caught at the thought. The guilt was too much and closed off his airways. When he was able to breathe again, he knew he should have gone to the police or done something about Theodore's condition, but he hadn't done a damn thing but hide from the facts that were so obvious. This time he couldn't fail Theodore. He'd do whatever was needed to help his son.

Chapter Thirty-Four

Theodore felt better as he exited the freeway. He wasn't sleepy anymore. His mood was lifting a little. The airport was all about going places, seeing new things. The thought of adventure helped him to forget about his mother's miserable attitude. He opened his mind to more options.

Where will I go? Big city or small? Desert or the Midwest? Perhaps California would be nice.

As hope surfaced, he even imagined Paris. He saw himself checking out the Eiffel Tower with Daniel. It brought a small smile to his face as he drove towards the airport's parking facilities. Was it possible? Someday, could he and his brother go to France together? The idea filled his mind like a bright, shiny ornament on a Christmas tree. He quickly came back to reality as he approached the automatic toll station at the entrance to the parking garage. He stopped long enough to push the red button on the ticket dispenser. After he retrieved his ticket, he watched as the toll gate lifted and allowed him to drive through.

Maybe I don't have to work in a convenience store forever.

His weak smile broadened as the Land Rover began its ascent towards the parking levels. He'd only gone as far as the entrance to the first level when a movement from the side of the ramp caught his attention. Someone was waving at him. As he slowed down to barely a crawl, an older man in a brown jacket stepped forward and walked into his lane.

"Grandfather?" He put his foot to the brake and brought the Land Rover to a stop. He couldn't believe his grandfather was there. They usually only saw each other on special occasions, and those times were more than enough for Theodore. He knew his mother must have learned her obsessive need for order and perfection from her father. Whenever the gruff man was around, he took charge. He told his daughter what she was doing wrong. He always had instructions about the correct method for doing everything, including making chicken on the grill and bringing up Theodore properly. Strangely enough, Theodore's dad was usually away on business during his grandfather's visits.

"Did Mom call you?" he asked as his grandfather walked up to the driver's side window.

The older man smiled. "Yes, she said she'd been angry at you, said some things. But I want to talk to you about it all. Now let me in."

Theodore swallowed hard. He'd rarely seen his grandfather smile. He figured it was meant to put him at ease, but it made his skin crawl and the hair stood up on the back of his neck. "Okay," he said hesitantly as he unlocked the passenger door.

*　*　*

Following Amelie's orders, Prissy went back to bed. She felt like a kid being told what to do, but she knew her mother was right. If she didn't get her eight hours, she felt cranky the next day. After she was snug under the covers again, she gazed up at the ceiling and listened to her roommate breathing. The sound was too quiet to be called snoring, but it was loud enough to fill the room with a gentle hum of repose. It helped to ease Prissy's busy mind. She soon turned over, enjoying the warmth of the comforter.

Just about to nod off, she was totally unprepared for the flash of a gun going off. The vision ripped through her mind so abruptly and so unexpectedly she nearly screamed with fright. Panicked, her first thought was to call out for her mother. The second was to stop and breathe, to let herself tune into anything else that wanted to come through. Another shot, so real, so loud, followed the first and made her grab her ears to stop the blast from deafening her.

"Oh no, Theodore! Daniel!" she cried as she leaped out of bed. It took a moment to get her bearings and run for the door. Once in the hall, she sprinted to the kitchen. There was a wall phone near the entrance. She grabbed the receiver to make her call. Her hand stilled when she heard the gunfire sound in her head again. Its deadly report was so real, she momentarily forgot her father's cell number.

Calm down!

She made herself shut out the vision momentarily. When she did, the number surfaced. She was able to tap in the digits on the phone. After one ring, she heard her father's voice. She began to cry as she relayed her information. "I saw bodies and so much blood!"

* * *

Wolfgang prepared himself as he pocketed his cell phone. "Doc, if you can move any faster, do it."

"Bad news?" Doc asked.

Wolfgang nodded as he thought about Prissy's vision. His own abilities were lacking when it came to foretelling future events. Some of his kind, like his grandmother, were much more gifted. Some humans were also gifted. Wolfgang recognized Amelie's talent early on, but he'd never encouraged her to use it. She was already so sensitive he didn't want her burdened further by knowing things she couldn't prevent from happening. Their daughter, Prissy, had the gift from both sides. If developed carefully, it would probably become one of her most powerful abilities. But would it help them now? He gave Doc a quick glance. "Did you bring your other gun?"

"Yes, do you think we'll need it?"

"I don't know." Wolfgang stared at the road slipping by and at the sign for the airport. The exit was two miles ahead. "I just talked to Prissy. If she's right about what she's seeing, we might already be too late."

* * *

Karl Neumann gave Theodore instructions to drive the Land Rover to one of the upper levels of the parking structure. "We can talk in private. At this time of night, we'll have the place to ourselves," he said casually as they made their way upwards. When they got to the fourth level, he gave further directions. "Pull over to that area. It should be perfect."

"Do you want to talk about what Mom said?" Theodore asked as he drove to the far corner and pulled into a parking space.

Neumann stared back, studying him carefully. He'd never wanted to play the role of grandfather, but he had wanted to keep an eye on his experiment. Now as he examined his supposed grandson of many years, he wavered for just a moment. Was there any more to be learned from the thing that sat across from him? It looked like a human being. Yet underneath, in spite of all of his work to alter its DNA, a subhuman freak of nature blinked back at him. It was time to close the file on this one. "It's the end of the line, Theodore," he said with loathing.

"I know. I told Mom I was leaving, that I'd be on my own from now on. From what she said, I think she's happy to be rid of me."

"Yes, I know how she feels."

Theodore looked at him. "So you're disappointed in me too?"

Neumann opened his car door and got out. "It's time to finish this. So let's go."

Theodore shrugged, looking confused, like he'd expected more from Neumann, maybe a stern lecture. Then he obediently opened his door and climbed out too. "I guess I don't fit into Mom's or your perfect world, Grandfather."

"My world's not perfect," Neumann said as he took a revolver from his coat pocket and walked over to where Theodore was standing. "My world won't be perfect until all of your kind are gone."

Chapter Thirty-Five

When he arrived at the airport, Daniel went straight to the parking garage. He knew Theodore was close. As their connection strengthened, he was able to feel his brother's physical presence. He automatically drove past the first two parking levels and slowed. Something was wrong. Theodore wasn't alone.

"Oh no!" Daniel's heart almost stopped when he got a glimpse of the person Theodore was staring at. Swerving into the third level lot, he tried to catch his breath. "Oh god, not him, please!" he cried out as he accelerated across the floor's almost empty expanse. Nearing the far wall, he slammed on the brakes, stopping as close to the stairs as possible. He was sick and hardly able to get any air, but he knew he didn't have time for anything but saving Theodore.

"Keep it together!" he ordered as he fumbled with the latch on the glove compartment. It took all his concentration to manage the simple task. "Come on, get the gun!" His hand tried to obey, but it was trembling so badly, he couldn't wrap his fingers around the weapon. With sheer willpower and determination, he was finally able to grasp hold of it. He pushed open the car door and started to get out. His legs were as shaky as his hands. They gave way, unable to support his weight. Desperate, he had to grab hold of the side of the car to stay upright. As he did, reality slipped away, replaced by the feeling that he was twelve years old again and totally helpless.

He was in a bright, sterile lab. Stripped of his clothes, he was so cold. He almost blacked out as he felt himself being strapped down, saw the look on Karl Neumann's face as he stood waiting with a surgical knife in his hand. Facing this monster who claimed to be human, Daniel knew the truth. Neumann was utterly cruel and ruthless. All of the WKA were hoodlums, but their leader was by far the most inhuman.

Daniel started gagging as the memories he'd never faced came flooding in, filling his body with the horrors that it had endured.

"Help me," he pleaded, as he begged for some respite. "Help me, please."

His tormented cry had barely been offered up to the ethers, when he got a reply. It was Wolfgang, calling back to him.

"Daniel, is that you? We're almost there. Hold on."

The voice offered Daniel a lifeline. It was enough to break the spell of terror that overwhelmed him. He had to claw his way back to an upright position. He did it by holding on to Wolfgang's few words of support. Stumbling past the elevator, his intent to help Theodore wasn't enough. Even if his mind was willing, his physical body was stuck in the past.

"Not now! I can't relive what happened now." Taking steady, slow breaths, he finally succeeded in reining in his emotions, stuffing them back into his gut and slamming the door shut. When he did, there was an instantaneous change in his body. He almost cried out with elation as he felt his strength returning. His muscles became fluid and ready for action.

I'm here for you, Theodore!

As he announced his presence to his brother, he was able once again to go into stealth mode, that place where a wolf could slip through the forest as quietly as a silent breeze. He went up the stairs soundlessly, gripping his gun with both hands. When he reached the fourth level, he heard Theodore's voice from across the lot. It sounded so young, so scared.

Daniel knew why. His brother was facing his worst nightmare.

You maniacal fiend, you won't take my brother again.

This time Daniel's message was for Karl Neumann.

You're not dealing with children anymore.

Daniel tightened his grip on the gun. He went from slow and cautious to preparing for an all-out assault. He wanted to kill the heartless thug who tortured his brother. In that moment, he knew he wasn't one of the enlightened ones. He wasn't one who could choose peace over violence, and he didn't care.

"If it means my soul, so be it," he swore silently. He made his way across the parking spots, hiding behind pillars and then advancing forward again. He narrowed the space between him and his target.

* * *

Theodore blinked back at his grandfather, not knowing how to respond. "What do you mean when you say my kind? And why do you have that gun?"

Neumann shook his head. "Stupid animal, that's all you are when it comes down to it. Sure you act like one of us, but underneath, you're a threat to what the Almighty made. We're the perfect human beings. You're a work of the devil himself."

Theodore began to back up, holding his hands in the air. His mind was scrambling to put facts together, but a part of him couldn't see past the idea that his grandfather, at least his grandfather in name, wanted him dead.

"You want to kill me? Is that it? Why? What have I done to you?"

Neumann's watery, bloodshot eyes narrowed. "You've wasted my time!" he shouted. "I took you from your rat's nest! I tried to get rid of some of the beast in you, to see what would happen, but that was pride on my part. I can't change something that's an affront to creation itself."

Neumann paused long enough to step forward. He reached out and lifted up Theodore's shirt in a rough handed jerk. His lips curled back in a scornful sneer as he stared at the red, recently healed wound on Theodore's side. "I was hoping if you did change into your animal self, that you'd first seek out your brother, and then he'd take you to join the rest of the vermin. We'd get rid of the bunch. But I see you found the tracking device."

Theodore slowly pulled his shirt out of Neumann's hand. His words came out in a gasp. "You're with the WKA."

Neumann let out a contemptuous laugh. "Bingo. That didn't take long. You're the first specimen I've studied so extensively. I've always been amazed at how backward you are. How can your breed think they're superior? Superior to what, to a cockroach?" He pointed the gun and stepped closer, shoving it against Theodore's head. "But enough of this. I need some sleep."

Theodore took small steps backward until he was against the wall. His gaze was fixated on Neumann's eyes. He couldn't believe how cold and hard they looked. "Just like that? You're going to shoot me?"

Neumann's face brightened with an executioner's delight. "Just like that."

* * *

Arthur pulled into the first level parking lot, got out of the car and looked around. "Oh hell!" Across the lot, he spied his father-in-law's black Mercedes. He didn't see anyone in or around it.

"Think like a lunatic. Where is he? Where would he take Theodore?" Neumann would have to make his move outside of the terminal. That meant he and Theodore were probably on one of the other parking levels.

"I've got to find him before it's too late!" He rallied round the words with all the courage he could muster, continually reminding himself of the picture he carried in his wallet. It was the only one he carried. It was Theodore's picture. On a rare occasion, when Phyllis had been sick, Arthur had taken his ten-year-old son to the fair. Arthur smiled at the memory. Theodore had been so excited to spend some time together for a change, to have a real father-son day like other boys. At the end of it, they'd stepped into a self-service photo booth. In one of the shots, they almost looked like they were related. For a fleeting moment, they had both been happy.

For a moment, we were father and son.

Arthur had held onto the picture, but not to Theodore.

Phyllis was always there, always telling Theodore he was sick, always making me sick. I couldn't be around her. I just couldn't take it.

His face sagged again. He'd given up on his marriage and on his adopted child. But would it have been so hard to stand up to Phyllis? Was he afraid she'd tell her father?

What a spineless wimp I am.

He looked around the parking garage and brought himself back to his purpose for being there. He didn't have time for self-loathing. Running to the stairs, he decided to check the other levels on foot. He'd have the advantage of surprise. He began to take the steps two at a time. He wasn't in terrible shape. He did go to the gym a couple of times a week. Would that be enough to face down Neumann? He doubted it.

* * *

When Daniel saw Neumann put a gun to Theodore's head, he made his final move. Crouching down and using the Land Rover for cover, he was able to slip around it and up behind Neumann. He was so quiet he caught the old man totally unaware. "Drop the gun!" he ordered as he took the last few steps separating them. He put his gun against Neumann's head.

The old man never flinched. He stood there, rock solid, still gazing at his victim.

"Daniel!" Theodore cried out as his terrified expression changed to one of surprise and happiness.

Daniel's eyes brightened, but he kept his attention on Neumann.

Neumann grinned. He seemed entertained by the optimism in Theodore's voice. "Ah, this is an interesting development," he said in a relaxed tone. "Looking at this young, ignorant good-for-nothing, I suspect he thinks he's being rescued."

Daniel jammed his weapon harder into Neumann's skull. "I said drop the gun!"

The old man let out a quick laugh. "My finger is tight on the trigger. You can kill me, but I guarantee he'll die too. Still, I have an idea. How about this? I've heard you live by some kind of primitive pack code. How about your life for his?"

"No!" Theodore's shout filled the space.

Daniel knew what was going through Theodore's mind. His brother was ready to sacrifice his own life if it meant saving Daniel's. "Be quiet, Theo. Let me handle this."

Theodore shook his head. "Shoot me, Grandfather! That's what you want and maybe Mom does too, so get it over with!"

Daniel cried out. "No! Don't tell me that this monster's daughter raised you?"

In that moment, it all gelled in both their minds. Theodore's adoptive mother was one of *them*. She was connected to the WKA, the people dedicated to hunting them out and killing them.

Theodore looked at Neumann. "That's it, isn't it? Mom called you because she wants me dead!" His voice broke with emotion.

Daniel could feel the pain sinking in, making Theodore look like he wanted to cry.

Neumann let out an amused laugh. "Aw, look at you. Are you going to bawl? Is the big bad wolf baby going to howl for me?"

"Shut up!" Daniel screamed.

"No, you shut up," Neumann hissed back. "And make up your mind. Your life or his, choose one."

"Daniel, don't!" Theodore shrieked. "I'm the one he wants to kill!"

Daniel could see that Theodore was losing it. If he did, he'd be gunned down for sure. "Alright! My life for his," he yelled as he backed the gun away from Neumann's head.

Neumann grinned triumphantly. "That's more like it. Put the gun down and move over there where I can see you."

"First let Theodore go. Then I'll put down my gun. I give you my word."

Theodore began to shake uncontrollably. "Please, no, Daniel, don't, please!"

"Your word? The word of an animal?" Neumann glowered at the concept. "Put the gun down now, or I'll shoot him. And that's my promise."

Chapter Thirty-Six

When Arthur reached the fourth floor, he was out of breath. His eyes widened in panic when he checked out his surroundings. Across the garage expanse, in the far corner, he saw his father-in-law. He had a gun pointed at Theodore's head. There was another man there who also had a gun. This man was backing away, but he stopped and began to stoop down. Arthur realized he was relinquishing his weapon. Theodore was yelling at him. His cries filled the rooftop.

"No! Daniel, No! He's going to kill you!" Theodore screamed out in a choking voice.

Hearing him pleading, Arthur didn't think about what to do next. He just reacted to Theodore's voice. He began to run as fast as he could towards the group.

"Stop! Karl! Stop!" He shouted as loud as he could, as if the sound of his words might have some power.

"Dad!"

Arthur heard Theodore call out to him. The sound was so despairing, so plaintive, that he tried to run faster. His son's acknowledgement filled his heart with joy and sorrow. In that instant, he loved Theodore more than ever. Yet, somehow, he knew it was too late.

There were two shots fired. The first one hit the man who'd put down his gun. Neumann pointed and fired the second round in Arthur's direction. Arthur didn't realize he'd been hit too. He was thrown back, but he stayed on his feet. He fought to keep going.

"Don't hurt my son!" He screamed the words with what breath he had left in his lungs, but he knew it didn't accomplish anything. The last thing he heard and saw as he fell to his knees was Theodore. His son was shrieking hysterically and attacking Neumann, shoving him off balance as Neumann got off the third shot. Arthur heard the zing as it went past him. Crumpled on the floor, trying to get air, trying to see what was happening, he heard a fourth shot.

* * *

The bullet from Neumann's gun hit Daniel with an explosive force that threw him backwards, slamming him to the concrete. Sprawled on his back, he was stunned and unable to move at first. He'd heard someone shouting from across the garage, but he hadn't had time to find out who it was. His only thought was to save Theodore. Flailing his arms and trying to get his legs under him, he realized his body wasn't responding to his demands.

A second shot rang out. The words, 'Don't hurt my son,' filled Daniel's ears. For a brief moment, he thought it was his own father. Hadn't he been told his father begged for mercy for his children?

Theodore's screams brought him back from the memory. Using all his willpower, he was able to move just enough to lift his head. He saw his brother jump towards Neumann. The old man faltered, but he got off another shot. With his strength failing fast, Daniel struggled to watch Theodore fighting with the old man, trying to get the gun out of his hand. A fourth shot was fired. Daniel's strength gave out just as he saw Theodore falling. The thought that his brother was dead filled Daniel with a rage that went beyond anything he'd ever felt before. But he couldn't move from the spot.

* * *

Theodore couldn't believe how fast everything happened. He tried to stop Daniel from surrendering his gun, but his brother wasn't listening to him. Simultaneously, a shout came from across the garage. Theodore looked over in time to see his father running towards them. He was ordering Neumann to stand down.

"Dad!" Theodore called out as if this man was really his father. For an instant, it felt like it was true. Arthur was acting like he cared, like he thought Theodore mattered. He was trying to stop Neumann. But the old man didn't hesitate. He fired at Daniel, and then at Arthur. That's when Theodore finally took action. Up until then, everything was too chaotic. He was in too much shock to know what to do. When he did react, it was instinctive. He lunged at the old man, fought for the weapon in his hand. He might have succeeded if Neumann hadn't got off another shot. Everything went instantly black.

* * *

It had been a long time since Neumann felt so elated. As Theodore's hands loosened their grip on his wrist, as the young dog that dared to call itself human, fell to the cold, hard floor, he smiled victoriously. Within his position in the WKA, it wasn't often that he had the opportunity to personally annihilate the animals he'd hunted for so long. He stared down at Theodore and marveled at how well this aberration could mimic the look of a real boy. But he had to remain focused. He glanced at the other one called Daniel. The would-be savior was barely moving. Finally, he scowled in his son-in-law's direction and walked a few feet towards him.

"Stupid of you, Arthur! Very stupid of you to think you could ever go up against me. But you're going to make it easy. I'll tell the police I saw Theodore, your troubled son, shoot you and a bystander. Then he tragically put a bullet in his own head." He laughed. "How convenient you've made it for me."

Neumann walked back to where Theodore lay unconscious and crouched down. All that was left was to put the gun in Theodore's hand, put it to his head, and fire. "My daughter wanted it fast and painless. She's going to get her wish."

A low, rumbling growl made him freeze. A cold shiver went through him when the ominous snarl came again, but this time it came in stereo. He recognized the source. He'd hunted wolves in the Ukraine. When his party had cornered a pair and their pups, they made the same noise as they faced their doom. But those wolves were thirty feet away. These animals were close, *very* close.

Easing back, grasping the gun, he was about to turn when he was attacked. Powerful teeth clamped down on his hand, making him drop the gun.

* * *

Theodore was only out for a few moments. He regained consciousness in time to witness an incredible sight. The two wolves that had helped him fight the WKA in the field were close enough to touch. They were attacking Neumann. One had the man's hand, and the other was trying to go for his throat. Theodore glanced over and saw Daniel move slightly. Next, he saw his father trying to move too.

They're both still alive!

His heart nearly exploded with happiness. Rolling over and onto his knees, he slowly got to his feet. Neumann's bullet had grazed his head and blood ran down his face.

"Help me!" Neumann screamed when he saw Theodore get up.

Theodore knew he should be relieved to know the old man was going to die, but a part of him hesitated. He abhorred the violence. Violence was what Neumann and the WKA were all about. All they knew was how to hurt people. Yet a rising hatred for what the old man had done to Daniel and his father was outweighing his peace-loving nature.

Let him die! He deserves it!

Theodore's mind was torn as the man who'd pretended to be his grandfather begged for mercy.

"Stop them, please!" The sound of Neumann's voice wasn't cocky or domineering anymore. It was pitiful and filled with terror.

"You're going to hell where you belong!" Daniel cried out from a few feet away. There was a smile of relief on his face when he glanced at Theodore.

Theodore kicked Neumann's gun as hard as he could, making it slide across the concrete and hit a pillar twenty-five feet away. He turned to the animals, knowing he'd made a decision in spite of his hatred. "Get away from him!" he yelled at the wolves. "You don't want his blood! It's evil and tainted!"

His command stopped the silver wolf as it was about to clamp down on Neumann's throat. It stood immobile, but every muscle in its body was taut, ready to finish off the man.

"What are you saying, Theo?" Daniel shrieked out in pain.

Theodore turned to Daniel. "We're not like him. We're not killers. We don't want his murder on our hands."

"He tried to kill us!" Daniel's rebuttal came in panting gasps. "I thought you were dead!"

"Call them off, Daniel, please."

Daniel stared at him. "Me? They're yours!"

Theodore shook his head.

"No, they're not mine. Please Daniel, I know I'm right."

* * *

Daniel let his head drop to the floor. Every cell in his body, every part of his mind wanted retribution for what he'd lost and for what had been done to Theodore, to him and to so many others of his kind. Then he remembered Prissy's face as she stood holding the rock over her head, ready to kill Theodore. She'd been eaten up with hatred too. It was infecting all of them. If he helped to promote it, fighting and killing the WKA might eventually become the prime motive driving the entire pack. "Oh hell," he sighed despondently.

As soon as Daniel decided to give in to Theodore's wish, the two wolves backed away from Neumann. One stood guard in front of Theodore and one in front of Daniel. When the old man realized what was happening, he acted quickly. As fast as he could, he scuttled backwards, using his bloody hands and feet to move away from the wolves. When he'd gone a short distance, he got to his feet and began to lurch towards an exit. Once he was gone, the two wolves disappeared too.

Soon Theodore was kneeling by Daniel's side. He tried to focus on his younger brother, but he felt like he was going to black out. With determination, he was able to hold on to the joy of seeing Theodore's young face and knowing he was safe. It was enough to ease his pain a little.

* * *

Theodore rushed over to Daniel with relief and gratitude. "Thank goodness you're alive," he whispered as he put his hand on Daniel's chest. He needed to know how badly his brother was hurt. After a few moments of tuning into Daniel's condition, he smiled weakly. "You're going to make it, but you have to hang in there while I check on my dad."

Daniel stared back. "That guy who tried to save you is the man who adopted you?"

"Yes, and I have to check on him. I'll be right back," he promised.

Theodore got up and ran across the expanse that separated him from the man he'd called father for most of his life. After he closed the distance and had a chance to see Arthur close up, his heart sank in despair. He dropped to his knees, trying to calm himself enough to speak. "Dad, can you hear me?" He pressed down on Arthur's chest, trying to stop the steady flow of blood that poured out of a grievous wound. "Dad?"

After a moment, Arthur opened his eyes. He blinked repeatedly, trying to focus on Theodore. "Are you alright?" he asked as he reached up. His hand barely touched Theodore's cheek and dropped back to the cement floor.

"I'm fine," Theodore replied. He tried to give Arthur a reassuring smile when he realized his face must be bloody from where the bullet grazed him. "I'm okay, but I'm going to get help."

Wait . . . wait—" Arthur paused, trying to get his breath. "I want to talk to you, to tell you I'm sorry. I haven't been much of a father."

"Dad, what are you doing here? How did you know—"

"I heard your mother. I wanted to help. That lunatic who pretended to be your grandfather—" He started to cough. When he spoke again, it was in short, choking spurts. "I let him hurt you . . . we all hurt you. Forgive me . . . please."

Theodore stared back, noting Arthur's graying hair and the deep lines etched in his face. The man who was confessing his sins hadn't had a happy life either. "Shh, save your strength."

"Forgive me, son."

Theodore felt his heart ache with an old feeling. When he was a young boy, all he wanted was to have a father like other boys, a father who was there for scouts or school events, a father who wanted a son. Now he could feel Arthur trying to be that person. "It's alright. You did your best . . . I guess."

Arthur's face was ashen as he tried to reach up again and didn't have the strength. "I wish that was true. You were the only good thing your mother or I ever had in our marriage. Remember that when I'm gone. You were always a good boy." He grimaced and closed his eyes. "A good boy," he whispered with his last breath.

Theodore's chest tightened. He started to cry. He couldn't help it. The tears came from so much desire to be loved by this man. Now he'd had that love for only a few moments. The sound of a car coming up the ramp interrupted his feelings of loss. Frightened that it was the old man coming back, he looked up. He started to cry again, this time with relief. Doc Leonard and Wolfgang had arrived. They parked halfway between Theodore and Daniel. Doc Leonard quickly got out of the car and ran to Daniel. Wolfgang hurried over to Theodore.

Theodore knew Wolfgang was reading his thoughts and felt his grief. But Wolfgang didn't say anything. Instead, he turned his attention to Arthur. He held the man's wrist with one hand and put his other hand on Arthur's chest. He shut his eyes and remained very still. When he looked up, he shook his head.

"I'm sorry, Theodore, he's gone."

Theodore nodded, not knowing what to think or do. His world was spinning, and he didn't know how to make it stop.

Wolfgang stood up and held out a hand to him. "We have to leave. The police will be here soon."

Theodore let Wolfgang help him up, but his mind felt frozen and unresponsive as he was guided towards the car. After he was seated behind the wheel, Wolfgang offered some words of comfort.

"I know it's hard, but it's going to get better, I promise."

Chapter Thirty-Seven

Wolfgang, Daniel, and the doctor drove the Land Rover, while Theodore followed them in Doc Leonard's car. Both vehicles headed towards another medical facility run by the pack. Theodore kept an eye on the back lights of the truck, but he was on auto pilot, maintaining visual contact with the Land Rover, and dutifully keeping up with it. Once they got to the facility, his own wound was bandaged. Daniel was examined and hospitalized. His brother had been shot in the chest, but the bullet missed his heart, barely. He was stable. He'd make it.

When Amelie and Prissy arrived at the facility, Amelie was quick in asking Theodore how he was. "Maybe you should come home with us," she said quietly, putting an arm around his shoulders.

Wolfgang joined her. "She's right. You need to rest."

Theodore blinked back at them. He was having trouble focusing on what they were saying. "Yeah, I guess."

"You're not planning on going anywhere, are you?" Wolfgang asked.

Theodore shook his head. "No, you don't have to worry about chasing me anymore."

Prissy gave him an encouraging smile. "Daniel will be alright. Don't worry."

Theodore looked at her mutely. How could he tell her he wasn't worried, that he wasn't even thinking of Daniel? His mind was pulling away from everything, retreating from the outer world and the craziness he'd just experienced. The part of him Prissy was addressing was just going through the motions.

* * *

Bunked out in Doc Leonard's library, Theodore slept for two days straight. Amelie tried to wake him a couple of times, but he begged her to let him go back to sleep. "I'm so tired," he insisted.

Doc Leonard checked on him and agreed. "He's exhausted, and he's had multiple shocks in a very short amount of time. Let him recover."

On the morning of the third day, Prissy tried to wake Theodore again. Her voice was filled with excitement. "Theo, I have great news."

Theodore opened his eyes and shielded them against the sun streaming through the window. "What?"

"They've arrested Karl Neumann for the murder of your father. They found his gun at the scene of the crime with his fingerprints on it. And when the police questioned your mother, she admitted her father had bullied your dad in the past, even threatened him. When she was asked about you, she said you were staying with an out of state relative."

Theodore closed his eyes again, but he didn't comment. Nothing felt real. Prissy, the strange house he was in, everything that had recently happened to him felt dreamlike. But when he closed his eyes and let sleep take over, he went to a place that cushioned him with its nothingness. The hazy retreat felt good and safe. He liked staying there.

Prissy shook him as he started to drift back to sleep. "Theo, aren't you glad they caught your dad's murderer?"

His eyes barely opened again. "Yeah, it's good. Now please, close the curtains. I'm still tired."

Prissy frowned but did as he asked. "If you need anything, call me," she said as she went to the door.

"Yeah, sure," he mumbled back.

* * *

By the end of the third day, Amelie could see that Doc Leonard was worried about Theodore. Standing next to the pull out sofa bed where Theodore was sleeping, he had his arms crossed and was frowning. She pulled him aside. "What's going on with Theodore? It's getting almost impossible to wake him."

"He seems to be withdrawing further and further into himself. He needed to recuperate, but now he's gone past that point. I don't think he wants to wake up."

"Poor thing, he's been through so much in his young life. He needs someone he can feel safe with. How is Daniel?"

"He's doing well, but I don't know if he's strong enough to deal with his brother's situation yet. At this point, I think they're both running on empty emotionally."

Amelie went back to the sofa bed and sat down next to Theodore. She pushed back his dark, unruly curls, bent over and kissed his forehead. "I'm going to stay with him from now on. He's lost so much, even the person he's known himself to be. Somehow, he has to be coaxed into taking a chance on life again."

"I'll help!"

Amelie looked up and saw Prissy standing in the doorway. She smiled back. "Okay, we'll both stay with him, but it could be boring, and I can guarantee that it'll take patience."

Prissy came over and looked down at Theodore. "Not a problem. I want to help. We can take turns."

* * *

Prissy offered her services quickly, without thinking about what she was taking on. Watching Theodore involved long hours of simply sitting next to his bed, doing nothing. Now, when it was her turn, she realized she'd been hasty. Patience was her least favorite word. She barely had enough of the elusive virtue for her own life. How would she have enough if Theodore needed loads? She'd probably be tested beyond her limits, but she needed to start proving herself.

"I can take care of this," she told her mother as she practically pushed her out of the room. "Go get some tea. See how Dad's doing."

Amelie gave her a last look of concern. "Theo's in a fragile state. You have to remember that. If you talk to him, only say things that are positive."

Prissy nodded. "Yes, trust me. I'll do exactly what you did." Again, she mouthed off the words without reflection. Again, her assurances were more talk than belief. Heaving a sigh of boredom, but filled with a determined sense of commitment, she closed the door after Amelie. Her mother was the queen of gentle words. Prissy, on the other hand, was more of a scullery maid.

"But really? How hard can it be to say a bunch of nice stuff?" she said as she sat down in an overstuffed chair by the bed. She crossed her arms and stared at her patient. That was how she thought of Theodore now. He was a shock victim, and she'd be the wonderful nurse who'd help him recover. When she noted his body language, he did appear to be severely shaken. His arms were clasped across his chest and there were deep, furrowed lines between his brows. Even in his sleep state, he seemed to be waiting for the next bad thing to happen to him. But looks could be deceiving as Prissy learned in the past. Doc Leonard explained that Theodore could probably hear everything being said around him.

Prissy sighed. "You're always listening, aren't you? But this time I'm going to redeem myself. You'll see. I'll help you, Theodore, whether you want to be helped or not."

She uncrossed her arms and got up. Amelie had only left the room minutes before, and Prissy already felt fatigued by her task. She approached the sofa bed and climbed unto the mattress. She sat down close to Theodore. With her legs crossed, she leaned forward and began to examine her patient more closely.

"You're rather attractive in spite of your scowl. If you really can hear me, I mean that as a compliment." Her brows arched as her eyes traveled to his hands. Putting one of her small ones over his for comparison, she laughed. "Did you know you have puppy hands? They're too big for your body. You haven't grown into them completely. I think you're going to be taller, aren't you? Probably like Daniel."

Theodore moaned at the sound of his brother's name.

"Sorry, Theo, I didn't realize you didn't want to talk about him. But to set the record straight, the doctor says he's recovering nicely." She touched his fingers lightly. "Dad said your real father was at least six-three. Who knows, you might end up like him."

Theodore groaned again.

She pulled back. "You don't want to talk about any of your family, do you? Well that's fine. I guess there's too much unhappiness there. But Theo, you're not the only one with problems. I've got loads of them."

She repositioned herself, lying down on her stomach with her chin cupped in her hands. "I know what you thought about me when we met in school, that I was always so confident and strong. Well, there's more underneath. I kind of grew up thinking I might be pack leader someday. So I had to be tough and act like leadership material. But I get scared sometimes. It's hard not to. Sometimes I wonder if any of us will survive."

She stopped herself. "Oh, I'm not supposed to talk about that stuff. But no matter what Mom thinks, maybe you need to talk about it. I know I have to, sometimes. You're going to find this very strange, but I don't have many friends. There aren't many in the pack who are my age. I guess you're the closest I've come to having a person to confide in. Maybe that's why I didn't know how to treat you when we first started talking to each other. I've never had a good friend before."

She laid her head down on the bed. "But I need someone, Theo. So don't leave, okay? Stay here." As she voiced her request, she felt really tired. "Good lord, I sound pathetic."

She sighed and began to relax when she felt a hand touching her arm. She looked up and smiled. Theodore's eyes were open ever so slightly.

"Your mom said to tell me nice stuff," he whispered.

She sat up quickly and blushed. "I'm sorry."

"You didn't let me finish. I'm glad you said what you did. I don't feel so alone when I know you want me as a friend."

She reached out slowly and touched Theodore's hand again. "I do want that. But sometimes, if I act, you know, kind of bossy, try not to take it personally."

"You want me to see the sweet, wonderful you underneath?"

"Yes! That's exactly right."

Theodore's dark eyes widened slightly, and his smile broadened. The moment was interrupted by a loud growl coming from his stomach.

The sound made Prissy snicker. "And I thought your snoring was bad. But I'm not surprised. You haven't eaten for days. Doc Leonard tried to set up an IV so that you'd get some fluids, but you fought him off like a wild animal."

"Can I have some toast?"

Prissy jumped off the bed. "I guess so. I'll get you something if you say the magic word."

"Please—"

"No, you're supposed to say, 'Can I have some toast, friend?'"

He nodded. "Friend."

Chapter Thirty-Eight

Amelie stood outside the door of the library, listening to Theodore and Prissy as they laughed and yelled at each other. They were playing cards and both insisted the other was cheating. Amelie was relieved and a little surprised that Prissy was able to reach Theodore so quickly. After only a day, he was fast returning to a somewhat normal state. When she opened the library door and peeked in, Theodore stared at her expectantly, waiting for her to ask an important question. Amelie didn't make him wait very long. "Do either of you want lunch?" she asked.

Theodore's face lit up. "That would be great."

Prissy rolled her eyes at Amelie. "Theodore's turned into a food addicted maniac. I've never seen anyone eat so much."

Amelie walked over to the bridge table where they were sitting. "It's understandable. Theodore is making up for all the meals he's missed."

Theodore scowled. "Yeah, Prissy, I'm not usually this hungry. In fact my mother—" He paused and looked down at his cards. "Never mind."

"Forget about all that," Prissy said quickly. It was evident she was still acting out her role as nurse and counselor. "I'm glad you're eating. And do you know why?"

Theodore looked up. "Why?"

"Because I don't want you to have any excuses when I beat you at tennis." She turned to Amelie. "I'm going to teach him how to play."

"I loved the game when I was in college," Amelie said. "Your dad and I played a lot."

Prissy grinned. "When I get Theodore into shape, we'll play you and Dad. That'll be fun."

Amelie groaned. "That sounds like a challenge. Your dad and I will have to start practicing as soon as he's back to normal." She paused as she was about to leave. Her face brightened when she looked at Theodore. "Guess what, Theo, Daniel is coming to see you this afternoon. Is that okay?"

Theodore lowered his cards to the table. With downcast eyes, he slowly rubbed the tabletop in a back and forth motion. "I'd rather he didn't."

Amelie could feel his unhappiness, but she didn't know what to say to him. The two brothers had problems they needed to work out with each other.

As Theodore continued to explore the smoothness of the wood, his face became even more desolate. "Tell Daniel I'm fine, that we can catch up some other time."

"What's wrong with now?" a voice asked from the doorway. It was Daniel's voice. He stood quietly, looking drawn and pale, but well enough for someone who'd been severely wounded recently. "I got here sooner than I expected."

Theodore didn't acknowledge his brother. Instead, his hands slowly closed into fists. He began to take short breaths. After a moment, he stood up. "Excuse me, everyone. I don't feel well." The words were barely out when he started running from the room. He passed Daniel without looking up.

* * *

Daniel watched with surprise as Theodore ran to the bathroom. When the door slammed shut, he looked at Amelie. "I thought he was fine, that he was eating you out of house and home. Is his stomach off again?"

"I didn't think so," Amelie replied as she walked over to hug him. "I'm so glad to see you up and about."

Prissy came over to join them. She hesitated before throwing her arms around Daniel. "We've missed you."

Daniel hugged her back with relief. Prissy seemed to consider him part of the family again. "I'm happy someone feels that way."

Prissy stood back and smiled shyly. "You and Theodore share a lot. You don't show it as much, but I think you both are kind of—"

Daniel frowned. "Kind of what?"

Prissy looked up, letting her eyes meet his for a brief second. "You're both sweet. There, I've said it."

Daniel felt his face go flush. He didn't know how to respond.

Prissy broke in before he had a chance. "Theodore needs you, but I think he's afraid. He won't talk about anything that's happened."

* * *

Theodore knew he was going to throw up in the small bathroom, but he didn't want to spoil the décor with his version of vomiting. When he felt an urge coming on, he practically buried his head in the toilet. Strangely enough, when the vomiting began, it wasn't the projectile type he was used to. This time he threw up like a normal person. It was a relief, but it didn't make the horrible nausea any better. He couldn't stop heaving, even when there was nothing left in his stomach. As he hung over the fixture, he felt something cold on the back of his neck. He looked up and saw Daniel.

"I thought a wet cloth might help," his brother said as he held the compress in place.

Theodore hesitated, feeling Daniel's energy and the cooling effects of the cloth. "Thanks." When his stomach settled a little, he stood up, put the lid down on the toilet, and flushed it. He quickly moved to the sink and washed his face. His nausea was better, but a powerful wave of emotion took hold in its place. Just like when he cried in the airport, tears streamed down his face. "I feel like such a baby. I'm sixteen, and I'm still crying all the time. How's that for a brother? Just the kind you always wanted, huh?"

He felt Daniel's hand on his arm. When he turned around, Daniel's eyes were softer than usual.

"There's nothing wrong with crying. It means you can feel, and that's good."

Theodore winced. There was a pressure inside of him. It started to build with the shootout. "I don't want to feel this. I guess that's why I wanted to sleep. Every time I think about you, I start to think I hate you!"

"You hate me? That's great." Daniel's brows narrowed. "But why, because I pushed you away before? I'm sorry about that. But I thought being there, getting shot to save your life, might make up for my ignorance."

Theodore felt his stomach lurch again, but his mounting anger was stronger. "Did you think for one moment about what it was like for me when we were in that parking garage? My supposed grandfather, who turns out to be a crazy madman, shot you and would have killed you! And do you know why? Because you have to always be the hero! You always have to sacrifice yourself. Do you realize that if you had died, your decision would have destroyed me too?"

"I wasn't trying to destroy you. I was trying to save you."

"It's my life, Daniel! Mine! You had no right to do what you did? I begged you to stop interfering, but you wouldn't. You insisted on getting yourself killed!"

Daniel stiffened as he glared back. "What are you talking about? I couldn't stand there and watch that monster blow your brains out."

"That's not the point!"

"What is the point?"

"Daniel, when you look at me, what do you see?"

"I see my little brother."

"Exactly. You still think of me as that baby you tried to protect. But I'm not that child anymore."

"I know that, and I'm sorry if I treat you like a kid."

Theodore turned and faced the vanity mirror. "Do you know what I see when I look at myself? I see the person I've always been. I see the person who couldn't stand watching you get hurt when I was a little baby any more than I can bear it now. It doesn't matter what age I was or am, I've always loved you."

"Yes, I know—"

"No, you don't!" He turned around to face Daniel. "When we were there the other night, in the hands of that killer, I was my brother's keeper as much as you were. I had as much right to plead for your life as you had to plead for mine." He felt the tears coming again, and he didn't care. "But you didn't hear me or pay attention to what I was saying. You didn't realize how much I value you because you don't value yourself."

"And I suppose you value who you are? After what they did to you, you should—"

"And to you! They abducted both of us! They tortured both of us! Do you know how horrified I was when I saw them hurting you, how much it hurt in here?" Theodore poked at his chest. "Well, I remember! And when we found each other again, I did start to value myself. I moved on. You haven't. Maybe that's the point. When I was standing there with a gun to my head, and then I saw you, I knew I was loved, that you truly cared. You didn't have to prove it to me. If I died in that moment, I would have died with that assurance."

Daniel backed up to the wall and leaned against it heavily. "So I should have let Karl Neumann kill you? Is that what you're telling me?"

"I'm telling you that your death was just as horrifying a thought for me, that's all. It's your attitude that's so wrong. To negate my feelings because you're trying to correct the past is wrong." Theodore stepped forward. "You're not responsible for what they did. Both of us need to stop worrying about all that. We need to let go and just be ourselves, brothers who care and support each other now. That's what I'm trying to say."

Daniel looked away. "I don't know how to do what you're asking. I've lived with the guilt of not being able to save you for so long. I guess it's what made me push so hard. I tried to excel in the pack. Somehow, I wanted to make things right after I failed you."

"Let it go, *please*. We both have to let it go."

Daniel's eyes flickered with uncertainty. After a long moment of contemplation, his gaze steadied. "You really would have been okay to die at that moment? I mean you did feel I loved you?"

"Nobody wants to die, Daniel, but if I have to leave this planet, it wouldn't have been the worst way to go. I'm not broken. Believe in me. That's all I'm asking."

Daniel reached out and put his hand on Theodore's chest. Finally, he let it drop away. "You're right, you're not broken."

Theodore grinned back and embraced Daniel in a brotherly bear hug. "Neither are you."

Daniel groaned. "Whoa, not too tight! I'm still a *little* broken."

Theodore released him at once. "I thought our kind healed fast. Is there something you're not telling me?"

"We do heal fast, but you seem to be particularly able to work miracles with your body. I'm not quite as gifted."

Theodore shrugged. "I haven't been able to change since that night. You don't think I've lost the knack, do you? I mean, if I have, that's okay too. Amelie is a human, and she's awesome."

"It's not something you can lose. It'll take time for the change to become permanent."

"That's good news."

"In the meantime, I'll try to do what you want, but I'll always be older. That's just the way it is."

"Yeah, I suppose."

Daniel straightened up and pulled back his shoulders. He seemed intent on showing Theodore the facts. He was still a few inches taller.

"And as your older brother, it'll be my job to teach you things and to yell at you when you grind the gears on the new Corvette I'm planning on buying someday."

Theodore heard the teasing tone in Daniel's voice. He stared back with raised brows. He remembered what Prissy had said when she was taking care of him. He'd been half asleep, but he'd heard her label his large hands as puppy hands. "I guess you'll have to do what you have to do, brother, but eventually I might be taller than you, and probably stronger. And you know what they say about payback."

Daniel grinned. "I'll take my chances." After a moment, he sobered again. "But Theo, if the scene in the garage was happening all over again, if Neumann had a gun to your head, I don't think I could act any differently. However, after what you said, I do know I'd feel differently about you. I wouldn't think I'd be saving my baby brother. I'd be saving a person who's probably a lot wiser than I am."

Theodore sobered too. "Maybe that's all I need, your respect."

Chapter Thirty-Nine

Theodore sat on a leather couch in Doc Leonard's family room. He was hunched down with his stockinged feet on the large, oak coffee table. Wolfgang sat across from him in an upholstered chair. When Theodore looked up at the pack leader, he noted his drawn features, how he still looked tired and worn. "Are you feeling better physically?"

Wolfgang's eyes brightened when he smiled back. "Every day I'm more like my old self. I'm sure I would have died if it hadn't been for Daniel."

"I guess that makes two of us."

"Amelie told me Daniel came over today."

Theodore crossed his arms and sighed. "Why does he have to be so stubborn? He acts like all of us have sheep in our DNA, and he's the only one who's strong. He thinks he has to protect us all."

"Give him time. You're his only real family. It's natural for him to care deeply. But you're right, he does seem to think it's his duty to constantly take care of the lot of us."

"He's talking about taking me to Europe, to see Paris, maybe live there. I suppose I'll have to go. Somebody needs to keep an eye on him and lighten him up."

Wolfgang laughed. "You both remind me of your father. He was stubborn too, but I couldn't have a better friend." He paused. "Speaking of fathers, I'm really sorry about your adoptive father. I understand he was trying to help you."

"Yeah, I guess he tried his best. And I think he saved us in a way. He distracted Neumann enough to make his aim go off a little. The old man didn't hit Daniel's heart. But my dad paid the price with his life."

Theodore thought about those last few minutes they'd had together. As his father ran towards Karl Neumann, his face was filled with anger and fear. There was also determination and courage. Maybe he was trying to prove himself to the person he regarded as his son. But his last words, "You were always a good boy," left Theodore feeling more sad than anything. He looked up at Wolfgang again, wishing he could feel some resolution. "Before he died, he said he regretted not being a better father."

"How do you feel about that?"

Theodore shrugged as he took his feet off the coffee table and sat up. "I suppose I could be really angry about my childhood. But when I think about the people who adopted me, I know they were miserable. My father seemed incapable of dealing with anything."

He stood up and walked to the slider. He gazed out at the well kept yard and woods beyond. Finally he glanced back at Wolfgang. "But he was there in the end. That counts, doesn't it?"

"What counts?" Prissy asked as she came in from the kitchen carrying a tray of drinks.

Theodore turned and looked at her. "Nothing."

"Wow, you sound cheery. I guess I'll have to beat you at cards again this evening."

Theodore smiled back. "You wish."

Prissy walked over to her father and offered him a glass of lemonade. Next, she joined Theodore. "I thought we could go outside and enjoy the sun."

* * *

Theodore sat next to Prissy on a lawn glider on Doc Leonard's patio. They were both holding glasses of lemonade. "This is nice. Thanks for the drink."

"You're welcome," Prissy said curtly.

Theodore gave her a sideways glance. She had a serious expression on her face that made him a little nervous. She didn't scare him like before, but she could still make him edgy when she was in a mood. "Is everything okay?"

"I overheard you say something about going away with your brother." She paused. "Sorry, I wasn't trying to listen."

Theodore took a sip of the lemonade and had to put a hand to his mouth, trying to cover the face he made.

Prissy wasn't fooled. She took a sip of her drink and grimaced. "Yuk, I think I forgot to add the sugar."

"No, it's good." Theodore said in a firm voice. He put his glass on the side table. "I'm just not thirsty right now."

"You are way too nice," Prissy giggled, but her eyes lost some of their sparkle as she paused. "So you might live in Paris? That's exciting. I guess you'll be glad to get away from here."

"No, I love it here." It was true. He was happy staying with Prissy's family. However, Prissy was right about Paris. It sounded exciting. He'd even started to imagine what it might be like to see the Arc de Triomphe. He'd read the monument was commissioned by Napoleon, and it took two years just to lay the foundations.

He'd barely begun to indulge in his daydream when the late afternoon rays of light highlighted Prissy's long, golden blond hair. When a breeze lifted it off of her shoulders and exposed her pretty face, a crazy thought popped in his mind. He wondered if anyone had ever kissed her. "Geez." He groaned out the word like it was a desperate plea.

Prissy went on instant alert. "What is it? You're not getting sick again, are you? I hope it's not the heart thing."

Theodore sat up straighter. Red faced and embarrassed, he avoided Prissy's eyes. "No, I'm fine."

"Theodore, you can't moan like that and expect me not to want to know why."

"You'll laugh at me. I know we're friends, but—"

"I will not. We have an understanding now. So don't be obstinate. Talk to me."

"I used to really have a crush on you."

"Oh yeah, that. I know."

He gave her a fierce look of dismay as his face reddened even more. "Forget it."

Prissy smiled. "Do you still have a crush on me?"

"I said forget it."

She got up and put her glass next to his. "I will not forget it. Do you like me or not?" Her tone was insistent, and she put her hands on her hips. "Yes or no."

He narrowed his eyes, avoiding hers. "Fine, I like you."

"A lot?" she asked more softly.

"Maybe." In spite of Prissy trying to bash in his brains with a rock, he knew he did have a crush on her. He hated to admit it, but he might even still love her. He didn't know if it was real love. He was still learning about such things when it came to girls. He lifted his gaze and barely made eye contact.

It was enough for Prissy to see what he was trying to hide. It made her smile. "I might kind of like you too," she said in a quiet tone she never normally used.

Theodore picked up his lemonade and took a large gulp. This time he fought his desire to make another face. Instead, he blinked several times.

Prissy started to laugh. "You're really strange, but I guess I'm going to miss you when you leave."

"You'll probably forget me as soon as I'm gone."

She took his glass and put it back on the table. "Listen, Theodore, I could never forget you."

"Are you sure?"

She leaned over and kissed his cheek. "You're very special."

He smiled. "Really?"

She pulled away and crossed her arms again. "You're very special and don't forget it. Promise?"

He felt Prissy shielding her thoughts, but her eyes were sparkling and happy when she looked at him. He grinned back. "I promise."

Chapter Forty

Paris was even better than Daniel had hoped, but he didn't have a lot of time to soak in luxury baths. Theodore wanted to be out and about. His brother devoured the city in the same way he devoured food. "I didn't realize feeding you would be more costly than our lodgings at a five star hotel," he complained as he watched Theodore eat his dessert.

Theodore glanced up. "I don't understand it either. But I suddenly have a voracious appetite."

"Yes, and you seem to have an uncanny way of picking out the most expensive restaurants."

"I guess I have good taste like my older brother."

Daniel leaned back in his chair and sipped his wine. "Why do I get the feeling I'll rarely win any arguments with you?"

Theodore swallowed another large bite of chocolate mousse. "You won't have to. We're on the same side, remember?"

"Right," Daniel said as he looked out the window. The restaurant was located four floors up, high enough to see the lights of the city spread out in front of them. "I love it here. We should start looking for a place to rent. Later, after we explore our options, we can decide on something to buy."

Theodore put his fork down and dusted a few crumbs off of his shirt. "I guess."

"You guess? Theodore, I'm talking about living in one of the most amazing cities in the world. How many people get a chance like that?"

"It's been great to see all the sights. It's been incredible. And if you want to stay —"

"I can't believe it. You don't want to live here." Daniel hadn't bothered to tune into Theodore's thoughts since all the misery they'd been through. He was acclimating himself to behaving like a normal human. Now, as he probed his brother's mind, he saw what he'd ignored. "You want to go back." He continued to scan. "Prissy? You like Prissy?"

"It's not just her!" Theodore's head jerked up with a flush of red coloring his cheeks. "I miss everyone. I miss our world. I was just beginning to fit in. But if you want us to live here, that's okay."

Daniel leaned across the table. "I'm doing this so we don't have to worry all the time. We can lose ourselves here. You'll be safe."

"Will that make you happy?"

The question hung in the air, a bird of the mind hovering over Daniel's emotions, waiting for him to look at his own truth. But he waved it aside with a laugh. "Sure, let's enjoy our lives."

"Does that mean we're running away from who we are?"

"You almost died!"

"But I didn't." Theodore leaned in too. "I thought you wanted to help the pack, help Wolfgang with the transition that's going on."

Daniel stared out the window again. He didn't want to think about the past. It was behind them. They were in a glorious city, safe from the WKA, safe from Daniel's previous ambitions. His dreams and desires to help the pack with fresh ideas and perspectives were tainted with ego and pride. He'd been an arrogant fool to challenge Wolfgang's position.

"I can read your thoughts too, Daniel," Theodore said forcefully. "As usual, you're being too hard on yourself. Wolfgang wants your help."

"He was happy when we left."

"That's not true, and you know it. He wanted you to have time to lift that burden off your shoulders, to put aside the pressure you put on yourself every time you involve yourself in something. You needed time away. You needed to get some balance back in your life. But you've had that. Now it's time to think of your future."

"Not just my future, Theo. I have to think of our future. Sure I have ideas that might help the pack. I want the best for everyone, but—"

Theodore pulled back and smiled. "Wow, I haven't seen you look that excited for awhile. Do you realize our eyes sometimes glow?"

Daniel looked away, but he was smiling too. It felt good to let himself feel passionate again. "I want us both to be happy, that's all."

Theodore scraped up the last bite of his dessert and swallowed it with a satisfied nod. "Yes, but you definitely need a place for all your energy. You can't just sit around and let life pass you by. As for my future, I like who I am, who we are. I don't want to run from that. If I can, someday I'd like to help the pack too."

"I see." Daniel looked down at the table and took his wine glass in hand. Swirling the rich, garnet red contents, his face went from tense to thoughtful to resolute. "You've thought about this a lot."

"Yes, but I'll do what you want. If you can't face going back—"

Daniel laughed. "Me? Is that it? You're worried about me? Remember what you said in the bathroom, that you weren't broken? I can't promise I'm a hundred percent, but I'm okay."

"So, you want to go home too?"

When Theodore said the word 'home,' Daniel felt something stir inside his chest. A warm, comforting feeling began to flood a space that felt empty. He put his glass down and dared to allow himself new hope. After all his years of feeling he'd lost a place where he could feel connected to family, now he knew he hadn't. That place was waiting for Theodore and for him. "Let's go back to the hotel. I'll check out flights back to the states."

Theodore's face lit up at the offer, but he snagged Daniel's hand before he could stand. "Wait a minute."

"What now?"

"I'm still hungry. Can we take a couple of desserts with us?"

Daniel blinked back. "I couldn't afford to stay here anyway, not the way you're eating. Maybe you picked up a tapeworm along the way."

"I don't think so, but I'm getting this funny feeling, like my body is getting ready for something. It's kind of exciting and scary at the same time"

"The only thing I'm picking up is an order for crème brulee and lemon-raspberry flan." Daniel raised his hand to hail the waiter.

"Daniel?"

"Yes?"

"Thank you for everything."

Daniel shrugged, but smiled. "When we get back, we'll both get a fresh start on life."

"No, let's enjoy the rest of the one we've started," Theodore countered. "I have a feeling we're just beginning to understand ourselves and what's happened to us. Someday I want to talk to you about those wolves you conjured up to save us."

Daniel froze. He didn't want to think about the wolves. "Conjured up? I don't know what you're talking about."

Theodore paused and tapped his plate with his fork. "I have some ideas about it. Maybe we can discuss them at some point, when I have more clarity about it all."

Daniel hated that his curiosity was peaked, but he was also relieved to put that conversation off, at least for the time being. When the waiter came over to the table, he was pleased that his brother had more important things on his mind.

Theodore's eyes were filled with anticipation when he looked at the waiter. "Can you bring the dessert cart back, s'il vous plait?"

The End For Now

Thank you for taking the time to read "In The Care Of Wolves - My Brother's Keeper." If you enjoyed it, please consider telling your friends or posting a short review. Word of mouth is an author's best friend and much appreciated. – S. S. Bazinet.

www.ingramcontent.com/pod-product-compliance
Lightning Source LLC
Chambersburg PA
CBHW050713180626
46814CB00002B/411